Entice

A Hearts of Stone Novel

By

VERONICA LARSEN

Editing by Lea Burn, Burn Before Reading
Proofread by Julie Deaton
Interior formatted with Scrivener for Mac version 2.5
Published by Veronica Larsen
authorveronicalarsen@gmail.com
Cover design by goudydesigns@gmail.com
Cover image: shutterstock.com #145079746
First published May 25th, 2015
ISBN: 978-0-9908253-3-3

This novel is for Ariane.
For your courage, humor, and grace.

Prologue

Owen

Music and laughter trickle past the open door, dissolving into the air as I peer outside, hesitant. The night is colder than I anticipated. There's an uncomfortable chill that probably has less to do with the temperature and more to do with the way my palms have grown sweaty.

I scan my surroundings, but the front steps are empty, stained dark from the rain. As my ears hone in on the noises outside versus those of the prom celebration behind me, my stomach sinks.

She's gone.

I'm sure I saw her slipping out, the flash of a pale yellow dress as a figure disappeared down the hall like she hoped no one would notice.

I wasn't fast enough to catch her.

Fingers still wrapped around the edge of the door, holding it open, I take one last look around before turning to go back inside. I freeze mid-step when a soft sound reaches me. An intake of breath or maybe a sniffle.

She's standing a few feet away, back pressed to the brick wall of the building. Her arms are crossed behind her back, her head is bowed, and her shoulders, bare in her strapless dress, curved slightly inward.

"Hey," I say, awkward as always.

The only indication she hears me is the way she turns her face away, a strand of her light-brown hair falling over her cheek as she does so.

I swear, she looks like an angel. Her smooth skin glows in the night, like she's absorbing the light from the nearby lamppost and, in the process, dimming everything around her.

A lump forms in my throat at the silence that follows. And though I let the door close behind me, I can't seem to figure out what to do next.

I didn't have a plan when I followed her out here. She doesn't know me. We've never talked. I just...I hated to see her go through that. The way that asshole humiliated her back there, in front of the entire school. She wasn't exactly a pushover. The things she yelled back made everyone fall quiet. Then she stalked off, head held high, toward the bathrooms.

Voices rippled around as everyone who witnessed the fight immediately started their petty gossiping. But not me. I stood there watching the entrance of the bathroom. Waiting for her to come back out, wanting to know she was okay.

And now she's here, angling away from me, not wanting me to see her face, which is probably streaked with tears.

"Hey," I say again, taking a step toward her. "Are you okay?"

"I'm fine," she snaps, hurrying forward to sit on the steps, her back to me.

The urge to sit beside her is overwhelming, but she doesn't want to talk to me. Why would she? She has to think I'm some random guy trying to take advantage of her newly-single status.

That's not why I'm out here, at all. I'm out here because...because I want to hear her voice. I want to hear it directed at me for the first time. I want her to look at me, to *see* me, and know I'm not like that asshole in there. Know I'd never talk to her the way he did.

She shivers and I get the odd sensation of the cold creeping up from the cement and seeping through the thin material of her dress.

Stripping off my suit jacket, I hang it over her shoulders. She takes in a sudden breath and her eyes lift to meet mine. I try to speak but nerves wrench my stomach tight. All of her light is contained in those green orbs, and for the very first time, they're fixed on me.

I don't care about the black streaks of makeup running down her face, she's the most beautiful girl I've ever seen. I've thought so all this time I've watched her from a distance. But up close, she makes it impossible for me to form a coherent thought. Shifting away again, she brings a hand to the side of her face. She doesn't want me to see she's been crying. Right when I find the courage to say something else, the door behind us bursts open and her friends descend on her in a flood of words.

"*Are you okay*?"

"*Is it true*?"

"*Jonathan's such a fucking jerk.*"

I pull back as they surround her, displaying their concerns in various degrees of back patting and hair smoothing. She keeps her head down despite their questioning, not wanting her friends to see her face.

One of the girls snaps up at me. "Why are you lurking around like a creep? Go away."

Responding would be a waste of my breath. Anyway, I'm just glad Emily isn't alone anymore. Though her friends may be an obnoxious bunch, they seem to care about her.

Going back to the crowded dance, I try to ignore the blaring music. Try to hold on to the scene replaying in my mind: her eyes on me, my jacket on her. It's an image that I wish I could print out and hang on my damn wall.

A few minutes later, Emily and her friends come back to the dance but she disappears into the bathroom again with two of the other girls following closely behind.

I'm getting a headache from the music, as I attempt to block it out and focus on just one thing.

Her.

The first time I noticed her was during the fall assembly my sophomore year. The auditorium was packed tight with students and tense with the awkwardness of a new school year. Principal Warner's voice droned on, monotone, nearly putting me to sleep. He asked the crowd a question, which, not surprisingly, was met with silence. Until Emily piped up from her seat. She was a freshman, though she didn't act like one. Her raspy voice, dripping with sarcasm, drew everyone's eyes to her.

I didn't catch what she said, but it was funny enough to bring laughter rolling up the rows of seats to reach me. Her mischievous smile was what captured my attention before the rest of her did.

From then on, it was impossible not to notice her. How her confidence was simultaneously too large for her frame and yet tailored to her body. How her personality walked before her, breaking up crowds in the hall, people parting to let her through, like they were all trained to the same subconsciously choreographed move.

I should've known it was all too exaggerated to be real.

One day after school, I was in the middle of my shift at the diner when the sound of her voice trickled through the kitchen's open door. I froze, a plate slipping from my hand and sinking into the soapy water. No one from our school ever came into the diner. It was notoriously filled with a gray-haired, stuffy crowd.

I peeked around the doorframe until she came into view, sitting on a stool in mid-conversation with my father as he wiped down the counter. I barely recognized her. This was a different Emily. Visibly bare of her bravado, like she'd pulled it off and thrown over the back of the chair. A coat she didn't need while she was telling my father she didn't want to go home, that things were getting worse for her there.

I don't know what shocked me more. Seeing her talking so candidly with my father, or seeing her look so sincere. And genuine. And vulnerable. Her eyes flitted in my direction but I ducked back into the kitchen.

The damage was done. For me, anyway. I couldn't stop thinking about her after that. It was like glimpsing into another world. A world where the most arrogant, most beautiful girl I knew revealed herself to be someone else altogether. Someone that clawed at my damn heart. Someone I was dying to talk to.

I asked my father about her, as casually as I could. He said she stopped in every morning before school. If he saw the shock on my face, he didn't let on. I was glad Emily rarely came in during my after-school shifts. Because the times she did, I couldn't stop myself from eavesdropping on their conversations.

And I hated myself for it.

Drums erupt from the speakers as the music switches abruptly, reminding me where I am. Standing still as a statue, staring at the bathroom door in hopes of catching sight of her again.

For what? It's not like I'll be able to talk to her again tonight, not when she's constantly surrounded by her snotty friends.

Time is running out for me, graduation looming around the corner. I wasted the chance I've been waiting for when I let nerves choke me up like an idiot. I've never been good with words. That's why I wrote her the letter. A letter that's burned a hole in my pocket all summer. Not that I have it with me now. I decided, almost as soon as the school year started, the letter was a bad idea. It might have the opposite effect I want. Might freak her out instead of making her realize how I feel. It's too long...too much for someone who doesn't even know I exist.

That's what it boils down to. I'm the guy pining over the girl who not only doesn't know who I am, but is in the bathroom crying over another guy altogether. To say I'm pathetic would be an understatement.

It's time to leave.

As I cut through the groups of students, the girl who called me a creep glares at me like I did something else to offend her. Ignoring the way she turns to whisper into someone's ear, I walk past, not caring what she could say about me.

The side-exit door slams shut behind me as I hurry down the steps, the chill outside pressing against my button-down shirt. I'll have to explain to my father why the suit jacket he gave me is gone, but I don't care. Emily has it draped over her gorgeous body and that alone makes anything else seem trivial in comparison.

"Hey. You!"

I turn around, seeking the source of the deep, rough voice, and see the guy running to catch up to me.

It's Jonathan. I don't know him either, but everyone knows *of* him. Varsity wrestler, giant ego that somehow still manages to seep out through the ridiculous amount of gel in his hair.

My arms hang loosely at my sides, despite the way the hairs on the back of my neck prickle awake in anticipation of conflict.

He looms over me. "You fucking talking to my girl?"

What an idiot. He embarrassed the girl, called her white trash and a whore, broke up with her, and now, he chases someone down for talking to her? Who the hell does he think he is? Does he think she's his property or something?

I'm trying to think of something snarky to say, but words fail as irritation whips away at my skin.

I hate everything about this guy. From his blatant sense of superiority to the careless way he treats the girl I'd kill to be with.

I stare him down instead, to show him I'm unafraid, although, I'm not exactly convinced of that. I might be taller than him by an inch or two, but my lean build pales in comparison to his bulky frame.

"Relax," I say. "I was just making sure she was all right."

Not waiting for him, I turn to walk away. His hand clasps my shoulder and he whips me back around.

The way he does it--with the force and disregard of someone handling a rag doll--sends a blinding rage shooting through me. I swing a clenched fist but my knuckles barely graze his cheekbone.

Releasing my shoulder, his hand moves to where my class ring left behind a small cut on his cheek.

Dammit. I shouldn't have done that.

Jonathan's fist lands more accurately than mine did. It connects with my jaw and I stumble, falling onto my hands. He flattens me against the ground with his foot, my cheek presses to the cold, wet cement. The moment the pressure of his foot leaves my back, I pull up on my hands and knees.

"I've got a message from Emily," he says.

The sound of her name makes me stop to lift my head. The sight that greets me is his large foot hurling toward my side.

Chapter One

Emily

WALKING INTO THE OFFICE, MY fingers tighten over the deli bag containing my lunch. Adam looks up from his desk at the crinkling sound of paper. His response to my sarcastic smirk is a slow blink, his face as blank as ever. I know he has no idea my smile isn't really a smile, but a warning.

We've shared an office for months and I still know nothing about him. Adam and I have trouble communicating both verbally and non-verbally, so we opt for ignoring each other most of the time.

He doesn't speak my language; sarcasm is the only way I know to weed out the robots.

I'm aware of the silent understanding we have not to eat in the office. The space is small and the smells linger. But if I don't bring this sandwich to my mouth soon, the smell of onions and ham will be the least of Adam's worries.

It's barely noon, but already my stomach is eating itself and speaking in tongues.

I'm not *me* when I'm hungry. Or worse, I *am* me when I'm hungry.

The last thing I should've done was skip breakfast. But my stomach turned at the thought of food this morning when I awoke to a notice from my landlord announcing the building had been sold.

While the new owner will honor current lease agreements, he will not grant renewals on any lease after it expires. Why? Because he's an asshole developer looking to turn the apartment building into commercial offices.

The notice may or may not have been sitting in my mailbox for a few weeks. Physical mail is something I've developed the bad habit of ignoring since I pay all my bills online. The only things I get in the mail are supermarket coupons, invoices of bills I've already paid, and random flyers. It doesn't help that my mailbox is on the other side of the parking lot. And it's been cold and raining here in San Francisco for the last two weeks.

What I have less of an excuse for is ignoring the signs on the elevator last month that announced an important tenant meeting. I dismissed it, thinking things that are really important aren't taped to elevator walls. They are shouted through loud speakers over blaring sirens while people run around panicking.

Not foreseeing a reason to worry, I procrastinated on renewing my lease, which expires in exactly eighteen days.

If that doesn't sound awful enough, I have a roommate. Another supposed grownup with whom I share responsibilities. I'm not sure how it's possible that we could collectively fail to muster the maturity it takes to check our mail or adhere to posted directions. Two simple life skills that apparently we've both failed to learn.

This morning, as we poured over the details of our impending eviction, Elle announced with thinly veiled excitement her decision to move in with her boyfriend for a while. I couldn't shake the feeling she was almost relieved by our predicament. Part of me wonders if she *did* read the notice in time, but opted to re-seal it with an iron and put it back, all to have a last minute excuse to play house with her man.

Not that it matters now. I have a little over two weeks to find a new place to live and, even more challenging, another roommate. Elle and I aren't exactly the best of friends, but we get along pretty well and have managed to avoid any sort of female drama over the past year.

A low growl rumbles in my belly as I set the deli bag down on my desk. I pull my coat off, tuck my hair behind my ears, and remember the brown roots I've been neglecting. My blonde dye is turning into an unintentional ombre look.

The door to the office swings open, forcing me to squeeze out of the way so I'm not pinned against the wall. Mona pokes her head inside. Her tense expression melts with relief when she sees me and she hurries inside, shutting the door behind her.

Nope. Whatever it is she wants from me, it needs to wait until after I eat. Walking around to my desk without looking at her is a challenge, but I manage just fine.

Mona is Bernstein's personal assistant. For Adam and me--associates, also known as bottom feeders--Mona is often the bearer of bad news in the form of tedious tasks that make me wonder if my profession is actually indebted servitude.

When I walked across the stage and received my law degree, no one called it a 'sort-of law degree.' When I passed the boards, no one said, 'You're almost there.'

No.

They said things like, 'Congratulations!' and 'You've made it!'

Made it where? To the filing room? To the coffee run? Not the way I envisioned my career panning out. From the time that I was a kid, I wanted to be able to slam my palm against a polished wood surface and yell, 'I object!'

That was the dream.

At some point, I allowed myself to be seduced by the notion of intellectual property law being the fastest growing specialty. As an IP, the only things I will ever get to jam angrily are keyboard keys. Not exactly exciting. But as a new associate, I don't even get to do this. I'm denied the simple joy of angry key jamming.

"*Emily...*" Mona says, realizing I'm ignoring her.

I'm already settled behind my desk, peeling the wrapping paper away from my sandwich. The creamy scent of mayo makes my mouth water. Almost at the same time, a pang rips through my stomach.

Oh, sandwich, come to momma. You're the light of my day and I'm going to make sweet love to you with my mouth.

"Collin Davenport's in the office," Mona blurts out.

My head snaps up and, from the corner of my eye, I see Adam look up as well. Even he isn't immune to that name.

"Is he outside the door?" I ask her, wondering what her secrecy is all about.

"No, he's in Bernstein's office."

"Okay, so why are you whispering?"

"I'm nervous!" She throws her hands up as though she can't understand how that's not obvious. "You need to go in there."

I bring the sandwich to my mouth but pause at her words.

"What--*me*? *Why*?"

Any other day, any other moment, I would be thrilled if not incredulous at the opportunity to carry out a real task. But something is off. Neither Adam nor I handle any real part of Davenport's civil suit. Bernstein seems insistent at keeping him away from the rest of the staff whenever he's in the office.

"Where's Bernstein?" I ask.

She lowers her voice to a whisper again. "Davenport wasn't supposed to come in today. His meeting was yesterday but he didn't show up. I think there was some scheduling mix-up, but I don't know how to tell him." She runs a hand through her hair and then fidgets with my stapler. "Bernstein's with the others at the promotion luncheon. I called him and he's on his way but he said to keep Davenport happy. The guy's already been waiting for ten minutes and he's super impatient."

"So you want me to stall him, until the real lawyers get back?"

She nods quickly then stops to bite her lip, realizing what she admitted. I give her a resentful look, which she returns with an innocent smile.

She gets me. I like Mona.

"Let me just finish eating this." I gesture toward my lunch.

She turns her head from me with an air of impatience. "Emily, it'll take ten minutes. Fifteen minutes, tops. Bernstein will take over as soon as he gets in. All you have to do is start going over the interrogatories that came in earlier this week. You've seen the questions."

"Sure, when I was *filing* them into the case file." I glance down, noting the onions poking out from between the two slices of sourdough bread. Damn it. I'll reek if I try to eat this right now. I swear, my damn vanity will kill me one day.

Sighing for dramatic effect, I set the sandwich down and rewrap it.

"Thank you," Mona says, the urgency fading from her voice. "He's usually really nice, but he's in such a bad mood today."

"Great, you're throwing me in with an angry puppy."

Her lips twitch before she mouths more thanks and disappears behind the door again.

Adam doesn't say a single word, even though I'm glaring at him, blaming him for the fact that I won't be able to eat for at least another fifteen minutes.

Why do *I* have to be punished for being the socially competent one?

With the stab of hunger now spreading into my veins, this is bound to be a lovely meeting, indeed.

Chapter Two

THE REVAMP OF THE *BATMAN* franchise is in production right here in San Francisco. The movie has yet to wrap filming and its star, Collin Davenport, is already garnering twice the tabloid attention he usually receives. For him, it's translated into a string of run-ins with the paparazzi. The latest of which is the reason he's in Bernstein's office oozing irritation, among other things.

Davenport gets to his feet when I enter. His companion, a blonde woman wearing a tight, black sweater dress, remains seated.

I've never met a famous person before but there isn't an ounce of awestruck giddiness in me. Maybe the growling beast in my gut ate it. While Davenport *is* nice to look at, I can't exactly eat him.

He's taller than I expected. At least six foot three, by my estimate. He wears a black peacoat over a tan sweater. His hair, which I always thought to be black, is in fact dark brown and longer than I've ever seen it, combed back in a sleek hairstyle. He's the spitting image of Bruce Wayne if I've ever seen one. The guy is as attractive as they come. Yet, I don't even picture myself sitting on his face.

"Good afternoon, Mr. Davenport."

I do my best to keep my tone even, trying to tune out my irritation, which, I try to remind myself, has little to do with his impatient demeanor.

"Hello." He's unsmiling as he shakes my outstretched hand, gaze moving past my face and toward the door behind me like he's expecting someone else to walk in.

His grip is loose over mine, barely taking the action seriously. It's not until I pull down firmly that he seems to correct himself at the last second to meet my purpose. I'm a fan of firm handshakes. None of that gentle bullshit.

His attention snaps back to me and I can tell I've caught him off guard. Good, little cock measuring contest, just for fun.

"I'm Emily Stone. I'll be going over a few things with you before Bernstein joins us."

We sit off to the left side of the room. An area designed to make meetings feel less formal. That's just code for *getting the client to tell the damn truth so we can cover our blind spots.*

He takes a seat on the couch beside his companion and I lower myself onto the armchair across from them. The blonde eyes me critically, throwing invisible daggers in my direction. I have no clue what her problem is, but I don't spend a second longer considering it.

Generally speaking, a woman who carries herself with her head high is something I admire. Just not when the reason her chin is pulled up is that she gets fucked by a more successful, famous man.

I flip through the case file. "Mr. Davenport, what I'm about to go over with you is a list of questions the opposing counsel sent for clarification--"

"Why couldn't this have been done over the phone or email?"

"It's best to do this sort of thing in person. You can...take your time to word your response. Off the record."

"And Bernstein?"

"He's running a little late and will take over once he arrives."

Davenport nods. "Let's get started then."

Truly, the meeting is a pleasure. And by pleasure I mean an experience akin to beating my face in with my own high-heeled shoe.

All I'm doing is asking simple questions that anyone could answer in their sleep. For the life of me, I can't understand why he insists on complicating the meeting.

"Where were you headed when you left the hotel and had the altercation with Mr. Qua--"

Davenport cuts me off for what has to be the tenth time in less than five minutes. "Calling him by his name somehow makes him sound like a decent human being. He's a paparazzi, a parasite."

I take a breath and repeat the question. "Where were you headed?"

"Out."

"Mr. Davenport, I need you to answer the questions thoroughly, please. Clarifying the details works in your favor."

Mona warned me he was in a bad mood. She didn't tell me he was a freaking grenade with its pin slipping off. The man's responses started off curt, quickly growing dismissive, and are now bordering on antagonistic.

Davenport seems peeved his actual attorney is not present and does not appear to take me seriously in any regard. Someone with twice the patience I possess would be worn thin by his arrogance and bravado.

Sure, I'm familiar with the expression 'the customer is always right.' And Davenport isn't the first difficult client to walk through the firm's doors. But on this particular day, all the forces have aligned to bring me over the edge.

There has to be someone up there, way up there in the control center for humans, pushing a bunch of buttons on a screen, throwing random obstacles in front of me. Waiting to see what tedious, seemingly insignificant event might be the one that makes me snap.

I'm almost there.

You hear that, Control Center? I'm almost there.

"This was blown way out of proportion." Davenport paces the office in long strides. I'm still waiting for him to answer the last question I asked regarding the presence of security outside of the hotel. But he's gone off on a tangent again. "The guy was laughing at me from the ground. He's not hurt. Bernstein should've gotten this case thrown out already. These questions are a waste of my time."

The tension in the room reaches an intolerable level.

From Davenport interrupting me every few seconds to go on and on about how annoyed and bothered he is by the whole situation, to the blonde giving me *what the fuck are you looking at* eyes.

Her presence is annoying enough, given I've already been exposed to her face plastered all over the tabloids. Davenport is known for his carousel of women, each one plucked from a mundane job, paraded around like a royal princess, dressed in expensive gowns, and walking all the red carpet events at his side. Until the day she slinks back to obscurity, replaced by a similar looking blonde.

My tongue aches from the dozens of times I've had to sink my teeth into it. A dull ache creeps in between my eyes, throbbing to the tune of the growls in my stomach. All the while, I struggle to the very inch of control to remain outwardly calm against Davenport's beam of hatred unfairly aimed in my direction. I struggle to suppress my temper, which is now pulsating in my ears, picking up speed, as Davenport interrupts me. Yet. Again.

Jesus, go choke on a dick.

The blonde gasps, as though suddenly choking on the very dick I imagined for Davenport. Cold sweeps through me as I realize my thoughts left my lips in actual, spoken words, cutting Davenport off in mid sentence. I shut my eyes in vain before opening them again to chance a look at my client.

Davenport seems stunned silent, a tightness creeping into his face, before he manages to ask, "What did you just say?"

Unchecked anger pours out of his eyes. And I--forgetting in the moment that I'm the culprit of the sudden, ice-cold hostility--set my jaw. Rage blinds me. Rage at the look on his face, an expression more infuriating than his attitude, than his tone, or even the hunger clawing at my insides. A look that says, quite simply, I should've asked his *permission* to dare speak.

Grasping around for my professionalism, I discover it's not where I last left it. In fact, it's nowhere to be found.

I clear my throat. "What I meant to say was, your lawsuit isn't going to disappear. You should really cooperate with us so we can help you. I paraphrased it the wrong way, that's all."

My tone could've been more apologetic and less hostile, but fuck him.

He half-turns away and raises his hand in my direction, as though dismissing my words. "Rebecca, let's go."

His companion rises from her seat as though his words pull on strings attached to her limbs. The sight is so bizarre and unexpected that I literally choke on my own snicker, which brings Davenport's attention back to me.

We have a stare down that lasts a few seconds, or a few hours. I can't tell which.

"You are...obscene," he says.

I swallow back the dread of how much worse I've made things for myself. First, I tell him to go choke on a dick, and then I laugh at him.

Davenport walks to the door and I'm rooted to the

spot, feeling as though the entire meeting might have been an ominous daydream and I'm actually still sitting behind my desk, contemplating whether or not to take a bite of my sandwich.

But no, it's all real. The proof is in the clunking sounds of Rebecca's heels as she rushes past to follow him out into the hall.

I've just fucked up. Big time.

Chapter Three

IF THE MEETING WITH DAVENPORT is any indication, hunger isn't just a physiological state for me. It's an actual, legitimate emotion. A mutant love child of unreasonable frustration and dangerous irritability.

There's nothing left to do now but settle back behind my desk and eat my sandwich without tasting it. As I wipe my mouth with a napkin, Mona pokes her head inside once more.

"Bernstein wants you see you. Right away," she says, her sights angled toward the carpeted floor.

"Hey?" I call out before she can rush away again. She makes eye contact with me, hesitant. "Did someone call, or something?"

Mona nods.

"Davenport?"

"No. His girlfriend."

Adam shoots me a curious sideways glance, probably wondering what the hell is going on.

As I get up from my chair, I'm acutely aware the heaviness in my stomach has nothing to do with my lunch. Hearing my boss wants an impromptu meeting is not comforting on any day, let alone on this day. Worse still, when my boss is Donald Bernstein.

In the months I've worked here, I've witnessed Bernstein only as an enigma of sorts. Tall, white-haired man, who looks the way you'd expect a wizard to look: grim and intimidating with his overly thick eyebrows and large nose. He's had very little to say to me, but the times I've heard him speak, the implication of silent mockery lay evident in his tone, though his actual words are always short, measured, and never decisively offensive. In fact, aside from clients and Snyder, his partner, Bernstein treats everyone with blatant disinterest. My impression is he underestimates those who yield less power than he does, and merely tolerates those who feed it.

As I sit before his massive desk, drumming a finger along the handle of the chair in a slow, steady beat, I try to push my swirling thoughts back. The worst thing to do is assume I know why he wants to meet with me. If I did, I'd be more likely to blurt out something that could bury me into further trouble. No. I have to keep a clear head and see where this goes.

There could be another reason Rebecca called, something completely unrelated to me. Far-fetched, but I need to hold on to that hope, however slim. Davenport's been gone all of twenty minutes. Bernstein could just be curious as to why his client isn't waiting for him.

Taking slow, deliberate breaths to calm myself, I squint in the direction of the wall-to-wall windows. The natural light assaults my eyes, but the view beyond the haze is of the harbor and Oakland Bay Bridge. A view I can stare at forever and find comfort in, most days.

But the scene fails to comfort me now. I have an odd, existential sensation of being at a crossroads in my life. I've felt this way before, as if I am standing on the cusp of something and about to topple over.

"Emily," Bernstein says, walking into the room.

He sits behind his desk, setting down the small memo pad in his hand.

"Good afternoon." My tone is clipped. I don't mean it to be, it just is.

I've never been good with authority, especially authority wielded by a man, as it often is. For some reason, it makes me resentful and defensive. I'm no shrink, but I'm sure my aversion has something to do with suppressed daddy issues.

There's already an air of impatience clinging to Bernstein as he speaks. "I understand you met with Davenport earlier?"

I nod. The whole meeting lasted maybe eight minutes, the longest eight minutes of my life.

Bernstein tilts his head forward, watching me closely, his fingertips touching. "Is there anything you want to tell me about the meeting?"

Just by his tone, it's obvious that Rebecca called to report me. My heartbeat should pick up. My hands should grow damp. Nerves should tie my gut in knots. But all I feel is numb as though the real me is floating overhead, watching all of this play out like a movie.

My boss asks me to recount the meeting to the best of my memory. I do so but I'm careful, of course, to leave out my parting words.

When I finish, his tone grows sweetly patronizing.

"Emily, I'm just going to come out and say it. I've been informed you hurled a crude comment at our client. Do you recall what that was?"

I shake my head but touch a hand to the base of my neck. I'd lie through my teeth if I could get them to unclench.

Bernstein glances down to the notepad in front of him and hesitates. "Our clients can be difficult, at times." He sounds simultaneously bored and disdainful, as though he's explaining something to a small child that requires him to reel in his patience. "We have to remain understanding that each of them is going through stressful times in their lives, or they wouldn't need our help. Davenport is headstrong, sure, but I've never known him to be hostile. I can't imagine what would compel you to say...this..." He looks down at the paper again and all I can think about is that the words 'choke on a dick' are scribbled there in Bernstein's handwriting. And he keeps glancing down at them.

It occurs to me that Bernstein, for all of his biting attitude, has never uttered a single word of profanity around the office. I wonder if he's one of those people that never curse at all. The man is old enough to be my grandfather, but carries himself with the pretentious swagger of an aristocrat, someone far superior to the average person, far too good to degrade himself by uttering nonsense.

Go choke on a dick.

I wonder, idly, if the phrase is circled. Or maybe underlined, for emphasis. Are there asterisks in place of the last three letters of the word 'dick'? Did Bernstein keep a careful hand over the note, as he walked to his office, worried someone might glimpse it?

Just like that, the numbness falls away to a rumbling, building inside of me. I keep it back, but just barely, and it tickles at the base of my throat.

I know what the rumble is. It's an insane, destructive, ill-timed laugh threatening to erupt.

I cough, trying to stifle the urge, realizing there is something deeply wrong with my reaction. A beat of silence follows in which it completely escapes me that I may be expected to speak. I'm too busy pressing my tongue to the roof of my mouth and trying to pull some horrific image into my mind's eye.

Something sobering or serious. Though obviously, the man sitting in front of me should be serious enough. This man is my boss. Everyone in the office walks on eggshells to please him. But right now? He's anything but daunting. He's a prude old man, trying to find a way to avoid repeating the vulgar words before him.

"Please tell me, Emily. Did you really say this? This...I mean--" He cuts off to readjust his glasses. I've never known Bernstein to look so uncomfortable. "Emily, do you want me to say it *out loud*?"

Oh, please say it.

"No. No. *Don't* say it." I hide my face in my hands, throat trembling with the pressure of holding back the laughter.

What is wrong with me? My boss is having a serious conversation about my misconduct and I am desperately fighting the urge to burst out into hysterical laughter.

I'm wondering if the sham is up, if this is the day everyone will realize I'm faking the whole *being an adult* thing. Wondering if it's possible to wield a get-out-of-jail-free card in exchange for a day of immature mistakes. And then be allowed to resume my adult life the next day. A do-over.

I need a do-over.

"Emily?" Bernstein's voice is impatient. "Emily, there's no point in crying."

He thinks I'm *crying*.

Oh. My. God...

My shoulders start shaking. I lower my covered face to my knees, in an attempt to compose myself. I try to breathe. To breathe instead of laugh, but I'm about to burst at the seams. I take in sharp breaths and hold them in for a few seconds at a time.

Don't laugh.

Don't laugh.

Don't laugh.

The more I tell myself not to laugh, the more the urge to do so builds. A snort escapes my nose and I inhale quickly to cover it.

"Oh, for God's sake. This is ridiculous. Just tell me whether or not you told Davenport to go '*choke on a dick*'?"

The dam bursts. *I'm* choking. Not on a dick, obviously, but on the sound of my laughter, gasping for air, trying to recover, but finding no sanity to hold on to.

I've lost my fucking mind.

"Are you--" Bernstein's chair creaks as he gets up.

"Are you *laughing*?"

"No...no," I say between gasps. Mustering a somewhat serious expression, I finally look up, wiping tears away from my face, only to be betrayed by the laughter that just won't end.

And that's when I get fired.

Chapter Four

THERE ARE A FEW THINGS I expected from the experience of being fired. For one, I thought I'd make the walk of shame clutching a box full of my belongings. Like in the movies. But as I reach my desk, with Bernstein hovering over me, I realize I have nothing to put in said box. I've never been one to keep personal items at work. There are no picture frames on my desk or motivational posters brightening the walls. Just my degree, hanging on the wall, inside of a frame that belongs to the firm. I pull out the diploma, stick it in a manila folder, and slide it into my purse.

Second, I expected to have a few minutes to clear my internet browsing history. At the very least, I envisioned myself being fired in a more dramatic way, going out in a blaze of glory, telling everyone to go fuck themselves. But I've got nothing to say as I pull my purse strap across my chest and follow Bernstein's outstretched hand gesturing toward the door.

Outside, the cold air flows over my face, stinging my skin. I tilt my head down and pick up my pace, walking past my car. I see it, but somehow barely register it. Some days I take the trolley to work and this morning, my body operates on autopilot, moving down the sidewalk without my brain having to consciously direct it. But instead of stopping to wait for the trolley, I cross over the rails and wait for the all clear to cross Embarcado Road.

The traffic light turns red and the cars halt on the other side of the crosswalk. The people in them watch me as I pass and I know what I must look like to them. Another business prick in a suit, walking with purpose. I'm sure they see me and think, *that lady looks legit. She has it together.*

When I was a teenager, I would look at people in their twenties and think they had everything figured out. Then I got to my twenties and realized it's an illusion. It's people in their thirties that are the *real* grownups; they're the ones that have their shit in line.

I turned twenty-seven in August, so I'm close enough to thirty now to know that's bullshit, too. I keep hearing that people grow up. I've just yet to meet a single, real life grownup under the age of fifty.

The light turns green and the cars whip past me before I even clear the sidewalk.

Sons of bitches.

I'm nearly at the Ferry Building when I stop in the middle of the sidewalk. The tall, white clock tower looms overhead and sounds of traffic rush to my ears louder than before, prompting me to look around. I'm disoriented by how far I've walked without direction.

"Got some change?" a deep voice asks.

A homeless woman sits on a bench a few feet away, facing the street. She's holding a piece of cardboard with a handwritten word in black marker. *Hungry.*

She's a middle-aged, thickset woman with deep eyes and blotchy skin. Dirt, or maybe soot, stains her dark-washed jeans, frayed at the edges and torn in places. Her puffy gray coat reminds me of that material people use to stuff packages with.

A car horn blares in the distance and, in a flash, I see my own face on the homeless woman's body. Her sign now reads, *Obscene.*

The vision is gone in a blink, and I'm left still standing in the middle of the sidewalk. The woman stares at me, her thin brows pulled tight over her eyes as if she finds me suspicious. Before I know what I'm doing, I've made my way over to sit down beside her.

I don't look at her and instead stare out at the road, at the cars and--through the gaps in between--at the trolley coming to a stop across the road.

Beside me, the woman clutches the worn backpack on her lap, like she thinks I'm going to yank it from her and run.

Her voice is hoarse when she speaks. "What are you doing?"

I'm guessing not very many people approach her, but sitting beside her feels like the most natural place for me today.

"I'm so fucked."

I hear myself say the words, but even then, I'm not sure if the sound is coming from inside or outside of my head.

She throws her head back and laughs, a deep throaty laugh. "What's the matter, little girl?"

Well, she *did* ask...

"I'm losing my apartment because I couldn't be bothered to check my stupid mail. Wouldn't be so bad except I got myself fired so I can't exactly take on rent until I--"

"Got any change?" the woman calls out to someone else walking past. It's a lady pushing a baby stroller and she shoots me a quick, sideways look.

"...until I can find another job," I finish.

My bench-mate looks down her nose at me, a clear sign that my problems don't impress her.

"Listen, little girl, you need to get the fuck off my bench. You're scaring away my money."

"Seriously?" I start laughing, so forcefully that I'm nearly choking on it.

This is how I lost my job. Saying the wrong things. Laughing at the wrong times.

The woman eyes me, half smiling, half grimacing, like she smells something nasty or perhaps senses I'm bat-shit crazy.

"I'm not kidding," she says. "You need to get the fuck off my bench."

"Fine." I get up and smooth out my pants, though obviously I've got nowhere important to go and it doesn't matter if my clothes are wrinkled. "You're fucking rude--" Another car horn blares and I bite back the urge to argue with her, realizing she's not the source of my frustration.

Here I am standing beside a woman who's clutching everything she owns on her lap and I'm complaining to her? This has to be the lowest I've sunk today.

Maybe ever.

And yet, standing in front of her makes me realize some key things. I'm not homeless. I'm not broke. I still have so much. I have my degree. My health. I've got a car. A really nice fucking car that can take me away to my safety net. My sister. I'm privileged to have fallen and not hit rock bottom.

"Thanks for the pep talk," I say. I mean it. She's pulled me out of my pity fest, flooded me with a sense of gratitude for everything I still have.

"Got any change?" the woman blurts out just as I turn to walk away.

I pull out a fifty-dollar bill, two twenties, and four ones from my wallet. It's all I have on me at the moment. "Do you have change for a fifty?"

A redheaded woman marching past shoots me a disapproving look, not realizing I'm kidding. I wave away her concern, saying, "It's okay, we're friends."

Red increases her pace without looking back. I don't blame her. Folding the bills in half, I hand them to the homeless woman, whose jaw drops.

"Damn, girl. Thanks," she says, counting the cash with a huge grin on her face. "Hope you get your shit together real soon."

Yeah, me too.

Chapter Five

THE SCENT OF NEW LEATHER and polished wood paneling fills my lungs. This car smells like luxury and drives like it too. It's last year's BMW 4-Series, black with tan interior, and it drives the way cutting through butter feels. This baby melts under me, responds to the smallest of movements, and has enough buttons and blinking lights to set up a mission to space. And I have no idea how much longer I'll be able to afford it, the only luxury in my otherwise student-loan-fueled austerity.

Frowning in this car is something I never thought possible. But that's exactly what I'm doing. I'm frowning as I drive over the Oakland Bridge and leave San Francisco, altogether. I have a long ride ahead of me. It's only...12:45p.m. *Seriously*? The longest day of my life was over before noon? This is just...I mean, it's fucking poetic.

Digging my phone out of my purse, I call my sister but it goes straight to voicemail. Her curt and professional tone fills my car.

"You've reached Alexis Stone, please leave a message."

Hearing my sister's voice is like having solid ground

to stand on again. Her exaggerated seriousness always, by default, brings out my playfulness.

"Hey, sexy *lady*," I singsong, "I'm coming to see you. Hope you're not in the middle of fucking because that'll be awkward and I left my eyeball pliers at home. Call me."

I hang up and feel a smile tug my lips when I picture my sister cringing when she hears my message. Lex has always been a bit uptight and I honestly have no idea who she modeled herself after.

Our mother is as tasteless as she is classless. Never the type to hold her tongue around us or think twice about what wouldn't be appropriate to discuss around her children.

Seven hours later, I find my sister under the shriveled up, lumpy blanket on her bed. A pair of feet sticking out from underneath, toes pointed toward the mattress.

I'm relieved and annoyed. Relieved because I grew worried when she didn't answer the door. Annoyed because I had to dig around the bottom of my purse to find her spare key, and then walk hesitantly into her condo, not having any idea what to expect in the darkness.

Whatever is going on with Lex manifests into an almost tangible presence in the room. It crowds my own worries into a corner. Because while me having issues is nothing new, Lex isn't often the one in need of comforting.

We sit in the dining room. My sister twirls her fork around in the pasta I made for her, despite her insistence that she wasn't hungry. She looks more like a cavewoman than the beautiful brunette I know she can be when she brushes her hair.

"I'm just worn down," she says. "Work and stuff."

I don't have to guess what the 'stuff' is. The stuff is *Leo*. It's obvious my sister's state of disarray has something to do with him. I met the guy last time I was down here. He's one fine piece of ass. Sharp blue eyes, short blond hair, and clothes that fit tight in all the right places.

I don't blame her for wanting to jump his bones. I just wish she'd been smarter about it.

He and I didn't exactly get off on the right foot. There was something about him that instantly rubbed me the wrong way. Now I wish I'd been more vocal about my opinion of him. It might have saved my sister the trouble of finding out for herself.

From what she tells me, it sounds like Lex assumed she had a stronger handle on the affair than she actually did. In the end, she got burned.

That's how these things tend to end; there really isn't another way. Trying to keep a man in a relationship is like trying to keep a lion as a pet. You know they are inherently wild beasts, dangerous even. But when they come up and sniff your face, you start to think they're just misunderstood. They make you feel good about being able to tame them, feed them, learn their moods. Except they're never *really* tame. They're waiting for the moment when you leave the gate unlocked so they can eat you and run out to terrorize the neighborhood. It happens all the time. Okay--maybe not *all* the time. But it *does* happen.

Whenever I see something like that on the news, I think to myself, *Idiot, you don't keep lions as pets*. And I think the same thing whenever a woman whines about getting her heart broken.

Idiot, you don't keep men as pets.

"I promise I'm fine." She runs a hand through her hair. I expect it to get stuck, or maybe for her crazy hair to eat her hand, but neither happens. "I need a few days to--"

"Mope around?"

"I'm not moping around," she snaps, defensive.

"If you say so."

She dives into her food and it seems to be so she doesn't have to respond. When my sister starts speaking again, it's to ask me why I was fired. I tell her about the meeting with Davenport. About the demon giggles that possessed me at just the wrong time.

"God, did they have to fire you this time of year?"

I almost laugh. My sister has a parental blind spot when it comes to me, extracting from my story only what was done to me and not everything I did to deserve it.

But she does have a point. It's nearly Christmas, a shitty time of the year to be out of a job. I don't mention the part about my lease expiring, not seeing the point in bringing it up tonight.

"Yeah, well. It's done," I announce, with as much maturity as I can muster. I'm on my feet, walking back to the kitchen before I have a good reason to. "And now...I need a drink. What do you have?"

Ignoring the assortment of wine bottles on her counter, I go to her fridge and see, to my surprise, a six-pack of beer in there with four bottles left. Lex doesn't drink beer. I grab one and make a mental note not to ask if these are remnants of Leo's presence.

Lex goes off to sleep and I stay on the couch watching television. After draining the second beer too soon, I'm left wanting something stronger. I've had a long day and would love something to help ease me into a dreamless sleep.

With reluctance at the limited choices, I sort through the wine bottles on the counter. These are the ones Lex doesn't care much for. The stuff she actually drinks awaits in her small wine cooler. I don't care for wine. Lex loves the stuff because anything stronger knocks her on her ass. Of us two, I've always been able to hold my liquor better. I'm not sure if that's something to be proud of, but there it is.

My fingers trace the curved labels absentmindedly until, pushing aside a large bottle of red wine, I find a frosted bottle full of crystal clear liquid. It's the vodka I bought for Thanksgiving dinner a few weeks ago, but never got around to opening it. What a sight for sore eyes.

Hello, gorgeous.

I know we just met, but I need you to help me not feel feelings anymore.

I pour myself a shot and down it in a gulp. Rummaging through the refrigerator, I search for something to mix with a second shot. Lex doesn't drink soda. However, she has an almost completely full bottle of ginger ale. I don't want to know how long it's been there. Probably from a time she was sick and needed to soothe her stomach.

Left with no viable alternatives, I pour myself a glass of straight vodka and sip on it slowly while letting my brain numb to the nonsense playing on the screen.

The next thing I know, it's after midnight and I'm jarred awake by an unnecessarily loud commercial blaring from the television. I shut it off and slink into the guest room. My thoughts hazy, I slip slowly out of consciousness, desperate to ignore the dread of dealing with my predicament in the light of day.

Lex stands in the kitchen, securing the lid on her coffee thermos. When she notices me in the doorway, I make a show of pretending to stumble backward in surprise.

Her electric-blue button down is tucked into a black pencil skirt, showing off her legs, lean and smooth. The outfit is amped up by sleek black heels, and her golden brown hair is pinned up into a bun, not a strand out of place. I've never seen Lex wear this much makeup before. The skin on her face is velvety smooth, her lips a deep red color, her eyes lined with a rich black that brings out the piercing color of her green eyes.

"Holy shit. You clean up nicely."

"Can't let them see you sweat." She takes a sip of her coffee. "You're up early."

"Hard to sleep in on a day I should be at work."

She takes in my appearance. "I see you found the

stuff you left here."

"Yeah, well, it's not much. A pair of jeans and the workout stuff I wear when you force me to go running with you." I tug at the baggy t-shirt I've paired with some running shorts.

"Feel free to go through my closet, grab whatever you want."

I nod. It's what I intend to do, but looking at Lex now, I'm reminded her runner's frame is a jean size or two smaller than I am. Finding something in her closet that fits me might prove challenging.

Lex grabs her phone and starts looking through it, checking her emails. In an offhand sort of way, she asks me what my plan is for the day. The question rubs me the wrong way. Because I know my sister and what she's really asking is, *What's your plan? What are you going to do to fix your jobless state? Do you have a list of contacts you can call? Do you need help with your resume? Do you even have a resume? Do you even have a plan?*

I don't answer her right away, opting instead to walk over to the refrigerator and grab a bottle of water. There's a dull throb between my eyes, the result of my drinking last night. My plan, I tell her, is to update my resume and start my job-hunting as soon as possible.

"Emily. Don't take this the wrong way, I love that you're here. I seriously do. But wouldn't it be easier to job hunt from San Francisco?"

I had the same thought first thing this morning. "Either way, I'd be back down here for Christmas. A week of online job hunting isn't going to hurt me.

Especially since, you know, no one is gearing up for interviews this time of year."

"I guess you're right," she says, eyeing me the way she does when she knows I'm not telling her the whole truth. "Take my laptop. Use anything you need. Let me know if you need help."

She grabs her keys and purse, and heads out the door.

The whole truth is that I wasn't thinking straight when I got in my car and drove south. I was simply putting as much distance as I could between my problems and me. Now that I'm here? Well, there's no point in making another seven-hour drive north when I can rough it here long enough to spend the holidays with my sister.

After several minutes of rummaging through Lex's closet, I pull out some day dresses that look like they will fit me. I dress for the day, thankful Lex and I wear the same shoe size, at least. Even in mid-December, the weather in San Diego is pleasant during the day, nothing like the biting chill of San Francisco's winter.

Back at the dining room table, I sift through old emails, pulling up contacts that might prove useful. A television morning news program hums in the background, on for the sole purpose of drowning out the stillness of the condo.

Am I imagining it, or is the silence here thicker than in my own apartment? It's so dense the hum of the television can't cut through it. Somehow, I can still *hear* the silence. The muted static of dead air.

It's hard to focus. The slightest fluctuations in sound

yank on my attention. A bird ruffling past outside the window, or a car door closing out front. All followed by that same, intense silence. It's deafening.

I stuff the laptop into a shoulder bag and, before I leave, I grab my jacket from where it hangs behind the door.

The moment I step outside, the air rushes to my lungs as though I've been slowly suffocating without realizing it. Smells of cut grass linger in the crisp air. There are lawn workers out, trimming hedges, and they tilt their big sun hats in my direction. I manage a small smile as I pass them, feeling a stupid, guilty throb that I'm not heading to work. That I am heading to the slick, black BMW I won't be able to afford for much longer.

For the first time, the thought of my car turns my stomach. I decide to walk instead. The closest commercial center isn't far, maybe a mile away at most.

Lex's condo is in a community built around a golf course, tucking the structures away from the surrounding areas of Carlsbad, and giving her and her neighbors a view filled with trees and rich-green, sloping lawns.

Carlsbad is as far north as I'd ever like to live in San Diego county. It's a chill beach town just a thirty-five minute shot down the I-5 from downtown San Diego.

I was in town last month, but this visit feels different. As I walk, the laptop bag strapped to my back like a school bag, I'm transported back to the mornings I'd walk to school, though from a completely different neighborhood.

The cars swoop past on the street beside me. A

woman gets on a bus, tugging at the hand of her small child. Everything around me feels oddly nostalgic. As if my past is right behind an invisible veil I could accidentally walk through at any moment and find myself face-to-face with the person I used to be.

Or, worse, the people I used to hurt.

Chapter Six

THE BELL OVER THE DOOR chimes as I enter the diner. I'm soothed by the familiar surroundings. It's been years since I've been in here. Ever since I moved up north for school, I haven't made the time to drop by whenever I visited Lex.

How could I have forsaken this small haven? It's quaint and homey, smells of pancake syrup and bacon, and instantly puts me at ease.

I pass the section of squared tables. A handful of people sit among them, engaged in light conversation. One or two glance in my direction.

The man behind the counter isn't the person I expect to see. I expect to see the owner, Lucas. But the man in his place is a much-younger, handsome version of Lucas.

I see attractive men all the time, but I can't remember ever once doing an actual double take. My subconscious craves an instant, closer examination. When my sights swing back, his eyes meet mine, and our gazes lock with an almost audible click.

Well, hello...

He's in his late twenties, with dark hair, long enough to finger comb into its easy, disheveled state. He wears a long sleeved, dark gray thermal shirt. A casual style that somehow serves to exaggerate the broadness of his shoulders and muscular build of his arms. His features are a shade too intimidating to be considered handsome. Never mind the beard growing in, whether it's a few days old or purposely buzzed short.

Rough around the edges. Just how I like them.

I'm convinced this man's presence is a roughly packaged gift from the universe.

Sorry you had such a shitty day yesterday. Here's some eye candy for your viewing pleasure. Enjoy a tingling in your groin with your breakfast.

You're welcome.

I settle for a seat at the counter. There's a kid on the stool beside me, a dark blue backpack strapped to his back. One hand cradles his face, elbow resting on the counter. With his other hand, he lazily scoops scrambled eggs in his fork and flings them into his mouth.

He looks at me from the corners of his eyes as I pull the laptop open over the counter. I can tell by the way his head shifts in my direction. But he doesn't say anything and neither do I.

A minute later, the dark-haired man stands before me on the other side of the counter, pulling back a sheet of the small note pad in his hand, pen at the ready.

"Morning, what can I--" His voice, which is as gravelly as I'd expect it to be, cuts off abruptly when I look up from the menu to meet his strange, fleeting expression. His head turns a fraction.

No. That can't be recognition dawning on him. I'm

sure his features are only vaguely familiar because he's obviously related to Lucas. I'm sure I've never met this man before. How would I forget a face like that?

"Do I know you?" I ask, setting the menu down.

"I'm Owen. Lucas' son."

He says it like it should ring a bell, but it doesn't. I didn't even know Lucas had a son. I mean, I assumed he had kids, but he never mentioned them, if my memory serves right.

I sit up because this Owen guy is watching me so closely it'd make anyone self-conscious, eyes darting across my face like gears clicking memories into place. When his sights fall on my blonde waves, his eyes narrow ever so slightly, as though encountering an impostor to their memory.

I can almost see what he sees in their place. Golden brown hair pulled back behind my ears. A pale face and pink cheeks. Big green eyes.

Holy shit. He really does recognize me from somewhere.

"I'm Emily," I say. We've yet to break eye contact but neither one of us seems to mind. "I used to come in here all the time but I don't remember you. Which I find strange because--" I lean further in so our faces are maybe a foot apart "--well, you're sort of ridiculously good looking."

"That's interesting." He straightens up, creating extra space between us. "I remember you."

There's no mistaking the impassiveness of his expression. The notes of resentment in his tone, though subtle, are like the early, seemingly harmless winds of a storm that's not too far behind.

I want to know where it's all coming from.

"You worked here when you were younger?" I ask, not knowing if this is the case, but compelled to break the stiffness between us.

"After school and in the summertime. I washed dishes. Sometimes filled in waiting tables." He looks at the tables behind me. "Business was better back then."

Makes sense now, I wouldn't remember him if he worked here after school. I'd come in early mornings, rarely ever after school. Yet, as soon as he says it, my eyes are drawn toward the doorway behind him. A memory loosens and flashes before my eyes. A tall, thin, dark-haired boy clad in a white apron, darting back into the kitchen when he saw me noticing him. It's a hazy memory, blurred at the edges. I'm not sure if I'm making the whole vision up.

Memories aren't the reliable archive of the past people assume they are. Memories can be altered by biases and new information. It's why eyewitness testimony is notoriously unreliable.

"What will it be today?" he asks again, telling me in not so many words he's not here to make small talk with me.

I order and watch him walk off without another word.

The kid sitting beside me lets out a short sigh and I remember he's there. He looks miserable. So much so, in fact, that I want to laugh aloud. What the hell does a kid his age even know about being miserable?

"Are the eggs not good?"

The kid looks at me. "Huh?"

"Just wanted to know if the eggs are making you miserable. So I know to stay away from them."

"It's not the eggs."

Watching him, a few details come to me at once. He can't be older than thirteen, middle school age. And he seems to be alone.

"Shouldn't you be in school?" I ask, glancing at my watch.

He sets down the fork and sits up. "Shouldn't you be at work?"

My hands are over the keyboard of my laptop, resting there. I tap a finger over one of the keys without pressing it. "Maybe I am working."

"Are you?"

I can't help but laugh. "Fine, you got me. I'm not working."

"You're from out of town, aren't you?"

"Yeah, I guess I'm technically from out of town. How can you tell?"

"It's always the same people here. Usually super old people this early in the morning."

"It's always been like that here. A good place to hide from the school crowd."

He watches me with a little more interest. "And how do you know that?"

"I went to the high school up the street. I used to come in here all the time, actually."

"Oh," he says with blatant disinterest, "that's cool."

There's something familiar about this kid, something tugging at a memory. Or maybe he reminds me of myself at that age. That thought alone is enough to give me the impression he is up to no good.

Though the logical assumption is that he's headed to school, the backpack strapped to his back makes me wonder if he's a runaway. I know I shouldn't ask him too many questions. A kid his age has been conditioned not to trust strangers. Still, I can't help it.

"Are you here with your parents?"

"No. My parents are dead."

Well, things just got awkward.

I turn to face my laptop screen, unsure what to say to that. The way he said it, the solemn tone, his downcast eyes--I somehow, instinctively, know he's telling the truth.

"I'm sorry," I say. "That sucks."

"Yeah, it does." The kid wipes his mouth with a napkin and stands up. Without looking at me, he closes a hand around his glass of orange juice and shoots back the remainder of it as though it were something much stronger.

Maybe it's because of what I learned about his parents, but his body language and mannerisms seem mature. He digs into his pocket, pulls out a ten-dollar bill, and slaps it on the counter.

"Hey, Owen," he calls out with an exaggerated casualness that wasn't there a moment before. Owen looks up at the sound of his name and his face falls slightly in a tired way. The kid's tone twists into blatant sarcasm. "Thanks for breakfast."

The bell over the door chimes and cool air rushes inside as the kid heads out onto the street. I hope he really is headed to school.

Owen places a cup of coffee in front of me, along with my food. He reaches for the ten-dollar bill and stuffs it in his pocket. I find it strange that he pockets the kid's money, but he doesn't even seem embarrassed or secretive about it so I'm left to assume this must be normal.

Rolling up the sleeves of his thermal shirt, he reaches for the dishes the kid left behind. Plates clink as he gathers them and his gaze lifts to meet mine.

I expect a smile. A fake, customer-service smile.

He doesn't smile. But he *does* look at me for a few seconds too long, curiosity in his eyes, as though noticing something about me he didn't before. He catches himself and switches his focus to wiping down the space beside me.

Owen moves around behind the counter, carrying the plates, and I can't help but notice there's something exaggerated about his posture. The type of intensity you wouldn't expect from a man working in a diner, but from someone about to draw a gun. And that's exactly the energy he emits, a treacherous one. Rocky cliffs and pounding shores. The type of landscape you wouldn't trek if you were cautious.

I'm a lot of things, but cautious isn't one of them.

I'm not the slightest bit subtle about the way I gape at him as I sip my coffee. It's been a while since I laid eyes on a man I could consume with my eyes and he looks far more appetizing than my food. The type of man you can't look at without imagining yourself doing things to him. Or better still, imagining him doing things to you.

He doesn't notice, or pretends not to. It's not until he takes the stack of dishes and disappears through the doorway that leads into the back that I'm finally able to fully take in my surroundings.

Some things are different.

The menu, hanging on the wall, for instance. It looks crisp--not the old worn lettering I've looked up at since I was a teenager. The tops of the stools are also new leather. Not fringed at the edges with small tears in them, the way I remember.

A dark worry creeps across my chest. It occurs to me that maybe Lucas is gone for good. That's how it happens. You get used to people, they become a staple, and you sort of forget that they're growing older. You don't notice the lines growing on their faces or their hair slowly peppering away into white. It happens slowly and then one day they're gone, washed away by time. The spot where they once stood scraped clean and taken up by a newer, younger person. Change is the only real constant in life.

Owen reappears only a moment later and I slide off my stool to meet him. "Where'd you say Lucas is?"

"I didn't say."

Is that supposed to be the end of the discussion? He seems to think so, moving along the counter, arranging the condiments sitting in front of each stool. I follow, walking parallel to him, the cold slate of granite separating us.

"Is it a secret?" I ask, my gaze flicking upward. His blasé responses will grate away at my patience pretty quick.

He stops and looks at me. "He's in the hospital. Scripps Mercy."

"What happened? Is he sick?"

Closing each of his hands over the edge of the counter in front of him, Owen leans into the space between us as though to make sure we aren't overheard. My eyes are drawn to the outline of his muscular arms beneath his shirtsleeves. "He had a massive heart attack a few days ago. Still recovering, but doctors say he'll be fine."

"I'm sorry to hear that. I'm really fond of him. He's a good man."

"Sure he is," Owen says, too quickly. I get the sense of an implied, 'what the hell would you know?' And he walks away once again without the slightest warning.

I'm well aware of the discernible sting of rejection as I'm left standing there, my mouth parted in anticipation of what I was going to say next.

I get the urge to laugh, but not out of humor. How has this place not gone out of business with him behind the counter?

Sliding back onto my seat, I bring my attention where it should be. The laptop screen. My resume. My job hunting research.

I decide I've had enough of Owen's antisocial demeanor. Because fuck this guy. He's not eye candy delivered by the universe. He's a dark cloud shading my safe haven, stripping it of all the things I expected when I walked through the doors.

A part of me had hoped this little haven of mine

remained untouched and sacred, even while so much in my life was uncertain.

What used to be a symbol of normalcy to me, a place I could escape to, is now just another thing that isn't what it used to be.

Chapter Seven

THE SOUNDS AROUND ME ARE comforting: light chatter, silverware clinking, soft ambient noises. Nothing that should distract me. Yet my attention is divided, half on the embellished list of phrases on the screen before me and half on something else in my immediate surroundings.

When Owen comes to collect my empty plate, I finally admit to myself what the real distraction is. It's him. I'm aware of him even when I'm trying not to be. I know when he is closer to my end of the counter or further down. I sense when he passes by me to bring people their orders or when he's behind the register ringing someone up.

And now, I'm trying to *not* be aware that he is somewhere behind me. I'm trying so hard that his voice jars me when, out of nowhere, he says, "It's too long."

I turn in time to see him reach over, finger landing on the laptop screen and tapping on the spot right over the bottom of the file, which reads, *Page 1 of 3*.

"Your resume," he says. "It's too long."

"Do you mind?" I yank the screen down, stopping short of slamming it closed. I can't believe his nerve. It doesn't help that my glare meets the back of his head as he's already walking away and around to the other side of the counter.

But I guess he's not done with me because he turns to add, "No one has time to read a resume that long."

The short laugh I let out is as humorless as the fake smile that accompanies it by default. "Okay, *what* is your problem?"

"My problem?" He's across from me again. This time behind the drink machine. The way his hazel eyes scan my face, with a sliver of amusement, reveals he knows exactly what I'm talking about.

"The massive stick you have lodged up your ass." I make a general gesture in his direction. "Ring a bell?"

He folds his arms over the counter and tilts his head the way a person does when they genuinely don't understand a question.

"*Oh, come on.* Your customer service skills? They suck."

"Do they?" he asks, straightening up again to fill two glasses with soda. "I don't consider them skills, really."

He heads off to bring the drinks to a nearby table. I watch carefully. The customers don't appear put-off with his indifferent mannerisms. They give him a smile and mumble what I think is 'thanks,' though I can't hear it.

Owen doesn't look at me when he returns to his spot. Even though I'm sure he knows that I'm watching him through narrowed eyes.

"You know," I say, "I thought you were being an asshole by mistake, but maybe it's entirely on purpose."

His head hangs down, eyes on the glass he's drying

with a towel. "I don't do anything by mistake."

A beat.

I don't have a comeback and am breathing a little harder than I was a few seconds ago. To say I'm annoyed is an understatement. The universe is fucking with me, subjecting me to psychological warfare. It wants me to become a ridiculous news story that goes viral on social media: *Female Attorney Beats in Man's Head with Resume Bearing Laptop at Local Diner.*

I get up and pay my bill without saying another word. Owen runs my card through the machine and I'm not even sure if he looks at me because my gaze burns a hole into the back of the cash register. The all too recent memory of the last time a man got under my skin weaves, tauntingly, like a bobble head in the forefront of my mind. That situation didn't end well, and I've reached my quota for how many assholes I can handle without setting the feminist movement back a few notches with a PMS-cidal rampage.

Crossing through the front door, I glance back without reason and find Owen's sights darting up from behind me.

You've got to be kidding me. This motherfucker was staring at my ass.

Distracted, I nearly trip over the door's threshold. I quickly recover, but not soon enough to soothe my ego, which gives me a subsequent kick in the throat. Great. There goes my graceful exit. I wish I would've fallen all the way and cracked my face on the pavement. At least then he couldn't have considered it funny. I grip the laptop bag's strap closer to my chest and continue walking, the morning air distinctly cool against my unusually warm face.

Chapter Eight

ONE SECOND I'M SLEEPING, THE next I'm bolting upright and panicked by the brightness of the room.

I didn't turn on my alarm and now I'm late.

Straightening up, I push away the gray bedcover from my body. Wait. I don't own a gray comforter. This depressing color is my sister's version of sophistication. I'm in Lex's guest room. And I'm not late because I don't have anywhere to be.

Stomach tightening, I fall back onto the bed and stare at the crack in Lex's ceiling. And as I lie there, the panic that jarred me awake looms. I can't seem to shake it.

When I finally head into the living room, Lex is near the front door, slipping on her heels and getting ready to leave for work.

"*Morning,*" Lex says, with almost sarcastic enthusiasm. I know she's mocking my appearance--which, though I can't see, I imagine resembles that of a creature emerging from a moat.

Dragging my feet on the ground for dramatic effect, I slink over to the refrigerator, grab a bottle of water, and proceed to chug it down, noisily, while the refrigerated air soothes my bare legs.

Lex reaches past me to grab the empty carton of beer on the second shelf. "We should probably throw this out. I don't think they magically re-stock."

I let out half a chortle into my water bottle.

Buttoning her jacket, she adds, almost as an afterthought, "How's the job search going?"

"It's going," I say, straightening up. When she fixes me with her hallmark, probing eye, I say, "Updated my resume and put in a few applications yesterday. Should make more leeway today."

Lex leans back against the edge of the counter, considering me for a moment. She starts to say something, then stops. Then starts again. "Do you need money?"

"I've got savings."

Her expression tells me she's battling the urge to ask me how much. I wouldn't mind telling her, but I know she wouldn't be asking to make small talk. She'd ask because she wants to do the math in her head, she wants to lay out a plan for me of how long I can live on my savings.

My sister's resisting the urge to offer to solve my problems because she doesn't know how badly I want her to, how much I can't bring myself to ask. But our relationship has gotten so much better since she stopped treating me like a problem that needs fixing.

Lex and I haven't always gotten along. Over the last few years, though, we've managed to build a friendship of sorts, the type of relationship I imagine sisters ought to have. Because before that, Lex wasn't my sister. She was a parent to me. The only parent I've ever had. It took moving to another city for me to convince her I'm not a little girl anymore. I'm still not sure she believes it.

Before leaving, Lex tells me, not for the first time, that she's here if I need anything. She means money. My sister is pretty well off in that sense, her business doing better than ever. But I couldn't take a cent from her. I already feel indebted to her for paying for everything when we were younger.

Anyway, what I said is true. I did manage to set some money aside. My bills are paid for this month, but my savings can only afford to cover me for another two more months without a source of income.

In truth, my real emergency plan is my credit card. I've managed to keep from using it but I could fall back on it if I ran out of all my other funds before landing a new job. I could never tell my sister this, though. She'd get upset if she knew my backup plan was essentially getting into more debt.

I eat breakfast at the condo, get ready for the day, and settle behind the living room table with the laptop. For hours, I submit application after application. My eyes stinging from staring at the screen, typing in the same information over and over again. Hitting submit dozens of times as the laptop speakers chime with confirmation emails.

Staring down at the list of my submitted applications fills me with little satisfaction. Because I know there are no guarantees, and I'm not the only person out there looking for a job. Many are likely to be more qualified than I am.

Every one of the jobs I apply for are in San Francisco, though I come across listings in San Diego as well. I don't bother with those, despite the twinge in my stomach telling me I shouldn't be so quick to dismiss them.

Staying in San Diego isn't an option I'm willing to entertain. The whole point of moving away was to start a new life. Staying here now would be like accepting defeat. Like moving backward. Failing. And I don't like to fail. Even if I seem to be pretty good at it.

The highlight of my life to date was getting into Berkeley Law. I packed up what I needed and left all of the heavy shit behind to move to the Bay Area. When I think back to that time in my life, I'm still flooded with how lightweight I felt. The world was new and teeming with possibilities. That was, to me, the beginning of my adult life.

People looked at me differently then, as though they suspected I was going places, going to be someone. And I felt the same way. I imagined a life for myself. A life as a fancy lawyer in a fancy condo overlooking Fisherman's Wharf. Maybe there's still a chance I can get that life I envisioned for myself.

Lunchtime rolls around and I shut the laptop, needing a break. It goes without saying that I don't have any urge to go back to the diner. The whole point of me going there in the first place was to feel better. Instead of a pleasant trip down memory lane, I got a six-foot-something chastising man.

It occurs to me now that Owen didn't agree with me when I called his father a good man. Not to mention, he referred to him as Lucas instead of 'my father.' Both of which stir in me something I recognize as contempt toward someone you are supposed to love and admire. This doesn't make sense to me. The Lucas I know is a genuinely kind and heartwarming man.

I distinctly remember feeling as though I gained an ally in that diner. Someone who didn't just lend a willing ear but cared enough to ask questions. Adults never ask kids questions, not the right ones, the ones they don't already know the answers to.

I settle into my car and push back the guilt the wood trim of the lush interior threatens to pull out of me. There are a few things I need to pick up, like underwear for starters. Going to the mall, knowing it's going to be crowded with holiday shoppers, is oddly exciting. Being around people has a way of energizing me.

My car radio plays Christmas music, which I was listening to my last few days in San Francisco, trying to will myself into the spirit of the season. It didn't work so much then, but I wasn't in need of cheering up as badly as I am now.

As I head south toward Fashion Valley mall, the music seems like the antidote to the heaviness brewing in the pit of my stomach, bringing a comfortable warmth over me, making me feel light though nothing has changed about my situation. The anesthetic effects of Christmas music. It's too upbeat and over-the-top until the moment it's not. Until the moment you believe it.

I pass the exit for the mall and take the one to Scripps Mercy, instead. When someone you know is hospitalized, isn't the proper thing to do to pay him or her a visit?

Parking is a pain in the ass, but fifteen minutes later, the nurse is asking me for Lucas' full name after I requested his room number.

I hear myself say, "Grant. Lucas Grant."

How do I know that? No clue, but I'm right. As I lean back on the elevator wall, watching the lighted numbers tick past, I try to decide when I first came to learn Lucas' last name. Maybe he mentioned it at some point and I filed it away in my brain cabinet?

Yeah, that's possible.

But then, why does the word tug at something else in the back of my mind?

Chapter Nine

LUCAS GRANT SITS UP IN bed wearing a light gray hospital gown. He doesn't see me walking in, his attention fixed on the newspaper in his hands. He looks a bit different from the last time I saw him. Thinner and a bit worn. The hard lines and coarseness of his features seem to bring a tense seriousness to his face that anyone who didn't know him might find intimidating. But I know that when he smiles, all of his edges fall away.

"Good God," he blurts out when he finally notices me beside him. "Are you trying to give me another heart attack? I never thought I'd see you here."

Smiling, I take the seat beside him. "Had to see if it was true. Sounded like you were playing hooky and skipping work."

His laugh is a deep, hoarse cackle.

"I got you this," I say, handing him the card I bought from the gift shop on the first floor.

"That's very kind of you. Thank you. Your hair is different, again. Blonde. I think last time it was red?"

God, that was over two years ago. Has it really been that long? I pull on my ends absentmindedly. I'm flattered he remembers.

"It was," I say. "Anyway, how are you? How long will

you be in here?"

He straightens up, as though needing to prove to me that he's fine. "Discharging tomorrow, just waiting on some test results."

"That's good news. Are you going back to the diner, or taking it easy for now?"

"I won't be going back for a while. My daughter insists I move in with her--"

"And I'm left figuring out what to do with his place."

Lucas' gaze moves to the doorway behind me.

I peer over my shoulder to see Owen walking into the room; steps hesitant, eyes fixed squarely on me.

"Emily," he says, surprise evident in his tone.

Beside me, Lucas juts a finger in the air in a gesture of eureka. "*Emily*," he says. "It was on the tip of my tongue."

Something in my chest deflates a few inches at the realization Lucas didn't remember my name. If my face shows my disappointment, no one in the room reacts to it.

"She's the girl," Lucas says, "that used to come in the diner all the time--"

Owen's response is quick, cutting his father off. "Yeah. I know."

Lucas starts laughing at some internal joke. "Oh boy, Owen was *obsessed* with you when you were kids."

I fold my lips inward to keep from smiling, but my eyebrows creep up in amusement anyway.

Lucas goes on, as if unaware of the awkwardness his words create. "You'd think he'd get over his nerves after seeing you all day at school. But whenever you walked into the diner, he'd disappear. Wouldn't come out of the kitchen if you were around. Finally, I figured out he didn't want you seeing him in his apron. Like he had a chance, anyway. Right?" He slaps my arm playfully. "Owen, do you remember that?"

I expect Owen to seem embarrassed, but he's visibly impatient, instead. He holds up a questioning hand that asks, '*why are we even talking about this*?'

"Just bringing you the clothes you asked for, for your discharge." He sets a plastic bag on the bedside table then looks at me.

I'm caught in the shocking afterglow of an embarrassing realization. Owen and I went to school together. I guess I should've assumed this. If he worked at the diner, reason suggests he lived close by and attended the nearest high school. Mine. Yet, I can't seem to muster up a single memory of him at school. Not surprising, I guess. It's not as if I could possibly know every single one of the fifteen hundred plus students I went to school with. There were four or five hundred people in my graduating class alone. Not to mention, I was one of the mean girls back then. Not caring about anyone outside of my circle of friends.

I stare back at Owen, not immediately registering there may be a subtle hint behind the silence that fell over us. Realizing it, I get to my feet. "Okay, so...I'll get going."

"No, you're fine," Owen says. "I've got to go, anyway."

We share another lingering look where, perhaps, we both consider what to say to get the other to stay. But before either one of us can speak again, a short woman with braided black hair strides into the room. A nurse. She announces in an overly sweet tone that she needs us to clear out for a few minutes.

That settles the matter; neither Owen nor I can stay. We say our goodbyes to Lucas, both quick and surprisingly impersonal. I'm battling more than a slight sting to find that Lucas didn't even remember my name. As it turns out, I spent my adolescence putting too much stock on innocuous interactions with a complete stranger whose job was to humor me with conversation and remember my face enough to greet me as an old friend when I walked in. Business. That's all it ever was. Even while I stupidly thought this man was a significant part of my life at the time.

Owen and I reach the door at the same time. He falls back a step so I can take the lead. But in one brief instant of near contact, he places a hand, almost automatically, on the small of my back.

All of my senses hone in on this simple gesture, his touch warming my skin through the fabric and pulling my pulse to that very spot. Just as soon as he does it, he pulls his hand back.

We walk down the hall, side-by-side. "It was nice of you to come," he says. "Thank you."

"It was nothing, really. I was in the neighborhood."

Chancing a glimpse in his direction, I consider how he seems less uptight today. Just yesterday, at the diner, every inch of his posture emanated a bad mood, a silent warning to stay away.

Now, outside the diner, he seems less threatening.

Not exactly friendly or laid back, but not completely unapproachable. I wonder if he's overcompensating for what his father just revealed to me.

"So...what was that about back there?" I ask.

"Not sure what you're talking about." There's the slightest hint of sarcasm there in his tone.

"Oh, you know," I say, letting my words inflate with egotism. "You were *obsessed* with me, apparently."

"Allegedly," he corrects. "You're supposed to say allegedly."

I don't immediately catch his meaning but then remember he read my resume over my shoulder yesterday and knows I'm an attorney.

"Hang on, was that--" I blink a few times, feigning disorientation "--was that a *joke*? And here I thought the giant stick up your ass interfered with humor reception."

"No. I get pretty good service."

I almost laugh and he nearly cracks a smile, and though we both resist the urge to show our amusement, he seems to take it further. I get an odd sense of him reeling himself inward, reminding himself of something.

A strange beat of silence passes. Followed by another, and then another, as we take the last few steps to reach the elevators doors.

"You don't have to be embarrassed," I say playfully, trying to ease the sudden tension.

"Do I look embarrassed?"

My body goes still as he leans toward me, reaching past my side to press the call button. The subtle scent of his cologne takes me by surprise. It's crisp and clean. He straightens again, sliding his hands into his pockets and watching me, waiting for my response.

"I imagine it must sting," I muse. "I wouldn't blame you if you're a little embarrassed."

Owen eyes my lips for a beat before answering. "I'm sorry? Am I supposed to enjoy talking about you as much as you enjoy talking about yourself?"

I let out a low whistle. "Wow, you're really holding a grudge, aren't you?" The elevator chimes and the doors open in front of us. "Why is that? Got burn marks on your palms from beating off to me every night?"

"Don't flatter yourself," Owen says. "It wasn't every night."

He holds out a hand toward the open doors in a gesture of *ladies first*, ignoring the way I cock an eyebrow in surprise at his words.

I get onto the elevator, and as I turn to watch him press the button for the lobby, my hands closing over the bar on the wall behind me, I'm distinctly aware of the shift happening between us. It's like there's a sudden crack of familiarity in his otherwise impassive wall.

Usually, people are visibly taken off guard by the things I say. It's something I enjoy. But the way Owen lets my antics bounce right off of him, and leaves me scrambling for a comeback, is surprisingly fun.

"Glad we got that out of the way," I say, as the doors close again. "Confession is good for the soul. You should really let it all out, though. I mean, since we're here and everything--"

In two fluid steps, he's standing in front of me. And though it's not an aggressive proximity, it's deliberately close enough so I have nowhere to look but into his eyes. He stretches out his arm, laying his palm flat against the wall behind me, and every pore on my skin seems hyper-aware of how close his arm comes to my side.

"What do you want to hear, Emily?" His gravelly voice is low and serious as sin. My lips part and my face tilts upward, both on their own accord. "You want me to tell you that I wanted you? That you were all I could think about? That I spent two years trying to find a way to tell you? Tell me, is that what you want to hear?"

I almost nod but manage to remain still, refusing to take his bait. Because it's clear now. He's holding something over my head. Taunting me with some unspoken strife. Keeping us stiff and formal even while a tangible attraction spins in the air between us.

The elevator comes to a stop. He watches me in the seconds before the doors open. "That was a long time ago," he says.

"Then you shouldn't be thinking about it," I respond, just as evenly.

His hesitation is so subtle I almost miss it. It's not until he gets off the elevator that I realize how close he really stood in front of me, and the empty space around my body feels exaggerated. I forget to move, my back against the wall as though held in place by his words, long after they've disbanded into the air. Except they are no longer questions, they are statements, loud and clear.

I wanted you. You were all I could think about.
I spent two years trying to find a way to tell you.

Chapter Ten

NEVER GO UNDERWEAR SHOPPING WHILE horny. That's a lesson I never thought I'd need. Everything I buy is suspiciously lace and see-through. Not sure who my subconscious is planning on banging, since the only guy I've got my eye on seems to hate me because he couldn't screw me in high school. Ah, petty first-world problems.

When I return to the condo, I devote the rest of the day to my job search. Though I've barely moved from the dining room table all afternoon, my energy seeps from me anyway. Job hunting is exhausting. Trying to not appear desperate for work is exhausting. Wording your resume to make yourself sound incredibly awesome is...well, that part I always enjoy.

I'm proud of my resume. It paints the picture of someone who's known from early on what she wanted. I worked for UC San Diego's legal department as an office aide to their IP attorney, all the while getting my undergraduate degree there. My second year at UC Berkeley law, I landed a spot on a competitive summer associate's program. My resume, in short, looks *legit*.

By the time Alexis comes home, I have to make a point to straighten my posture because my head is buried in my hands after a long day of submitting applications.

Lex walks over to the kitchen and pours herself a glass of water, her demeanor shows the signs a long, tiring day. She's been at work all day with *him*. If being around Leo is so draining for her, I'm not sure if she's going to make it to the end of the week. My sister likes to bury herself in work when she's going through something emotional, but this time--the very thing she's avoiding is part of her work life. Complications she should've foreseen. Penises have a tendency to disrupt normal thinking patterns in even the smartest women.

"What?" she asks at the way I've been watching her.

"Nothing."

If I were Lex, I'd make his life hell. She *is* his boss. She could do it if she wanted to. And my sister's smart enough to do it in a way the poor guy wouldn't know which way he was getting fucked. That's the best type of revenge, the subtle type that leaves the person questioning the root. But my sister is not vindictive enough for that.

She disappears behind the door of her bedroom. I turn down the music playing from the laptop to a volume she probably can't hear through the walls. But not even an hour later, I knock on her bedroom door, starving, hoping to drag her out to eat somewhere.

Lex must not hear me because she doesn't respond. I crack the door open and peer inside. Her room is dimly lit by the last rays of light on the horizon. All I see on her bed is a circular lump under the covers and an arm thrown over the pillow she keeps over her head. I hesitate, feeling guilty about even considering waking her up.

"Hey, Lex?"

She doesn't stir. I take a few steps, but halt at the sound of a chime that cuts through the silence. Lex doesn't stir to that, either. I walk over to the cellphone on her bedside table with the intention of turning off the sound. Then I accidentally on purpose read the text messages on the screen.

[You know what just occurred to me? Keeping me in the friend-zone requires some maintenance.]

[You've got to talk to me once in a while, remind me how you're immune to my good looks. Or I might get my hopes up and send you flowers again.]

It's from Jacob.

A friend of mine, Julia, tried to set Lex and Jacob up on a blind date a while back. My sister was already too starry-eyed over Leo to even give Jacob a shot. Now look at her. I've never seen my sister like this. I mean, sure, she takes things kind of rough. But I've never seen her act like this over a guy, not even when her marriage fell apart.

What is it about this Leo guy that has her so torn up?

As I look from the messages to the pathetic heap under the blankets that is my sister, I decide Jacob is perfect for Lex. Though I only met him once, I instantly liked him. His carefree personality could really rub off on my sister. The guy is smart and it doesn't hurt that he's an insane combination of hot and adorable. I mean, he has dimples for Christ's sake.

Lex obviously made the wrong choice in dismissing him. If she'd had given him a chance, she might not be curled up under her covers in the fetal position right now. She might not have an awkward mess of a broken affair to deal with every day at work. She might be in a healthy relationship, for once.

As I chew on my bottom lip, my thoughts quickly merge into a decision. I'm taking matters into my own hands. I have to. I owe it to my sister.

Phone in hand, I slide out of her room as quietly as I can manage. Then, leaning against the kitchen counter, I try to think of how to respond to Jacob's message.

[I think you're right. Join Emily and me for dinner?]

I go to set the phone down on the counter but his response is immediate.

[You're in luck. Just so happens I canceled plans I didn't have for tonight.]

I smile because he's maybe a tad too enthusiastic. And that's probably what Lex doesn't like about him. Lex is the opposite of enthusiastic. My response to his message is a time and an address.

Two thoughts come to me as I set the phone down. First, Lex is going to be pissed. Second, I've invited Jacob over to a dinner I haven't even started cooking. I rifle through the cabinets and refrigerator and realize Lex hasn't gone grocery shopping in at least a week or two. I meant to earlier, but got caught up in job hunting.

There isn't much to work with in this kitchen and so I decided it's pasta for dinner once again. I've got a half an hour to live before my sister wakes up to kill me.

It isn't funny, none of this is, but I laugh anyway, like an evil witch as I stir the simmering sauce.

Chapter Eleven

LEX DAMN NEAR STRANGLES ME when she finds out what I've done. It's a good thing that I'm trained in the art of persuasion because I manage to convince her to take a shot of vodka and eat dinner with us like a good host. By the end of the night, Jacob's charm melts the icebox that is my sister. She ends up enjoying his visit enough to invite him to her company's Christmas party on Friday. Well, he technically invited himself. Jacob seems like the type to do that a lot, wedge himself into the tiniest of holes. Like a sexy little chipmunk.

The next morning, my mood lifts a notch with the familiar chime overhead and the prominent sweetness enveloping my senses. The scent of powdered sugar and cinnamon.

An elderly couple sits at a table by the door, the woman cutting up a large plate of French toast. Nearby, a middle-aged man, dressed for construction site work, is hunched over a plate of pancakes. The kid from the other day is here again, sitting on the same stool and picking over an identical looking plate of eggs.

Owen is behind the register, standing beside a guy I've never seen before. From the way the two are hovered over the machine, with Owen gesturing to the buttons, it looks like the new guy is being trained.

At the sound of the door, Owen's eyes rise to meet mine and though neither one of us outwardly reacts to the presence of the other, our gazes remain unbroken until I take a seat on my favorite stool, beside the kid, and pull out my laptop.

The kid looks as disgruntled as ever, his head resting in his hand like before.

"How's your day going, so far?"

He peers up at me as though surprised. His face, which was crinkled between the eyes, relaxes a bit but his voice is flat when he speaks. "Not that great."

"*That's the spirit.*" I smile at him, taking his words to mean he's not a morning person. He sort of smiles back, more like he shrugs at me with his lips, before breaking eye contact.

The new guy takes my order. Owen goes back into the kitchen and I wonder if he's progressed to full on avoiding me.

Bringing my attention to my laptop screen, I pretend not to notice that the kid is watching me.

"Is it a girl that's got you all mopey?" I ask, without glancing at him.

He takes a deep breath, like my words pressed on a bullet hole in his stomach. "Maybe."

I'm typing now, logging into my email account. I can tell it's easier for him to talk to me when I'm not looking at him. "What's your name, anyway?"

"Landon."

"I'm Emily. How old are you?"

"Fourteen."

I raise an eyebrow at him.

"Okay, I'm nine."

I'm surprised. I knew for sure he wasn't fourteen, but I wouldn't have guessed he was so young. He comes across much older. Twelve, maybe. Maybe because he's tall.

"How old is the girl?"

"She's ten."

"Want to know a secret? Women are not as complicated as they seem."

He leans in and I don't think he realizes it. I meet his eager eyes and tilt my head forward as though I'm about to reveal a sacred secret that men are not meant to hear.

"She wants to be flattered, but not too much. She wants to know you like her but wants to feel unsure of it at the same time. Does that makes sense?"

"I think so. What do I do?"

I hesitate. I know what I'm *supposed* to tell him. I'm supposed to tell him to be himself. To tell her the truth about how he feels. And if she doesn't appreciate him the way he is, she doesn't deserve him. That's what I'm supposed to say. But, of course, it's not what I'm going to say.

"You do something sweet for her. But make sure it's in front of her friends, otherwise it won't count. Then you ignore her for a day, maybe two. Then do something else sweet for her. And repeat."

"That's it?" he asks, incredulous.

I shrug. "I give her a week before she's in love with you."

I'm going to hell. But it's true.

The kid may be cute but he carries himself like an old man, dragging his body from place to place. His shoulders slumped, head tilted down. His lack of confidence makes him forgettable. He's not the type of boy that gets the girl. The truth is even a grown woman is wired to want a difficult man. The obsession starts with not knowing what he's thinking.

Does he like me? Is this a game? Why didn't he call me? Why hasn't he looked at me?

I'm trying to do Landon a favor by telling him the truth. He would learn it on his own eventually but a kid like him would probably end up friend-zoned every time before he realized that a small, healthy streak of asshole is what girls secretly like.

It's not my fault. It's not like *I* was the one who infected the subconscious of women everywhere with this twisted notion. It is what it is.

He squints at me. "That sounds like a trick. Way too easy."

"Try it. Let me know if it works."

"It's a deal," he says, glancing at his watch.

I'm impressed the kid even owns one. Landon gets up, digs into his pocket, slams down a crumpled up ten-dollar bill, and calls out to Owen as he did the other morning.

I get a sensation of déjà vu, searching Owen's reaction. It's the same measured expression as he watches Landon walk off then stuffs the bill unceremoniously into his pockets before his eyes lock onto mine.

"Good morning," he says, automatically.

There's no sense of familiarity between us. No remnants of the banter from the hospital yesterday. Owen is cold and distant again, as though I've walked through those doors for the very first time and he secretly wishes I'd go away.

He wipes down the counter beside me.

"All right, Owen. I just have to know. What is it about me that turns your smile upside down?"

He stops to stare at me and I can tell he thinks I'm being ironic. Thinks I know exactly what his grudge is against me.

"I believe it's called classical conditioning," he says.

My response is a small shake of the head, signaling my confusion.

"When you crush on things that get your ribs broken, you learn not to crush on them anymore," he explains.

"Are the ribs a metaphor for something?"

"I don't know," he says, not missing a beat, "was you sending your boyfriend to break them a metaphor for something?"

I'm not sure if he's kidding. He seems to have the driest sense of humor I've ever encountered. He delivers his words deadpan. And though his face is serious now, it's too serious.

"Okay--" I put up a hand "--let's stop right there. What are you talking about? Who broke your ribs?"

"You mean, you don't remember?"

"If I did, I wouldn't be asking." As I say this, something cold grips my stomach because the answer dawns on me before it leaves his lips.

"Varsity wrestler, stocky blond guy."

Jesus Christ.

"Jonathan broke your ribs? When the hell did this happen?"

Owen turns slightly away from me. "Really, let's not bother having this conversation now. My ribs healed fine."

His words carry the insinuation something else didn't heal so well.

I shoot up in my seat and grab his arm before he can move away.

"Look, I'm not sure what you think I did, but I had no part in whatever happened to you."

"Are you sure about that?" he asks.

I release the hold on his arm and let my hand fall to my side, certain he doesn't believe me. "Wait, did Jonathan tell you I did?"

Owen looks out past me like he's recalling something. "I think his exact words were, *this is a message from Emily.*"

I'm aware of how every inch of my expression falls as I struggle to keep my tone from revealing how mortified I am. Because I remember clearly just how ruthless Jonathan could be.

"He lied, Owen. I swear. I would've never asked him to hurt you. Or anyone."

Owen watches me as though the truth is evident in my reaction, and his reluctance dissolves before my eyes. It's as though a realization crosses over his face, illuminating it like a passing headlight.

"Right, of course," he says with a slow blink. "I'm

sorry I implied otherwise. Shouldn't have brought it up."

Relief floods me and I realize how important it is to me that Owen believes me. The guarded way he crosses his arms and looks over toward the door gives me the suspicion that he's embarrassed.

"No, I'm glad you did," I say. "We've been having this silent turf war. Only, I had no idea and have been sitting here sipping coffee. Probably pissing you off."

"You do nurse a cup of coffee for hours."

"I'm jobless. You have free WiFi. And a hot guy behind the counter."

He keeps his eyes locked onto mine but his lips don't so much as twitch. I still sense his resistance to react to me. He's so used to holding a grudge, he doesn't quite know how to let it go.

"Do you not like me flirting with you?" I ask, as casually as if I were asking him for the time.

"I like it just fine."

The energy between us softens right then. Like a glacier shifting a few inches as it begins to thaw. I smile and his lips twitch up at their corners. This entire exchange is a pleasant surprise for us both.

The new guy manning the register calls him over and, as Owen walks away, something becomes obvious to me. The reason Owen looks so out of place in this diner is because he doesn't belong here. He answers the new guy's questions patiently and I can tell he is trying hard to make the guy feel comfortable.

That's when it hits me--he doesn't typically work here and was left with no alternative when his father fell ill. Owen's presence in this diner is temporary. This new hire is his ticket out of here.

The disappointment sinking in my stomach is ridiculous. My presence here is also temporary. I'm a visitor, passing through. I've got a life elsewhere, a life that will take me away from this place for good. And soon.

Chapter Twelve

EVERY ONCE IN A WHILE, things go right. Friday starts off wonderfully. By nine in the morning, I get a phone call from Janie Lowe. She's the hiring manager for the firm where I completed my summer associate's program back in law school. They offered me a position after graduation but I turned it down for what I thought was a better one.

Luckily, they still seem interested in me. Lowe tells me the firm was pleased to receive my application and I should expect a phone call after the holidays to coordinate a formal interview. The wordage she uses makes me suspect they've already decided to hire me and the interview is a formality. And though I know it's nowhere *near* a done deal until I receive an actual job offer, the conversation leaves me feeling light and refreshed. The two ton weight that's been sitting on my chest over the last few days shifts and I'm able to breathe again.

But the next call I get is far less fun.

"Emily, you can't disappear like that and not answer any of my texts or calls. Where are you?"

My roommate's tone is so frigid the phone grows a few degrees colder at my ear.

"I'm fine, Elle, I'm with my sister for the holidays. I meant to return your calls, just lost track of time."

I'm talking through a mouthful of burrito. The truth is, I don't have a good excuse for why I never got around to returning her texts. I read them and avoided responding right away because her questions required explanations I don't yet possess. Like where I'm going to live.

"Okay, fine," she says, "but you've got to get all your stuff out of here. You do know that, right?"

"Yes. Obviously, I'm aware."

"Good. I don't want them holding our deposit--"

"Elle, I get it. I promise I'll have my stuff out after Christmas. I'll stick it in storage if I have to. Consider it done."

My friend Amelia's the only person I bothered to text when I arrived in San Diego Monday evening. But when she invited me out for drinks tonight, I didn't think she meant to a North County bar.

"Why'd you want to come here?" I do a slow circle to take in the crowd. "This place is a buzz-kill. My old high school is, like, half a mile away. I thought you'd want to head downtown."

Amelia leans in, her long, brown hair falling over her shoulder. "There's a conference going on up the road. At the Park Hyatt Aviara. Huge, conservative conference. We're talking half a billion in donations each year, all funneled to right wing projects. But here's the thing, no one really knows which ones. It's all insanely secretive, from the location to the guest list. But guess what? I had a source leak the location to me two days ago."

"I didn't realize you wrote political pieces."

"I don't, usually. But this information fell into my lap when I was working on another story. I need to sink my teeth into something meaty. Something that'll convince my boss I can do more than fluff pieces. I need to break the front page."

"I'm not following," I say. "How does us coming here help you with that?"

"There's no getting into the conference, obviously. Security is too tight. But, I mean, let's be real. This is the only decent bar in half a mile radius. Some of those overworked suckers from the conference are bound to end up here."

"I doubt anyone important will come to a place like this," I say. "This place is stuffy, but not *that* stuffy."

"Big wigs aren't the ones that leak information. I'm talking small fish. Assistants, crew members, stressed out security guards."

We scan our surroundings, where we stand, hovering around a pair of barstools. Protecting them like they are the sacred lands of our ancestors, all but hissing at anyone who tries to nonchalantly slide in and take one. We aren't even sitting on them. It's just nice to leave our options open.

"I guess this place will do," I say, shrugging. "At least the cab ride's cheap. Not to mention the drinks. I happen to be in a celebratory mood tonight."

My problems are far from resolved. I don't have a

job secured and still have no idea where I'll live. But this is where I'm different from my sister. She broods over things whereas I have the keen ability to focus on the tiniest rays of hope. At least long enough to enjoy a drink and dance to some overrated tracks.

"And what are you celebrating?" Amelia asks.

"My almost landing a maybe job interview."

"*That's right.*" Amelia holds up her beer to my glass of gin and tonic.

I tilt my head at her. "Since when do you drink beer?"

"Since I wrote a piece on all the ways your cute drinks can be ruffied at a bar."

"Nice." I take a hesitant sip of my drink.

I want to dance, but the music overhead isn't exactly the type I can shake my butt to. It's the sidestep and finger snapping music. Those moves don't exorcise stress. At least not for me.

Amelia and I drain our drinks before long and order new ones. The conversation turns to the nuances of my predicament.

"Let me get this straight," she begins, "you have to get all of your stuff out of your apartment in two weeks and you still haven't started looking for a place to live?"

"I've been looking for a job."

"You've been shelving."

"What?"

"You know...putting problems up on shelves. Pretending they aren't there. You do that."

"Okay," I say, casting my eyes to the ceiling. My friends have one thing in common; they are candid and unafraid to speak their mind. I love surrounding myself with that type of honesty, especially in a world where everyone goes out of their way to tiptoe around everyone else's feelings. But sometimes I'm not in the mood to hear it. A candid tongue isn't as amusing when it's lashing out straight at me.

I change the subject without preamble. "That guy over by the window keeps looking at you."

I should know better than to think Amelia will find a subtle way to glance over her shoulder. Instead, she turns on her heels and stares right at the guy, long enough for him to smile at her.

"Meh," she says, turning back to me. "Dude gives me serial killer-ish vibes."

"Really?" I eye him again, trying to decide what part of him leans toward homicidal. He's in his early to mid-twenties with short dark hair, dressed sharply in a light blue button-down. Not bad looking at all.

"He's got that tight-lipped smile," Amelia says. "You know? The kind that doesn't reach his eyes."

"He's cute," I muse.

"Ted Bundy was cute. In fact...." She turns to look at the guy again, eyeing him carefully. The guy's smile slips slightly, as though he's not sure if our conversation is working in his favor. "I bet he rents a basement apartment from his mother. And when he goes home every night, he takes off his shoes under a solitary light in the center of the ceiling. You know...the one that inexplicably hangs from a string and sways from side-to-side like there's a draft in the room. Then he goes and checks on the pieces of people's limbs he keeps in his refrigerator."

"You're so morbid."

"I'm a realist." She shrugs. "That's how I stay out of serial killer's refrigerators."

Half an hour and a few strong drinks later, I feel *nice*. I mean really, *really* nice. My cheeks burn under the strain of my constant, liquor-induced smile. The music, which was just bearable before, is now somehow exactly my type of sound. The words touch me in all of my special, sensitive, feeling places.

"Bingo." Amelia's wandering eyes widen when they land on a short blonde in a purple dress, standing on the other side of the room. "Look at that. Hair slicked back in a bun. Dress down to her knees. This girl came from somewhere super conservative."

"Or maybe she's just not into getting laid."

"I'll be right back," Amelia whispers before heading off in that direction.

With Amelia gone, I notice giggling noises coming from beside me. A group of three much younger ladies stand there, visibly wasted.

When my eyes lock with one of them--a brown-haired girl with bangs cut over her eyes--she stumbles forward and hugs me. I shrink back in surprise and try to resist the urge to knee this stranger in the stomach. She pulls away just in time.

"Your hair color is so pretty," she says in what is either an accent or a tongue weighted from the effects of liquor. "Lila, *look*--" she gestures enthusiastically to get her friend's attention, standing on wobbly legs as she towers over me in her giant heels "--should I get this brown-to-blonde color? Isn't it super cute?"

The one called Lila says, "*Yes!*" with exaggerated importance. It's obvious by the way her *Happy Birthday* crown sits crooked atop her head that she is drunk enough not to care about her appearance. We chat for a few minutes. Everything I say elicits hysterical laughter from her. She slams a fifty-dollar bill on the bar and announces that, in honor of *my* birthday, she's buying us all another round of shots.

It's December. My birthday is in August. But when Lila plops the crown on my head, that crescent-shaped plastic with rhinestones on it sends a surge of excited energy flowing through me. This crown is freedom. This crown is attention.

It's my motherfucking birthday.

I allow my tipsiness to overtake me, giving in to the urge to repeat the phrase "It's my *birthday*" enough times to elicit congratulations from nearby strangers, who proceed to buy us drinks.

I swallow back another shot and slam the glass back on the counter. Almost immediately, my eyes are drawn to a man further down the bar, speaking to someone I assume to be the manager because, as I slip around intoxicated people, he disappears behind a doorway marked *Employees Only*.

The second man does a double take as I approach, taking in the sight of the blue dress I'm wearing.

I slap his arm. "Rowan!"

He remains unsmiling. "It's Owen."

I know that. I do. But for some reason, I find it amusing to pretend that I don't.

"Oh, *that's right.*" I snap my fingers. "*Owen.* How are you, man? How's it hanging?"

"It's...hanging fine, thanks. I'm actually on my way out."

"But you just got here?" I squint. "*Didn't you just get here*?"

"I came to have a word with a friend."

I shake my head. "You should stay. It's my *birthday.*"

"I did overhear that."

"You did?"

"Yeah. I spotted you across the room and I thought, here we are running into each other again. It's all starting to feel a bit too...coincidental...." he trails off on purpose, eyes glinting with meaning.

"You--what? You think I'm stalking you?" Even in my drunken state, my pride bubbles to the surface. "Really? So, you think I go home to a wall covered in pictures of you and touch myself?" I pause for a reaction but he merely stares back politely. "Oh, yeah. I bet you wish that were true. Bet you wish I spent hours just...masturbating to you and trying to figure out where you'll be next. All so I can stage a convenient way to run into you because, you know, you're so fucking friendly."

"Is that a confession?" He doesn't allow himself to smile, but there's no denying he's enjoying this.

"Just so you know, coming here wasn't my idea. And if I hump my pillow at night, it's most definitely not to thoughts of you." That's a lie, but he doesn't need to know that. "Anyway, let's not forget who was obsessed with who here."

"Was. Past tense. Let's not forget who crossed the bar to reach the other."

Damn him and his perfect comebacks. Why the hell do I keep going out on a limb, trying to get him to warm up to me? What did I expect when I walked across the room to reach him? Did I think he'd suddenly be easygoing and friendly? Or do I enjoy the sting of rejection?

You know what? Fuck this. He is killing my buzz.

Failing to come up with anything witty to say, I turn to walk away without another word.

"Wait," he calls out.

I turn to him again, and catch various expressions chasing each other across his face. He takes in my features in a way that makes my skin flush, before turning his head for a fraction of a second, only to bring his eyes back to mine, shoulders relaxing in surrender.

"Stay," he says, and the word floats through the air, brushing the skin at the nape of my neck in a way that feels so good.

I pull my chin up. "Why should I?"

"I'm trying not to be a jerk."

"Well, try harder."

When I attempt to turn away again, his hands close over each of mine. And with a soft tug, he draws me back to meet his eyes once more.

"Okay."

"Okay?" I ask, gloating in the way he's all but admitting he craves my undivided attention. I crave his, too.

"I'll try harder."

"Good--" I pat the part of his chest between his open jacket. My hands meet the hard muscle under his shirt. Jesus, he's solid. An involuntary smile tugs at my lips. "Let's start over. I'll buy you a drink."

I flag down the bartender and order us each my favorite beer without even thinking to ask him if it's what he wants. Owen takes the bottles from the bartender and slips him a wad of bills before I can whip out my wallet. I scoff in protest but he hands me the beer as consolation and sets his down behind him.

"Happy Birthday," he says.

"*Thanks*." My cheeks warm under a grin as I remove the stupid crown from my head and toss it onto the bar. "Do you not like beer?" I ask, eyeing the way his sits forgotten behind him.

"I'm not drinking."

"Oh. Why didn't you just say so?"

"I have a feeling there's no stopping you tonight."

Before I can consider his words, a new song cuts on and its beat seems to infect my bloodstream. Somehow, though I barely recognize the song, I'm convinced it's *my* song. Excitement floods me, I resist the urge to cheer loudly and announce to the room that this song, this amazing piece of sound, is *my* song.

I need to dance.

My body is grooving before I decide to let it. Owen sits there at the edge of the stool, legs parted wide, watching me with undeniable amusement.

Of course, I don't understand why he isn't responding to the music in the least. Can't he feel it inside?

"Why are you so uptight?" I ask. "I'm sure you get laid a lot."

"I'm not uptight."

"Oh, yeah? Prove it. Dance with me."

He takes in the details of my face in a gradual, controlled way. The way a person does when they're allowing themselves to really look at something for the first time.

"Dance with me," I say, again.

His lips part and I'm sure he'll say yes. Instead, he says, "I don't dance."

"Well, I bet I can get you to move."

I start dancing in front of him, winding slowly as though I'm gearing up for a sensual move, raising my hands over my head to trail my fingers over the opposite arm--but then my arms wrench into sharp, mechanical movements as I start doing the robot.

He laughs. Actually laughs. His face lights up like a bolt of lightning shooting across the room, his features losing their edge in the momentary glow.

I realize I'm staring at him. Hard.

The alcohol is a warm blanket over my brain and I'm so distracted by the sight of his smile that I lose my footing, nearly toppling over. His hands fly to my waist to steady me, and in the process, I'm pulled between his parted legs.

I go very still, despite the erratic beating of my heart. Our proximity pumps my body full of whatever it is that makes you crave someone. He feels it too. I can tell by the way his lips part slightly but words forget to come out.

"Told you I could get you to move," I whisper, peering down at the crotch of his pants. Insinuating I'm referring to something else. Because I am.

"You've got me there," he says, hands still gripping my waist. The longer they lay there, the further the warmth of his touch spreads over me and the thicker the haziness that floats across his face.

All I can hear is the sound of my pulse. I'm unaware of our surroundings. It's just us. Just this.

He doesn't speak. Doesn't have to. Whatever is on his mind, he says it with his hands, one of which slides downward until his fingertips begin to trace the hem of my dress, drawing a line on the bare skin of my thighs where the fabric ends. Leaving a trail of sensations that spread across my body and crank up my internal thermostat.

The seconds lurch slower than my hazy thoughts. My senses sharpen beyond the alcohol's reach. I rest my forearms on his shoulders, aware of every inch of his body and the air that separates it from mine.

As he moves his face to meet mine, a small hand closes over my shoulder from behind and pulls me away. I stumble backward and see Amelia standing there. She wraps an arm around my shoulder and smiles at Owen. "Hi there. *Sorry*. I need to speak to my friend for a second."

I'm stunned and disoriented as she leads me a few feet away. My mouth takes a few seconds to catch up with my brain. "Why'd you do that?"

"The cab's here. Remember? You said two hours.

Didn't think you wanted me to leave you here."

I throw my head back. "You totally cock blocked me."

"Nope. I saw you dancing the robot in front of him. You cock blocked yourself."

"Whatever, just go. I got this."

She shakes her head. "Emily, I can't leave you behind. Drunk. With some random guy who...." She turns to Owen. I do the same and we see him sitting there in his leather jacket, looking right back at us. Amelia lowers her voice. "Who looks like he's either in the mob or part of some undercover FBI stint investigating the mob."

"He's not some random mob guy." I snort, aware of how heavy my tongue feels as I speak. "He's *Owen*...he serves me *breakfast* every morning. Well, twice. But he's beautiful. We like the same *beer*. And he's going to have my *babies*." I nod vigorously even as Amelia gives me a slow, but steady shake of her head.

She pats the side of my face. "Okay, sweetie, stop talking. You're drunk."

"Seriously," I say, mustering every morsel of sobriety I can manage. "It's okay. I know him. We went to high school together. He's not homicidal in the least."

Amelia fixes me with a serious expression as though trying to decide if she should really leave me. She's insanely overprotective of the people in her life and a bit on the paranoid side. I grab her phone from her hand and take a picture of Owen. The flash lights up the spot where he stands. His eyebrows pull together in a 'what the hell?' expression.

"Here," I say, handing Amelia back her phone. "Now you've got his picture as collateral."

"Fine. Text me when you get home--or...wherever," she finally says.

I nod a little too enthusiastically and watch her walk off. When I turn back to Owen, he's getting up and straightening his jacket as though he's gearing to leave.

"Did the impromptu photo shoot scare you off?" I ask as innocent as I can.

"No, not at all. I've just stayed longer than I was supposed to--" He looks after Amelia as she disappears beyond the front doors ahead. "Did your friend leave you? How are you getting home?"

"I guess in a different cab. Hers is probably taking off right now and I can't run in these heels."

"I'll give you a ride."

He says this like it's the most innocent phrase that could come out of a man like him. For the record, it's not. Hearing that combination of words leave his lips makes my mouth water.

"Yes, please. I'd like very much for you to give me a ride," I say, smiling wider than necessary.

Chapter Thirteen

THE MOON IS A CRESCENT overhead as we make our way out into the dark parking lot. Sounds of traffic are dulled by the hum of music and conversation pouring out of the bar's front doors. The cool air works to sober me up.

Owen hands me a motorcycle helmet. "Have you ridden before?"

I hesitate, weighing the helmet in my hands. I haven't. But I'm tempted to lie and say I have just because I hate admitting I'm inexperienced in any way. It's just...the way he asks, it's as if he's hoping to show me things I haven't seen before. And I'm left battling the excitement he stirs in me, like I'm some teenage girl.

I glance at the slab of machine, so open and exposed.

"No," I admit. "First time."

Owen must notice something on my face because, after asking me where I'm going, he says, "Don't worry, that's not far. The ride will be quick and easy."

I want to make a joke about preferring it long and hard, but I catch him looking at me for way longer than I think even he intends to. Somehow, in those few seconds, the residual noises of our surroundings dull a few octaves, leaving just the rustle of a breeze sweeping in to tangle a strand of hair in my eyelashes.

Owen's hand comes up to my face, fingers sweeping over my eyebrows, taking the strand of hair with them, and tucking it behind my ear. I freeze at his touch, feeling my chest rise on a sudden intake of air.

He removes his jacket and hands it to me. "Put this on."

"What about you?"

"I'll be fine," he says, pushing the leather into my hands.

I put the jacket on, distracted by the way it carries his scent in stronger and more intoxicating doses than I've ever experienced. The crisp, clean smell I recognize from before has notes of citrus and spearmint, which twist into something unexpectedly warm and sensual. I resist the urge to pull the jacket over my face and inhale deeply.

The helmet, on the other hand, is considerably less pleasant. I cringe internally at the way the hard material is snug around my skull, making me feel constricted and a bit claustrophobic.

He gets on the bike, motioning for me to do the same. I straddle the seat behind him and he turns his head toward me as he puts on his own helmet. "Hold on tight."

He starts the engine, it hums and purrs, vibrating between my legs and heightening my sense of arousal. When I wrap my arms around his torso, I'm taken completely off guard by how dense his body feels. Every inch of him is sturdy and compact. A wall of muscles meets the palms of my hands, which I realize too late have strayed across his abdomen in their curious examination.

I laugh into my helmet, hoping he didn't notice me copping a feel. If he did, he doesn't react to it and instead, pulls the bike out onto the street.

The movement brings flutters in my stomach. Suddenly, the constraints of the helmet don't matter. We are flying down the streets, nothing between us and the cool night air whipping against our clothes. I keep the side of my face pressed to his back, watching our surroundings turn to whirls of indiscernible shapes and colors. And every once in a while I catch another lungful of his scent.

Way too soon for me, he brings the bike to a park at the lot in front of Lex's condo and turns off the engine. The vibration ceases and, strangely enough, I instantly miss feeling the raw power between my legs.

He gets off the bike first, takes off his helmet, and extends his hand, which I don't see right away because I'm distracted by his hair. It's disheveled in a way that adds extra grain to his already rough looks.

He squints his eyes for a fraction of a second, as though he finds my looking at him curious. I take his hand and slide off the bike. When I pull off the helmet, I make a point to run my hand through my hair, self-consciously smoothing out some tangles, and letting it drape over my shoulder. Owen's gaze darts to the newly exposed skin on my neck. In a small, seemingly unconscious movement, he wets his bottom lip.

"Come on. Let me walk you to the door," he says, the corners of his mouth twist up a little to let me know he can tell I'm still impaired by alcohol.

We walk alongside each other and I can still feel my body holding on to the back of his. I get the urge to loop my arm through his, but I don't. He makes me nervous in an exhilarating way I can't get enough of.

He slides his hands into his front pockets and his arms seem to tense. I wonder if he's cold, if I should offer him back his jacket. But when our eyes meet in a sideways glance, I see something else there, firing up the caramel strands of his hazel eyes. He's not cold.

All I see is heat.

We reach the front door and I stare at him for a few seconds, wishing I could invite him inside without my sister finding out I brought a stranger into her condo. It's as if I'm a teenager again, with no safe place away from parents to entertain a guy and possibly dry hump in the dark.

"I'm staying with my sister," I say, a bit awkwardly.

He nods his understanding, but doesn't offer anything else, just watches me like he can't get enough of my face. I remember to take off his jacket and hand it back to him. He takes it and drapes it over his arm.

"I was surprised you didn't leave with your friend," he says, with the air of someone prolonging the seconds before a goodbye.

I take in a deliberate inhale of fresh air, willing the alcohol to hang back, just for a few minutes. Somehow, in my inebriated state, I'm acutely aware of Owen. More so than anything else around me. More so than ever.

The more I stare at him, the more I realize it's not so much his face that is stern, but the expression in his eyes. As though his eyes produce a tangible barrier that shrouds everything else.

I recognize that look.

"I'm curious...about you." My words sound steady, though my mind is anything but. Thoughts swirl lazily around my head. Thoughts of how good it felt to hold onto him on the ride here. Thoughts of how I could manage for that to happen again.

"I'll admit, I'm curious, too."

"Oh?" I lean back against the door and wait for the words about to trail from his lips.

"I'm curious what brings you to the diner, after you've been gone for years."

"I feel...good there." I laugh at the ease with which the words slip from my tongue. "That's the truth serum speaking right now."

Owen pulls my chin up with a finger until our gazes intersect again. "Can I tell you something you're not supposed to know?"

I try and fail to keep my tone even, my voice dropping down an octave. "Yes."

"I feel good with you there, too."

A smile tugs at the corner of my mouth. "And why am I not supposed to know that?"

"Because...I'm not sure I'm ready for you to know what I think of you. Or the effect you have on me. The effect you've always had on me."

He leans in and steals the breath I'm about to take. Right from my lips.

Hands running up the sides of my neck, he weaves fingers into my hair, pulling my face firmly to his. There's a contained sort of wildness about the way his mouth moves over mine, a torturous slowness that makes me suspect I'm only glimpsing the fire raging inside of him. A fire he's protecting me from. Letting me enjoy the heat without getting swallowed up by the whole of it.

The light moan that trails from my lips reveals how badly I *want* to burn. I want him to envelop me, to consume me until there's nothing left. My hands close over the fabric of his shirt at the waist. I bring my body closer to his, leaning my weight on him. But as I resign to the idea of letting him take me right where I stand, he breaks away to look at me. His eyes shining with a satisfied smile at the way I'm left stunned, angling for more, and pulling in a breath between my swollen lips.

Sirens wail in the distance and a car door shuts nearby. The cloudiness in his expression disperses as reality seeps, unwelcome, into our bubble. He waits for me to say something. My thoughts strap my tongue down and all I can do is stare right back.

I tilt my head back to get a better look at him, but the simple movement causes the world around me to lurch unpleasantly. I shut my eyes and press my head back against the door to ground myself.

My whole body must sway because Owen steadies me. I open my eyes to meet his again and notice his lips are now turned down. "Are you okay?"

"Yes," I lie and press my fingers to my lips as the burn of alcohol rises into my throat.

"You should get inside," he says, a slight disappointment noticeable in his tone. "Get some water in your system."

"I will...thanks for the ride."

He waits for me to unlock my door and step inside. "Goodnight, Emily."

I like the way my name sounds from his lips.

"Goodnight, Owen."

He stands there as I shut the door, watching him reduce to a sliver of color between frame and door. When he's obscured and the door shuts with a thud, I press my forehead to it as everything around me swims.

Chapter Fourteen

IT'S SO DAMN BRIGHT IN Lex's condo.

I pull the covers over my head, but the sun still penetrates the strands of the material, its warm rays lighting up the back of my eyelids.

Birds chirp outside but the sound is so sharp it cuts through walls and fabric and stabs at my eardrums.

Groaning, I pull the pillow over my head. There's nothing more infuriating than when the day insists on being obnoxiously happy instead of being appropriately gray and miserable. Like the headache rocking my brain against my skull.

Dear bright and cheerful day,

I need you to kindly pipe the fuck down.

Eventually, I drag myself out of bed, swearing to abstain from alcohol consumption for however long it takes to forget this awful feeling. Or however long it takes for me to want to repeat it.

I forgot it's Saturday. Lex is at the kitchen table eating breakfast. Her mouth hangs slightly open when she catches my appearance.

"What happened to you?"

My brain was ripped from my skull, run over by a semi-truck, I want to say. Instead, I groan. Like a bear.

Like a bear that's going to reach out of the window and snatch up those goddamn birds. And gnaw on them until they can't chirp anymore.

I squint to filter out some of the room's light and feel around one of the kitchen drawers for the bottle of aspirin I've seen in it before. Finding it, I pop two pills in my mouth, and dry swallow. I lay my head on the cold countertop and groan again. Lex laughs but I don't care. The cold granite feels good against my face.

"Drink some water," she tells me.

I drink two glasses of water, chugging them down noisily and without a break, then slink over to the table and sit beside my sister. I lay my head on the wooden surface, which isn't cold and soothing, but at least it's not moving like the walls are.

"Maybe you should cool it with the drinking," Lex says. "You've been doing a lot of it lately."

I narrow my eyes at her, not realizing what she's talking about, and she points toward the bottle of vodka.

"I didn't have any of that last night," I say. "Just a whole lot of other...beverages in tiny little glasses."

"Yeah, but what about every other night this week?"

"Cut me some slack. I've had a rough week. How was it with Jacob at the Christmas party last night?"

"It was...interesting," she says.

I open my eyes a crack and see the conflict on her face. She almost looks like she doesn't want to tell me. But she does. I keep my head pressed to the table and watch her expression as she tells me how Leo cornered her and tried to get her back. Swearing ending things the way that he did was all a big mistake. How he wants nothing more than to be with her.

Blah. Blah. Blah.

He used the 'L' word. *Motherfucker*. It's the commitment phobic's kryptonite. I imagine Lex toppled over and played dead until he gave up and walked away. I can't imagine how else my sister would react to him telling her he's in love with her.

I'm not good at consoling people, but breakups are fairly easy. All you have to do is agree the guy is an enormous asshole and the woman is better off without him. List out all the shit he did wrong and remind her why she should hate him.

Easy.

I really believe it when I tell her Leo's full of shit. He's messing with her and I'm not going to sit here and play the 'what if' game about this guy who's plucking away at my sister's bruised heart like she's a damn violin.

I don't play *devil's advocate*. I play *drag the motherfucker through the mud*.

These last few days have been awful for me to witness. My big sister trying hard to pretend she isn't hurting as bad as she is. The worst part is that I can't relate to what she's going through. I'm trying, but I can't. I've never been in her shoes, never missed someone the way she misses Leo. Never been in a position where I had the maturity to not be with someone when I realized he wasn't good for me. Lex is intent on keeping a broken heart over a man who isn't right for her.

I have to wonder what's going on in my sister's head. And as my worry for her grows, there's a thought lurking in the back of my mind: I'm set to head back to San Francisco, after Christmas.

It's not that I don't think she'll be okay on her own. I know she will be. Lex has always been on her own. I wish she'd allow herself to lean on someone for once. And I wish there was someone that could help pull Lex out of this funk. Who, I don't know. A Leo exorcist? Such a person ought to exist.

Perhaps it's me.

My headache's finally dulled by the time Lex finishes her breakfast. I go to fix myself a plate of eggs, but she does it for me. I pull the laptop out and set it beside my plate. I check the news to get some perspective. Someone out there is having a worse start to their day than me.

Oh! Flood, up north. People stuck in their cars. *Yes.* That really sucks.

Lex and I make light conversation. She tells me about Leo's ex-girlfriend Katy who showed up at the Christmas party like a crazed stalker. I mean, what is it with this guy? Why does his penis turn presumably normal women into nut jobs?

A chime erupts from my laptop's speakers, Lex pauses mid-sentence but then continues talking. I nod along, clicking open my email. Then my jaw drops.

"What is it?" my sister asks.

"Flood. Up north," I lie. "People stuck in their cars."

She nods then gets up. Says she's going to get some Christmas shopping done. I keep my expression steady as she walks away.

I turn back to my laptop and read the email from Leo Conrad.

—

From: Leo Conrad
To: Emily Stone
Subject: Alexis
If by some miracle, you didn't instantly delete this:
I need to talk to you about Alexis. In person.
It's important. Are you coming into town soon?

—

From: Emily Stone
To: Leo Conrad
Subject: RE: Alexis
Instantly delete this?

And miss an opportunity to tell you to go fuck yourself?

No way in hell.

P.S. Go fuck yourself.

—

From: Leo Conrad
To: Emily Stone
Subject: RE: Alexis
My mistake. I forgot I was communicating with a child.

Trust me, you're the last person in the world I want to talk to right now. Or ever. Yet here I am.

Let's cut to the chase. I'm going to assume a few things:

1. You are coming to town for Christmas.
2. You know what happened between Alexis and me.

3. You want your sister to be happy.
4. You know that she can be with me.

—

From: Emily Stone
To: Leo Conrad
Subject: Recap: Fuck off and die

I forgot I was communicating with an arrogant, self-absorbed pretty boy.

1. Did you really just make a numbered list?
2. You broke my sister's heart.
3. And so she hates you.
4. And so I hate you.
5. The best thing you can do is to forget anything happened between the two of you because trust me, she's way over you.

—

From: Leo Conrad
To: Emily Stone
Subject: RE: Recap: Fuck off and die

I hate that I have no idea what to use as bait to lure a vicious man-eater to meet with me.

What is it, anyway--your bait? Is it man blood?

I'm O-Negative.

—

From: Emily Stone
To: Leo Conrad
Subject: RE: Recap: Fuck off and die

Trust me, I'm the last person in the world you want to meet with. Because I can't guarantee I won't drive my very sharp heel into your crotch and puncture your balls--that is, if you even have any.

—

From: Leo Conrad
To: Emily Stone
Subject: RE: Recap: Fuck off and die

I honestly don't care if you like me or not. I don't get the sense that you are the sensitive type so here's the truth: the feeling is mutual. You may not like me, but this isn't about you and me. It's about Alexis.

—

From: Emily Stone
To: Leo Conrad
Subject: RE: Recap: Fuck off and die

I'm sure you miss her, blah blah. Want her back, blah, blah.

But it's time to own up to your shit, Leo.

You lost her. Now go after something that suits you, something cheap and easy. From what I've heard, you've got that department covered.

—

From: Leo Conrad
To: Emily Stone
Subject: Truce?

Here's the truth. I am in love with your sister. Insanely in love. Every second she slips further away from me feels like I'm losing a part of myself.

All I want is to make Alexis happy.

Please, hear me out.

—

Chapter Fifteen

TRUCE, MY ASS.

Lex and I spend the rest of the weekend together. I don't mention the emails and decide not to give Leo Conrad another thought. Lex's office is closed for the holidays and she won't have to see him until after New Year's. By then, I'm positive, she'll have gotten over him enough to where he'll be just a small splinter in her ass.

My sister treats me to a pedicure at a salon. It's my first time, since I usually couldn't care less about the color of my toenails. But to my pleasant surprise, the process involves so much more than I expected. It's not simple, mere nail painting. Oh, no. This is a goddamn experience. Why did no one ever mention the massage chair?

There're freaking industrial strength rods in there kneading all the muscles in my back as the salon woman massages me all the way up to my calves before layering on a mask that smells faintly of spearmint. I can't keep a straight face. I'm certain this chair is seducing me.

"Do you like it?" Lex asks from the chair beside me, laughing at the way my eyes threaten to roll into the back of my head.

"I need one of these. Holy hell, this is what I call a back massage."

"No kidding," she says, "I try to come every two weeks. But, I haven't been in for a while...." She trails off, then shifts and looks away, uncomfortable. I guess what's kept her away is she and Leo screwing like rabbits.

To distract her from thoughts of the asshole, I tell Lex about Owen. This topic peaks her interest, as I knew it would. She leans into my words as I describe how hard he is to read. I go on describing his appearance in obnoxious detail and even go as far as making a cupping gesture in midair, squeezing an imaginary ass. Then I throw my head back as though the description is getting me riled up and I let out a frustrated groan. "I want him so bad, you have no idea."

"I mean, since when are you shy about going after what you want?" Lex asks.

"I'm in no way shy--"

"Don't act like you're an innocent. We all know that ship has sailed. It sailed and it was ransacked by pirates, and those pirates burned it down..."

My sister erupts into a fit of self-indulgent snickering and while it's nice to see her laughing, I look on, glaring playfully. "It's not that. Trust me."

"What is it then?" she asks, rearranging her face to innocent curiosity.

"I'm not sure. It's like we're doing this seductive dance around the bush." I wave my arms around to demonstrate, ignoring the bewildered look the woman painting my toenails gives me. "All primal, caveman like. You know, daring each other to--"

"Screw the other's brain's out?" Lex offers.

"Well, yeah."

"Okay, so I get that you obviously like him. But what happens when you leave town? Do you really want to get caught up in a long distance thing?"

"Well...no."

"Just..." She hesitates. "Keep your focus on what's important. A man is never what's important."

I know she's right. San Francisco is where my future is. But where I'll be in the coming weeks doesn't change where I am now.

It doesn't change how I *feel* now.

I can't deny the real force pulling me back to the diner. It's not the food. It's not the ambiance. It's Owen. This mysterious, guarded man making me wish I had a way to access hints of his thoughts.

I know I shouldn't be curious. I shouldn't wonder what his body looks like lit from behind by the glow of a lamp, glistening with sweat as he handles me in all the ways I suspect he can.

What I should be doing is pulling my life together. Simplifying. Not lusting after potentially complicated things.

I know this. I do. But, dammit, I still want him.

Chapter Sixteen

I'M HUNG-OVER MONDAY MORNING, forgetting my sister will be there when I wake up. Having her off work for the holidays is an adjustment to the previous week when I had the condo to myself during the day. She makes another remark about me drinking too much and tasks me with helping her wrap Christmas presents. I don't get to sneak away to the diner for breakfast like I wanted, opting, instead, for helping my sister run errands.

Early Tuesday morning, I wake up to an unexpected call from the law firm that agreed to interview me after the holidays.

"A change?" I clutch the telephone tighter and try to keep my voice even. "May I ask what's changed?"

The woman on the phone, who isn't Janie--the one I originally spoke with--stays vague. Says there's been a misunderstanding. The interview is off.

They were perfectly interested in me just a few days ago. The change of heart is curious and, if my suspicions are correct, I'm in deep, deep shit.

Calling the dozen or so firms I've sent job applications to takes a surprisingly short period of time. Each call is almost identical, lasting two to three minutes. By the fourth one, I've got the steps memorized like a choreographed dance.

Ring. Ring. Ring. Receptionist's greeting, professional, distant. I ask for the status of my application and am asked to hold. Papers shuffling. Receptionist's voice returns, audibly awkward, as though glimpsing an embarrassing note on the file.

From then on there's a variation of responses.

"We apologize, we are no longer accepting applications for this position," and "Your application did not make the first round of reviews," and "Thank you for your interest but you are not in consideration at this time."

With each call, the disbelief, dread, and anger braid into themselves in the pit of my stomach.

I make one last call.

"Bernstein, Snyder and Associates, this is Mona."

"I need you to tell me what's going on, please."

A pause.

"Emily?"

"Just tell me."

Background noise trickles through the receiver but when her voice returns, it's slightly isolated. Like she's cupping a hand over where her lips meet the phone.

"Davenport dropped Bernstein."

"Because of me?"

"I don't think so. He came in the day after your meeting. Seemed fine. Even asked for you."

"What the hell for?"

"Said he wanted to apologize for being...uh, I forget the term he used. But it's like he didn't know his girlfriend put in the complaint--" As if on cue, the phone rings on her end. Mona puts me on hold; my hand tightens over the metal body of my cellphone until she returns. "Sorry, I really can't talk right now. But the gist of the story is, he and Bernstein got into it. Not sure what it was about, but the two never really liked each other, so honestly, this has been a long time coming."

"But Bernstein blames me?"

"Yes."

"I want to talk to him. Bernstein, I mean. Put me through."

"Emily..."

"Please?"

Mona exhales into the phone. "Okay, but I can't guarantee he'll want to talk to you."

Her voice cuts out to the 'hold' sound. A loop of three beeps followed by a brief silence. I shut my eyes and gather my thoughts.

"This is Bernstein."

My eyes fly open at the coarse voice, the bored tone. I was sure I'd be sent to his voicemail. Clearing my throat, I begin. "This is Emily Stone. I'm sorry for the way I behaved. It was unprofessional of me. I know. But I'm trying to move past that. Bernstein, I'm not asking for a reference, I'm just asking that you don't sabotage my job-hunting efforts."

"Sabotage?" His voice is slick and disingenuous. "What are you talking about?"

"I--" The anger I've been struggling to keep down closes around my neck, squeezing tight. "You're blacklisting me. That's what I'm talking about.

Blacklisting, by the way, is slander. Defamation. It's illegal."

"I am well aware of what's within the scope of the law, Ms. Stone. I'm also aware of what can be plausibly proven."

I shut my eyes.

A casual conversation he may have with some other firm's partner about the crazy associate who told Collin Davenport to 'choke on a dick' wouldn't be recorded anywhere. This wouldn't, technically be libel. But Bernstein's not just having casual conversations with friends. I'm positive he's making sure my application is rejected by every firm I apply to. How he's done this in just under a week, I have no idea. But it just goes to show his actions are deliberate enough.

Sabotage.

Bernstein's blacklisting me and he knows it. The problem is, I have no way to prove this. He'd be smart enough to cover his tracks which, for me, means no real chance at fighting him on it. Other firms' partners would protect him--thank him, even, for warning them away from the troublemaker associate.

I don't realize how long the silence stretched until Bernstein voice comes to my ear again, tone dripping with the smirk he is undoubtedly wearing. "Will that be all, Ms. Stone?"

I hang up and my arm jerks from under me, hurling the phone across the room. It bounces off of the opposite wall of the living room and crashes to the floor.

Cursing under my breath, I run over to make sure I didn't break it. The last thing I need is to delve out the money for a new phone. The phone is still functional, surviving my vicious attack for the most part. Except the glass screen now has a crack creeping halfway into it from the edge. Okay. I deserve that. And anyway, it felt pretty damn good.

Setting the phone down on the coffee table, I sit on the edge of the couch.

What a mess.

I'm under no delusion bringing Bernstein into a civil suit could give me anything but more problems. Even if I won, I'd lose. Because after it's all said and done, all I'd be doing is becoming a martyr for a cause that isn't going away. Blacklisting won't suddenly be a thing of the past. Firms in the area won't then feel inclined to hire me. I don't want to disappear into the wayside, blend away before my career really begins. There has to be another way. Some way that I can move out from under Bernstein's reach.

Options tick past the forefront of my mind like credits at the end of a movie. Firms are closing today or tomorrow for Christmas. The holidays stagnate everything and everyone; the world slows and churns to the same tune of enforced ignorant bliss.

I'm marooned on an island of twinkling pine trees, unable to do a damn thing about my situation until after Christmas. More than likely, not until after the New Year.

Needing to vent, I call Amelia. She's at work, of course, but gives me a solid three minutes to spew out profanities in the name of my vindictive ex-boss. As I speak, I fix myself another cup of coffee. My line of sight shifts without reason and lands on the bottle of vodka cradled between the bottles of wine on the counter.

I already want a drink.

Of course, this is ridiculous. It's just after ten in the morning. But as I stir sugar into my mug, I ask Amelia if the rules on appropriate drinking times apply only to people who have jobs or children to look after. Places to drive to. I have none of those things. All I have is time, an entire day stretched out before me to figure out my next move.

She agrees I'm allowed an early drink considering the circumstance. The tan liquid of my coffee rises gently in the cup with the introduction of the new substance. Giving the concoction a quick stir, I take my first sip.

Before we hang up, Amelia invites me over to her place tonight. Says she purchased a man-shaped punching bag, with a crotch and everything. Beating the shit out of it apparently works wonders for carrying out hatred of all phallic shaped things.

A bit discouraged and crestfallen, I leave the laptop closed for the day and spend the afternoon looking through my sister's storage shed, which is full of boxes I left behind when I moved north for law school. Can't believe it's all still here, collecting dust. Old college stuff, rare pictures from our childhood, the bicycle she bought me when I was twelve. And a ton of other crap she insists on hoarding.

I'm looking for a specific picture I remember of the two of us to frame as a present. It was the summer before I turned ten. My mother was dating a surprisingly decent guy at the time, one who probably had no idea what he was getting into. He took us to the county fair, at the Del Mar fairgrounds. There's a picture of Lex and me on one of the rides. If memory serves me right, it's hilarious. Lex looks terrified, holding onto my hand for dear life, while I sit beside her, hair standing on ends but otherwise looking positively unimpressed with the ordeal.

After pouring over the collection of random trinkets in the boxes marked vaguely--probably by me--as *old stuff* and *more old stuff* and *the last of the old stuff*, I finally find the damn picture in a small photo album. There are a few other good ones in there from that summer. I take the whole thing and tuck it under my arm.

A glance at my watch tells me it's nearly eight in the evening. I'm supposed to leave for Amelia's soon and I'm still not dressed to go. As I turn back to the door of the shed, a box plopped atop a ledge catches my eye.

HS Stuff--Emily

High School stuff? I can't resist taking a peek inside. It's mostly empty, which surprises me. I find two textbooks I never returned, a plastic bag full of handwritten notes my friends and I used to pass back and forth between classes, a bunch of hair ribbons from when I was in the cheerleading squad, and my varsity cheerleading uniform. Under all of that, a black square of fabric takes me by surprise. I pull on it to reveal a man's suit jacket, staring at it for a beat before the memory comes over me. A memory rusted from time, of a cold night, a kind boy, and a warm, innocent gesture.

On the inside collar, written in black marker over the designer's tag are two words: *Lucas Grant*.

Chapter Seventeen

HANDS WRAPPED AROUND THE STEERING wheel, I tell myself I'm headed to Amelia's place. But the jacket on the seat beside me indicates my intentions of a detour.

It's quiet. The car radio is off for the very first time because my thoughts are loud enough tonight.

This is ridiculous. The diner's closed, I'm sure it is. The clock on my dashboard says it's nearly nine and the diner closes at eight thirty. But as I drive past it, I catch dimmed lighting coming from the inside.

A detour it is.

All the window blinds are shut and the sign on the door is turned to *closed*, but when I try the handle, the door gives inward and the bell sounds overhead like it always does. The place looks deserted at first, chairs pulled up over the tabletops.

Owen emerges from the back hall that leads to the restrooms. He's dressed in a gray button down shirt and dark jeans, holding a small can of paint. When he sees me, he freezes but doesn't immediately say anything.

I take my time walking up to him, the sounds of my heels clicking against the tile flooring echo around me as his eyes sweep over my figure as though unable to look anywhere else. I'm wearing a dress, like I usually am. Because dresses are the only clothes I can borrow from Lex and, also, they are comfortable as hell to throw on. This one is a tight sweater dress that comes about mid-thigh.

"Kitchen's closed, you know. Wifi's been turned off," Owen says, smiling a little, as though suspecting I'm here for something else.

Holding out my hands, I pull on the material in them to reveal the shape of the jacket. "This is yours, isn't it?"

The jacket is obviously too small for him, it would fit a much smaller frame. He starts to shake his head but, slowly, recognition clicks into place and his eyes move up to meet mine. "Where'd you get that?"

"Storage. My sister has all my old stuff here. It's yours, isn't it?"

He nods after a few seconds. The silence that follows tells me he's unsure where I'm going with this, why I'd come here to give it back to him after all these years.

"My junior year, prom night...I was sitting outside. It was cold and I was shivering. Someone came up beside me and asked me if I was okay. I didn't want to answer because my makeup was running and I didn't want anyone to see. He put this jacket on me and I barely got a chance to look up before my friends came out and he disappeared."

He waits, as if knowing I'm not finished.

"It was you, wasn't it?"

"Yes," he says. "It was me."

"Was that the night you and Jonathan fought?"

"It was."

"I remember you," I say.

"I'm glad I finally ring a bell."

The brief moment that follows drapes a peculiar sensation over me. Relief. And in his eyes? Satisfaction.

It's like we are finally hitting the nail on the head, even when neither of us knew there was a nail to hit.

He eyes my smirk and I know he's thinking about our kiss. I'm thinking about it too. The tension I typically see pulling his eyebrows together dissolves before my eyes, seeping instead into the air around us, making the space between our bodies feel impossibly far and recklessly close.

"Can I ask you a question?" He nods to the jacket. "Why'd you keep it?"

His question catches me off guard and I have to look away to gather my thoughts. "At first I thought I'd find this Lucas Grant and return the jacket in person. I didn't like owing someone a favor. People always wanted something in return for their favors. I asked around, there were a few Grants but no Lucas Grant going to our school at the time. Obviously I didn't make the connection to Lucas from the diner...."

Because I didn't even know he had a son, I finish in my head.

"For the record, there were no strings attached."

"I knew that, somehow. That's why I couldn't bring myself to get rid of it."

We are standing closer than before, though I can't remember either one of us moving forward. His gaze trails downward in an 's' pattern, carving out the hollows of my body, the parts that swoop inward only to curve back out again. Then he says, "You look nice."

"Thanks." I lift up the jacket and slap it against Owen's chest. One of his hands rises to catch it, gripping part of my hand along with the material. I don't pull away, letting him hold it there for a beat before letting my hand drop back to my side.

As our sights hover unbroken, I wonder if we're playing a game. Daring the other to give into the force weighing on the space between us, pulling us inward.

A familiar voice pulls me out of my Owen-induced haze. "Oh. Sorry."

Landon is standing by the back entrance, his body half turned from us, unsure whether he wants to come in further or leave.

What the hell is the kid doing here?

"Are you ready to go?" Owen asks him.

I sidestep to stand beside Owen and I notice it for the first time. The resemblance between the two is undeniable: the straight eyebrows, the square chins, almond shaped hazel eyes, always slightly narrowed.

I blurt out, "Wait, are you two related?"

Owen looks surprised by my question. "I thought he would've mentioned it." A second slithers past, uncomfortable and leaving a trail of unspoken things in its wake. "Landon's my son."

I don't exactly think of what I'm about to say when I round on the kid. "You told me your father was dead!"

Landon doesn't miss a beat. "Well, he is. On the *inside*."

I know he means it as a joke. It would be funny if it weren't for Owen's reaction. His jaw is tight but behind the tired look of frustration is something else, something less edgy and more vulnerable.

"I'll just wait for Rob upstairs," Landon says.

Owen brings a hand to rub over his eyebrow. "Rob? I thought the plan was for us to go bowling."

Landon throws his head back. "I told you I'm going over Rob's tonight. You never listen to me."

Without warning, they both turn to me and I realize that instead of walking backward toward the exit like I imagined myself to be, I've been hovering by the entrance to the back hall, watching their awkward exchange.

Pivoting on my heel, I make a casual show out of examining the announcements pinned to the corkboard on the wall. Though I'm only pretending to be interested, one of the flyers catches my attention, for real. There's a loft for rent with an ocean view. The picture of it shows a cozy little place, an open floor plan, and a modern and fresh design despite the antique, attic quality of the slanted ceiling. Looking at this picture brings a flurry to my stomach. I don't care about square footage. I'd just love to get a little place like this, all on my own.

Owen and Landon finish their discussion and apparently, Landon is being picked up in fifteen minutes. "Can I go hang out upstairs?" he asks his father, as though already bored to be around us.

"Don't touch the trims, I just painted them." Owen says in a tired voice.

Landon mumbles something and I catch movement from the corner of my eye. As the kid walks past me, I swear he winks. I stare after him, watching him disappear down the short hall and go through a back exit I'm assuming leads to the upstairs.

Well, that was weird.

"Are you looking for a place?" Owen asks, noticing the ad for the loft in my hand.

"Yeah." When did I pull the ad off the bulletin board? "I mean--no. Just looks like a nice place."

"I see." Disappointment whisks past his face, as he turns his attention fleetingly toward the hall where Landon just disappeared.

I pin the page back to the board, quietly wondering if I could find a similar place in San Francisco on such short notice or if I'll end up having to settle for something much less appealing with a roommate who's a closet meth addict.

"Maybe we--" I'm interrupted by the shrill ringing of my phone. It's Amelia. The thought of leaving Owen now causes guilt to drum on me even though I'm not the one who ditched him. His son did. The little asshole.

Owen nods to my phone. "Is that your date?"

"It's--no. It's not a date, it's my friend. We're--"

Once again I'm interrupted by my phone, this time a chime of a text message.

[Are you still coming over?]

"We have plans tonight. But...." I pause in my answer to Owen in order to respond to the text.

[Something came up. Rain check?]

Amelia will be fine, she only asked me over because she's worried about me.

I go on, shaking my head at my phone. "But she

bailed on me."

[Okay, you flake. Just don't go gazing off any bridges tonight. You'll figure everything out. You always do.]

My stomach contracts when I realize she's talking about Bernstein blacklisting me. For a minute there, I'd almost forgotten about that.

Owen watches me as I slip my phone back in my purse.

"I guess we both got stood up," he says.

"I guess we did." I glance over at the doorway of the kitchen. "What are the chances I can order some pancakes?"

"Well, that depends. What are the chances you can get out of those heels and help me make them?"

Chapter Eighteen

THE FLORESCENT LIGHTS IN THE kitchen take a few seconds to buzz awake after Owen flips the switch. When light pours down over us, it reflects over the stainless steel table running down the center of the room. I walk around, seeing how incredibly spotless the place is, something serene about it despite its cold metal and white tiles.

The place is dead quiet. I slide my phone out of my purse. "Do you mind if I turn on some music?"

"Music?" he says it like it's the most ridiculous thing he's ever heard.

"Yeah, music. I promise it won't kill you."

He looks like he's about to tell me music isn't a good idea, but I pull my lips up into a grin and hit the play button. Upbeat music from my playlist pours from my speakers. Owen's narrowed eyes tell me he thinks it's unnecessary. I pretend not to notice him and do a small dance as I walk along, taking in the rest of the kitchen.

When I glimpse at him over my shoulder, I notice him watching me dance. We share a reminiscing look and I know he's thinking of the other night at the bar. And just like it did that night, his smile nearly knocks me on my ass. I have no idea why he spends so much time frowning when he could have women falling at his feet with a flash of that smile.

Owen's phone buzzes and after a quick glance at it, he says, "Landon left."

I walk back to Owen and lean over the countertop beside him, drumming my fingers as he pours batter onto the griddle. There are questions gnawing away at me and I'm not sure how intrusive they are.

"Landon said he's nine...so, he was born when you were...eighteen?"

It's clear that this topic is difficult for him by the significant pause he takes before adding more sections of batter to the griddle. "Nineteen."

"Must've been hard. Having a kid so young."

"It would've been hard, yes. If I'd known."

My eyes widen a notch, despite myself. "I don't understand. What do you mean?"

For a moment I think he's not going to answer me, but then he meets my eyes and says, "His mother and I, we had a thing the summer before college. We met during orientation. But first semester, she started missing a lot of classes, and then she dropped out and disappeared. Turns out, she moved back to Arizona with her parents because she was pregnant."

"Why wouldn't she tell you?"

"My guess is she was sure I wouldn't want it. I went through a pretty bad phase after high school. I was partying a lot, didn't really take anything seriously. I guess you could say I was reckless. Wasn't ready for a kid back then. But being ready doesn't matter." He sets the container down and runs a hand over the back of his neck as though the memory weighs on him there. "I would've gotten ready. I would've figured out how to be a dad if she'd told me. But she chose not to. Took away my chance to own up and be a man. Worst part is I can't exactly hate her for it now."

"What happened to her?"

"Car accident. I hadn't heard from her in almost ten years but when her mother reached out to me a few months ago, I thought it was to invite me to the funeral. I'd heard about the accident, from mutual friends. But the reason her mother called was to tell me I had a son. My name's on the birth certificate and everything. One look at the kid and it's obvious."

"Yeah," I say, feeling stupid for not noticing it before. "Can I ask--I mean, I get the sense you two don't really get along."

"It's been rough. We're strangers and nothing I do seems to change that," Owen says, wiping his hands on a towel, eyes cast to the circles of yellow batter slowly cooking. "He lets me know every day how much he hates it here. How he misses his life back in Arizona, but his grandmother can't look after him--and obviously, I want to."

I draw circles on the metal surface of the counter, absentmindedly. "Sounds like he's making friends. Making plans to hang out."

"Rob, you mean? No, that's his cousin. My sister's kid. I don't understand what they have in common. When you were thirteen, did you hang out with nine-year-olds?"

"Not really, but Landon seems pretty mature for his

age."

"I wish he acted more his age." Owen crosses his arms and I get the sense he is going to change the subject.

But this conversation is satiating my curiosity. "So you find out you have a kid, your dad has a heart attack...seems like an eventful few months."

"You could say that. I'm guessing there's a good reason you're job hunting right around Christmas?"

"Yeah. There's a good reason." I narrow my eyes and decide it *is* time to change the subject. "Do you keep in touch with anyone from school?"

"Not really. I've seen two or three people over the years."

He goes on to name a few people, none of whom I recognize. But he was a year ahead of me and ran in different circles, so that's not surprising.

"You know--it's funny. I don't have a single picture from high school. Not one. I'm not sure how that's even possible."

"You never took a photography class, then. I've got them by the dozens."

"Get out," I say, slapping his arm. The tinge of heat on my palm is something I should expect by now, but it takes me by surprise. "I'd kill to get my hands on a cheerleading picture. I didn't even buy a yearbook."

I don't tell him it's because I couldn't afford to.

"I have a box full of pictures," he says. "Back at my apartment."

"Trying to lure me back to your place, huh?"

A grin curving the corners of his mouth, he sets a

hand on either side of the counter, trapping me between his arms. "And what if I am?"

Our proximity makes my heartbeat pick up, but I pretend it doesn't. Even while my phone's speakers cut off to a song with slower tempo, fitting the mood a little too well.

"What exactly would we do? Back at your place?" I ask, squaring my shoulders.

He looks down at my chest in an obvious way, wanting me to see the way he takes in my cleavage. Wanting me to imagine his hands peeling away my dress.

"Anything and everything you'd like to do."

What a goddamn tease, this man. I'm distracted by the heaviness between my legs, the weight of my need for him. My skin tingles in anticipation of his touch. I can imagine what he would feel like, pushing inside of me. Sliding in and out as my naked body heaves under his. It's all so clear it might as well be a memory, but it's only a fantasy. A vivid one that gets me all hot and bothered.

"It's burning," I say.

His voice grows deliciously low. "What is?"

"The pancakes."

He spins around to the griddle. The smell of burning batter wafts overhead as he flips the pancakes over to reveal their charred backsides.

"You really, really suck at this whole running a diner thing," I tease.

"Yeah. Good thing I didn't quit my day job." He flings the spatula aside. "Forget the pancakes. How about I just show you what I've got back at my place?"

Hands down, the most appetizing thing I've heard all night.

Chapter Nineteen

OWEN'S APARTMENT HAS THE DISTINCT feel of a bachelor's pad. The furniture is modern and of functional design. There's minimal decor. No curtains on the windows, a few mismatched pieces of art on the walls.

"You should really close your blinds," I tell him, looking out the nearest window and seeing the street outside.

"You planning to show me something you don't want anyone else to see?"

"If you play your cards right," I say, after laughing louder than I normally would.

Why am I nervous?

Walking over to a large bookcase at the end of the living room, I take in the books brimming every shelf. At the very top sits a few boxes. Not moving boxes, but smaller ones, like for shoes.

"You read a lot."

"Yes. Yes, I do..." He sits down on the edge of the sofa, legs spread, forearms resting on his knees, and peering up at me with those insanely alluring eyes.

The man's not doing anything remotely sexual, just sitting and fixing me with an unassuming look--yet the sight of him floods me with lust.

I want to jump on him, right where he sits, tear away his clothes, and hurt him in all the best ways. I want to know what his kisses feel like down below. Fuck that. I want to smother him between my thighs...

Cool it, Emily. You don't want to go all Animal Planet on him and scare him off.

My urge for him is so overwhelmingly intense, I have to turn my back on him. Reeling myself in, I focus on running a finger along the spine of the books. Trying to sound unaffected, I say, "Crime novels. Why so many crime novels?"

"They're interesting. Do you read?"

I glance over my shoulder at his question. There's a genuine interest spiking in his eyes.

"Sometimes."

I rarely read. Every once in a while, I'll find my nose in a good book, consuming it quickly. I tell myself I should read more often, but I never get around to it.

Owen reaches to the table beside the couch and grabs a paperback sitting on the base of the lamp. "Here." He hands the book to me.

I hesitate.

"I think you'll like this," he explains. "The main character's a detective. Reminds me a lot of you, actually."

His last words pique my interest. I walk over to him and take the novel, spying the cover. There's a city backdrop, blending into an empty street at nighttime, crime tape spewed across it, police cars in the distance. In the foreground, a brunette kneels over a lump of white sheets, which I presume cover a dead body. The title is in blood red: The Dead of Night.

"Will you read it?"

"Yeah. I will." I put the book in my purse, which is on the coffee table, and sit down beside him. Our bodies are a foot or two apart. His arm is over the head of the sofa, body tilted to face mine.

"I had an interesting talk with Landon last night," he says, "about the advice you gave him."

I hang my head in pretend shame. "I was trying to get him the girl."

"That's not how you get the girl."

"Really, now? Doesn't sound like you were lucky with the ladies when you were his age."

He laughs and looks down. When he casts his eyes upward, there's a glint of mischief there. I swear the sofa slides sideways a few feet, but it's not the furniture that slides. It's my stomach.

I'm staring at him so hard I forget to take a breath. And, for the first time, we both seem to go still enough to hear the crackling in the air between us. The attraction whipping and lashing at us, demanding to be acknowledged.

"I want you, Emily. Bad."

"Nothing ever changes."

"You're wrong." He leans in. My body responds before I decide to let it, pulling away from where I sit to meet him halfway. I somehow feel every millimeter separating our lips as though the air between them was taken up by something tangible; tiny strings, pulling me in. Yet he holds steady, precisely where he is, stopping short of the kiss he knows I crave and says, "I can think of one thing that's changed."

I nod, somehow understanding exactly what he means. And I know what he's waiting for. Pulling up on my knees, I straddle him where he sits. Desire eclipses his expression, a fog of heat falls over us both. Holding his face with both hands, I say, "I want you, too."

In the split second before our lips part for the kiss, I feel his twist into a smile. Then his mouth commands mine, owning every curve, deliberating each taste. My dress is hiked up, almost all the way to my hips. His hands run up the sides of my exposed thighs, settling over my hips, tugging them inward, and pressing me as close to him as humanly possible.

The heat our kiss generates clouds my mind; all I see is need. And all I need is Owen. He buries his face in the nook of my neck and bites me slightly, making my nerve endings go haywire.

Hands holding me tightly in place, he gets to his feet with me still on top. My legs lock around him even though I feel weightless in his arms, unconcerned with falling.

He leads us into the bedroom, and the effortless way he carries me is an unbelievable turn-on. Every inch of my skin sears from the blaze raging inside of me. I don't realize where he's guiding us until my back hits the wall between his nightstand and dresser. He lowers me until my feet touch the ground.

"Put your hands up," he says, voice low.

I do as he asks, biting my lip at the way his words echo between my thighs.

He lifts up my dress, his fingertips dragging against

my skin from my thighs all the way up my arms as he pulls the material over my head. The moment my face is in view again, his lips are on mine. Much greedier than ever, bordering on ravenous, and he takes my bottom lip into his mouth as though biting into a supple fruit.

All the while, his hands explore my body, over my breasts, down my stomach, over my hips. And everywhere he touches, my skin revs up like an engine anticipating the ride. I unhook my bra and toss it aside as his fingers slip between the material of my panties and close over my ass, pressing me up against the bulge in his pants.

Why the fuck is he still wearing pants?

My underwear falls to my ankles and I kick it aside. A drunken sort of haze comes over me, naked and completely at his mercy. All I want is to feel him inside of me, but he moves without urgency, taunting me. Making me burn from the inside out.

If it's possible to die from horniness, I'm about to go code blue.

When he tosses his shirt aside and lets his pants hit the ground in a thud, I can't help but take in the outline of his hard cock through his underwear. Letting out an impatient breath, I reach around to pull his goddamn underwear off.

"Arms up." His voice is thick and sends a shiver of delight right down my spine. I oblige, resting my wrists on the top of my head. I'm about to ask him if he has a condom when he reaches into his nightstand drawer for one.

He brings his hand in for a sneak peek, and I

tremble as his fingers slide against what's waiting for him. Wrapper tears open. A sigh parts my lips as his warm hands come over my hips again. Thoughts are a desperate blur of anticipation, unable to wait a second longer to--

A moan rips through me as he plunges inside of me. No longer a tease, right when it matters most. I melt in relish from the delicious burn--he's unbelievably hard and I'm nearly bursting at the seams from him.

Owen fucks me there, against the wall. Holding and anchoring my weight on his arms again, his strokes long and steady. With a taunting slowness that I'm beginning to recognize from him. The burn drives me insane. But I can tell it's what he wants. He likes to watch me squirm under him, likes to see my body angling for more, quivering and begging for him to take me with everything he's got.

"Faster," I breathe out.

He picks up his pace, hands securing my hips in place. The frantic tempo is enough to send me clinging to the very edge of control. The sounds of his hard pounding echo loud around us.

"Can you take it?"

"God, yes." I'm breathless and trembling, the euphoric pressure building until it almost hurts to feel this good.

I'm overwhelmed by the way his body commands every inch of mine, making me delight in the midst of the building flurry of sensations. He plays me like an instrument, with complete control and confidence, stroking me in ways that make me whimper.

"Don't stop," I moan. "I'm close."

But he does stop. He spins me around to face the wall, wraps an arm under my breasts as though he knows I'm dizzy with pleasure, and pushes inside me again. "Damn, your ass is beautiful," he says.

He groans as I twist my back, pressing my lower half into him, and he sinks even deeper, still. And when he begins pulsing in and out of me, I shut my eyes and beg him to make me come.

"We're not done until the only word you remember--" he whispers, low and dangerous, matching his next words to each thrust. "--is my name."

Holy Fuck.

The power behind his voice, the tremble in his tone, vibrates right through me. I nearly come right then. When he reaches his other hand around to stroke my clit with his rough fingers, I let out an anguished cry and my knees buckle under me.

"Come for me," he growls.

The orgasm pounds through me with his next thrust, setting off every nerve ending in my body as I breathe out the only word I know.

Owen. Owen. Owen.

Chapter Twenty

THE HAMMERING IN MY CHEST slows as we lie back on his bed. Owen brings a hand behind his head, his other remains on the small of my back as though ensuring I remain where I am, on top of him.

A comfortable silence falls over us. Satisfied. And gives way to small talk a few minutes later. He makes me laugh without trying and we tease each other about unimportant things.

At some point, I veer off topic. "I never thought I'd say this, but I'm dreading Christmas," I say. "Bad."

"And why is that?"

"Not looking forward to facing the real world that comes after it's over. Looking for a job, a place." I drag my lips over his jaw as I speak, slowly taking in his scent, feeling it stir desire in the deepest parts of me. Owen lets out a small groan at the way I bear my weight on him until his newly forming erection pushes back against me right where I want it most.

"You don't like living with your sister?"

"Huh? Oh, no. I don't live with Lex. I'm just visiting until after Christmas. Then it's back to San Francisco."

Owen pulls me back slightly until our eyes meet, lips turned down. "You...live in San Francisco?"

Dammit.

"I thought--didn't I mention that?"

"No. You didn't."

A beat.

"Are you upset?"

"That you're leaving town in a few days? Or that I didn't realize this was a one-night stand?" He pauses then adds, "I don't do one-night stands."

How cute.

I bury my face in the crook of his neck and whisper, "We can do as many night stands as you want."

"I'm serious, Emily."

I prop myself up on an elbow to view him properly.

"I want you," he says, running his thumb over my swollen lips. The pause in his speech is punctuated by his hard-on, still pressing against me. But his voice floods with the wrong kind of conviction. "But not like this. Not when you're leaving right after and I don't even know when I'll see you again."

I can't help but smile at how endearing he sounds. Twisting my voice into an Australian accent, I say, "Here we have the *Male Monogamous*, thought to have gone extinct over two hundred thousand years ago--"

"Very funny." And in one move, he nudges my body off his and sits up on the corner of the bed, back toward me.

I'm surprised by how upset he seems and am unsure of what to say. I stare at the ropey muscles of his back, admiring the sexy hollows and contours, more pronounced as he pulls on his underwear and shirt.

"I'm sorry," I finally manage. "I don't mean to poke

fun. It's...I didn't realize I forgot to mention I was only in town for a little while."

"Don't worry about it," he says, evenly. "It would've been nice to know. That's all."

"Would it have changed anything?"

He stands to zip up his pants, looking down at me, eyes drinking in the sight of my naked skin. And I'm burning for him again, relishing in his admiration and refusing to shy away for a second, letting him see every inch of me where I sit on my heels.

"Probably not," he says with a small, resigned smile.

I like this man. A lot. I can't remember the last time I've liked a guy this much. I hate that the universe dangles him in front of me now, knowing damn well my life is somewhere else. Knowing we could never be anything more. Because, as much as I enjoy his company, I can't get into a long distance relationship. It wouldn't be fair. He wants more than I can give him from five hundred miles away, with so many aspects of my life needing serious repair. And honestly, I want more than the distance could give me, too.

He should know this. The sudden strain in the silence between us is building because he doesn't know.

"For the record," I say, "if you lived in San Francisco, I'd monogamize the hell out of you."

"Did you just make up that word?"

"Oh yeah. I'd monogamize you so hard..."

He grins, gazing at me for a second before holding out a hand to help me off the bed. I glance at the time on the clock and wonder when his son is getting back home.

"I should get going," I say as I pull my dress back on.

"You're leaving?" He sounds dissatisfied.

He brings his body close to mine and runs his hands down my sides as though to smooth out the wrinkles of my dress, knowing damn well what his touch does to me.

Our faces are nose-to-nose, and an almost palpable enthrallment tinges the air between our lips, drugging me with each breath I take.

I want him. And though I'm sure he wants me, too, Owen pulls his hands away from me pointedly and pushes them into his pockets, instead. A small, silent gesture indicating he isn't inclined to give into another romp.

It's like he's afraid it would only add to his disappointment of me leaving. Or maybe he, too, is aware his son might be on his way back.

"I should head back to my sister's place," I say, my lips nearly grazing his as I speak. "Take a cold shower. Hump my pillow--I do it every night, so don't flatter yourself."

His mouth pulls up. "Before you go, let me find the picture you wanted."

He leads us back to the living room. I sit on the sofa again and watch as he retrieves one of the boxes stacked over the bookcase. He sets it down on the table in front of me.

"Is this where you keep them?" I ask.

He nods and sits beside me as I start looking through the box. It's full of photographs. Some Polaroid, most print.

"*Oh my God*!" My hands snatch up a picture and laughter erupts from within my chest.

There's a young boy with a bowl cut. His eyes barely visible behind his bangs, though his sour expression is etched over his entire face. Judging by his outstretched hand, he doesn't want his picture taken. I wouldn't want my picture taken either, if I wore *that* awful outfit.

Owen snatches the picture from me, half smiling. "It was spirit week. Mismatched Monday. Remember?"

I nod. I do remember. The week before homecoming was referred to as spirit week. The school had a schedule to encourage students to dress in a nonsensical fashion. Mismatched Monday. Nerdy Tuesday. Pajama Wednesday.

I look through the other photos. They seem to be of Owen's friends. Fresh faced kids, smiling for the camera in ridiculous poses. A few with Owen in them, arms extended out. I spy the background of the photos, recognizing the halls of our school, see some familiar faces in there.

"This is hilarious," I say, flipping through. I freeze on one picture. Owen goes instantly quiet beside me, he tries to grab for the photo, but I turn from him, bringing it out of his reach so I can examine it further.

At first glance, it seems to be a photograph of the school's hallway, students at their lockers, some walking past. But it isn't a random shot. It is composed as to draw the eye to one subject in particular. A girl, in front of an open locker, face angled toward the camera but her expression far away. Her friends stand nearby and judging by the satisfied looks on their faces, they're engaged in a salacious conversation.

But the girl reaching into the locker stands out because her lips are turned down. Perhaps it was only for an instant, perhaps long enough for Owen to snap this picture. This girl dropped her guard and allowed the sadness to creep onto her face. But I know when she shuts the locker door, her face will lift with a grin that will fall short of her eyes.

"When did you take this?" I ask.

"Who knows." He reaches into the box to shuffle through the pictures, quickly. "Here it is." Owen places another picture over the one I'm holding, his fingers switching the photographs in my hand. I don't resist, but it takes me a few seconds to bring the new picture into focus.

The new picture in my hand is of the cheerleading squad, in the middle of a stunt. I recognize myself immediately, flying in the air in perfect form. It was my first time doing that stunt at a game. I can tell because the person spotting me was a girl who left the squad a week later. I remember how excited I was about the routine even though there was no one in the stands for me. Not my mother, because she didn't give a shit. Not my sister, because she had picked up a night shift three days a week and couldn't miss work. Her job was the only reason I could afford the expenses of the squad in the first place.

I'm aware that Owen's watching me and I get the sense he expects a positive reaction. Rearranging my expression, I tap a finger on the photograph and say, "Can I keep this?"

"Of course."

I reach over to my purse and slide it inside the book. "Thanks."

When I sit up again, I feel uncomfortable. Why did I want to take a trip down memory lane? Why did I think these memories would be anything but irksome? When I think back to that time in my life, I see smiles and laughter and carefree attitude. But when I think back to what was happening in my life at the time, I remember disappointment and heartache and emptiness.

"Strange to think, isn't it?" Owen says from beside me. "How long ago this was. How young we were."

I look at him and feel suddenly defensive. The irrational fear comes over me that he planned this moment to make me feel exactly these things. That he aimed to remind me of how awful I was and how little I've changed. That this is his revenge on me, for not noticing him. For making him feel invisible.

What he doesn't know is that I felt invisible too.

Even with all those eyes on me. Not a single person saw me.

"What's wrong?"

He seems genuinely confused by whatever expression he glimpses on my face. I pull my lips in for a beat then rise to my feet again.

"Bad memories. Anyway, I really should get going."

I left my phone in my car, so before we leave his apartment, Owen scribbles his number on a piece of paper and tucks it into my purse.

"Don't lose it," he tells me.

"I won't."

We're silent as he walks me to my car. A glance in his direction reveals his expression remains questioning from my reaction to the photograph. When we reach the parking lot, we stop to face each other.

Before I can say anything, Owen takes my face in his hands and claims my lips in a kiss. An intense, bittersweet, wildly tender, goodbye kiss.

Time slips from its natural flow and all the sensations his body drove through mine in the heat of passion bubble to the surface again. I already miss his touch and his hands have yet to leave me.

He pulls away and waits for me to say something, and though my lips part, I can't think of a single word. I smile at him, trying to convey in my silence all the things I can't think to say.

He lets his hands fall to my waist before dropping to his sides. "Goodnight, Emily."

I wonder if he likes the sound of his name on my lips as much as I like hearing mine from his.

"Goodbye, Owen," I say, taking backward steps to my car to keep my eyes on him for a few seconds longer.

Chapter Twenty-One

IT'S CHRISTMAS AND LIKE ANY product of divorce, I need to split my day wisely. I'm not referring to spending time with my father, of course. I wouldn't know him if he passed me on the street.

My holiday will have to be a strategic juggle between the two women in my life. Lex and my mother. My sister doesn't speak to our mother. They literally cannot have a conversation without it ending in a scream fest. It's something I've had to truly come to grips with recently.

I've come to accept that some relationships are toxic. Trying to maintain them for the sake of it is like allowing a disease to eat away at you when you hold the antidote. For Lex, the antidote is a communication blackout. For me...well, I haven't figured one out yet. And, as I sit in my mother's living room, I'm terrified there isn't one.

Guilt crawls around my stomach as I take in the dirty baseboards, the scuffmarks on the walls, and the worn carpet with stains layered on it. It disgusts me to sit here, on this couch, not knowing what's happened on it or why the room smells faintly like mold even through the pungent smell of cigarette smoke.

When I moved her in here, the apartment was decent. Nothing extraordinary, but at the very least it was clean. My mother's presence here dirtied up the place like vines crawling up walls, turning them into something else. Something wild and unkempt.

I watch as she opens the gift I brought for her, pulling the ribbon until it unravels before peeling back the wrapping paper. When she pulls out the picture frame, her face arranges into an automatic smile.

"Wow!"

She brushes a finger over the glass, tracing the image. It's one that I pulled from the album I found in Lex's storage. A picture of Lex, my mother, and me, all sitting at the edge of the fountain in Balboa Park. My mother looks good in the picture. Healthy.

Though I don't remember the picture being taken--I was a toddler--I'm certain my father was behind the camera. I've never been able to find a single picture of him. I think because my mother destroyed them all.

It's strange, but on some level, I feel this is the only family portrait we have. And it being out on a sunny day, in one of my favorite places in San Diego...all of it grounds me to the thought that things weren't always bad. We were happy once. We were a family.

"I didn't get a chance to get you a present," my mother says.

"It's fine, Mom. I just wanted to see you."

We all have areas of our lives we need to tend to from time to time, pulling the weeds before they grow to be a bigger mess. My mother is that for me. It's not that I don't love her. God knows I do. Some might argue she doesn't deserve it, I'd argue that's exactly why I have to. Because no one else will.

I ask her how she's doing and she fiddles with her hands in her lap. Her fingernails are uneven, chewed down to their beds, a sign that she's been fighting her demons.

She tells me she's been going to meetings. The guy she's dating is getting sober, on court orders, before being allowed to see his daughter again. That's motivated her to do the same, out of fear he will leave her.

For my mother, her own daughters weren't enough motivation. The ones cleaning up her vomit. The ones picking her limp body up from the cold, tile floor of the bathroom. Living in filth and opening the refrigerator to find it empty. Hiding under the bed when she and her latest boyfriend got into a blow out fight, and we were sure he would kill her.

I know I shouldn't fixate on her reasoning behind wanting to get better. I should just be happy she's trying. But it stings to think that all the times I cried at her feet as a kid weren't enough to motivate change in her. Yet the fear of losing a man is.

Of course this visit is a huge let down.

What else did I expect?

I nearly flinch when my mother puts a hand to my cheek. Her touch tugs at my heart in an awful way. I feel sorry for her. Really, deeply sorry for her.

Because even when she thinks she's changing, she remains exactly the same.

Lex and I spend Christmas with Julia's family. Her house is loud and energetic--not because of the kids running around, either. The adults are rowdy, their laughs hearty, and their voices carrying throughout.

There's not enough room for everyone at the table, so we eat buffet style, instead. Lex is in a better mood than she has been in recent days, but every once in a while, I can tell her thoughts carry her somewhere far away from the rest of us. I know she's thinking about Leo. She's missing him. I pretend not to notice, partly to save my sister the embarrassment, and partly because I'm not prepared to face the trickle of understanding coming over me of what it feels like to miss someone.

I already miss Owen, even though he was never even mine to lose.

There's enough going on with the kids squealing and the adults recounting stories for Lex's silence to go largely unnoticed. As I eat dessert, I fall into conversation with Giles, Julia's husband. Whenever he and I talk, it's usually small talk about UCSD. We both graduated from the university at different times and he still works there.

Giles is easy to talk to. He has an easy charm about him. But, being Julia's friend, there are things I know that could possibly make speaking to the guy a bit awkward. The type of graphic images you can't easily pry from your head.

It never occurred to me before to ask Giles what type of work he does for the university, having always assumed he was a professor. Turns out, Giles is the head of the Chancellor's Office.

A forkful of pumpkin pie freezes halfway to my mouth as I try to compose the surge of energy that comes over me. The university's chancellor oversees a cluster of departments, which includes the legal department. Shifting my line of questioning from the casual to the more specific, I prod into what type of legal work is available at the university. Giles tells me their research department has grown exponentially after receiving generous grants in the last few years. They have their hands full managing patents and making sure the research is protected. This piques my interest since intellectual property is, of course, my specialty.

Is this a sign? Of course it is. How can it not be?

I've been looking for jobs in San Francisco, dead set on heading back there. Then Bernstein blacklisted me. There's no telling how far his influence spreads in the Bay Area. There's no telling how many firms have already heard all about me. Moving out of Bernstein's reach may just mean moving out of the Bay Area all together.

The thought meets resistance even inside of my own mind. But the reality of my situation brings itself up to full height. I'm in no position to dismiss a job opportunity. I'm in no position to reject the notion of moving back here simply because...what? I left once before with no intention of ever returning?

What if I'm staring right at my shot at a second clean slate, another fresh start? The problem is,

Bernstein isn't backing off. Even if I apply for jobs here in San Diego, employment verifications will still go through his office. Is a fresh start possible when the noise from my old job, my old life, keeps creeping in?

Giles pauses mid-sentence to discipline one of his kids. "Blair, stop it. Stop it right now or I'm canceling Christmas for the rest of your life."

I try not to laugh as Blair looks horrified at his threat and promptly stops trying to pick at the tree decorations.

"That seriously works?" I ask Giles.

"It's basic kid-logic. The bigger, more ridiculous the threat, the more convincing it is."

My mouth opens to accept the forkful of pie I bring to it, lost in a sudden revelation. Giles' words tune my imagination into an elaborate fantasy on how I can free myself of Bernstein's ploy to keep me unemployed.

After dinner, Julia and I sneak off to the kitchen under the pretense of putting the food away into containers, a task no one else wants to be a part of. In fact, Giles takes the older kids and his mother-in-law out to see the Christmas lights.

Lex, Julia, and I stay behind. However, Lex sits in the living room, staring at the glow of her cellphone. Who knows what she's doing. Working, maybe? On Christmas day? I wouldn't put it past her.

Julia and I lean against the countertop island and sip on pumpkin flavored coffee. "Did you tell Lex? That you've been blacklisted?"

"Julia, look at her." I gesture toward the living room at the mindless, phone-scrolling drone that is my older sister.

Julia turns in the same direction as me. Both of our elbows are propped up on the counter, our hands cupping our mugs.

"I see your point," she says.

We sip our drinks in silence for a few seconds. Lex, who under normal circumstances would feel two sets of eyes fixed on her, seems unaware.

"That must've been some good dick," I say. "When's the last time you had dick so good you went into a catatonic state when you couldn't have it anymore?"

Julia holds up a hand as we gather ourselves again from our silent laughter. "Don't say the word dick to me. It causes me physical pain to even think of one."

I cringe at her statement and decide I don't want to go down the path of a postpartum sex life conversation.

"The word dick got me fired. Speaking of dicks...."

I pull up Leo's emails and hand my phone to Julia. Her eyes dart across the screen as she speed-reads the emails. She covers her mouth with her hand to stifle her snort of laughter.

"Yeah," I say. "I might have enjoyed it a little."

She scrolls down to the last email and her expression softens. "Man, he's really trying to hit a soft spot...Aw, this makes me feel sorry for him." She strokes her chest with her palm, eyes still glued to the screen.

I snatch the phone from her. "You can't be serious."

She looks at me, slightly pouty faced. "I don't know. That read heartfelt. You know, he stayed all night at the hospital with Lex, the night I gave birth. My sisters told me. Don't look at me like that...I'm only saying, it seems like he really does care about her."

"Did you even meet him? He's your typical God's gift to women type."

She shrugs. "Whether you like him or not is a different point. The question you should be asking is, can he make Lex happy?"

"I don't know. All I know is that not being with him makes her really, really unhappy. But Lex is too damn proud to give him another chance after he dumped her."

"Well, that's something."

"Is it? What if this has nothing to do with him?"

"That's not for you to decide. It's for Lex to decide. Look, it's obvious the guy's reaching out to you because he can't get through to Lex. Think about that. He knows you hate his guts, yet he is still trying. That says something to me."

I'm at a loss for words. I've been approaching the whole Leo situation from a completely selfish standpoint. I may not like the guy, but he obviously means something to my sister. He obviously regrets his decision. Enough to reach out to the very last person that's likely to ally with him. Me.

I pull on the ends of my hair for a moment. "You're right."

"Of course, I am. I'm always right. I'm still trying to convince Giles of this. He's waiting for the anomaly, but it hasn't happened yet. Actually, wait. I was wrong about Lex and Jacob hitting it off. That didn't pan out. I feel bad for Jacob. He really likes her."

"Don't feel bad for him. He'll do fine. The guy's got a

lot going for him." I make a general gesture to indicate my facial region.

She gives me a searching look. "You know, sometimes I wish I would've set Jacob up with you instead of Lex."

"Nope. He's not my type. I'm not into his whole..." I pause, trying to gather the words. "Enthusiastic, walking on sunshine, smiley sort of vibe."

"You like them broody, don't you?"

My thoughts swing to Owen before I can help myself. His face comes to my mind, the memory of his gravelly voice at my ear tugs at my stomach.

"Yeah. I guess I do. Come on, let's go join the zombie."

The baby monitor is a crackling hum in the background as Julia and Lex catch up in a way Lex isn't able to when everyone else is around. Though my sister hasn't been talkative tonight, her mood quickly improves under constant teasing from Julia and me. Finally, we nudge Lex to the point where she is dishing back the jokes.

The baby starts crying and Lex insists she wants to go soothe him. Julia shuts off the baby monitor as Lex disappears up the stairs. I set my glass of rum down and catch Julia eyeing me in silent amusement.

"What is it?" I ask her.

"Oh, nothing." She almost smiles but holds back, which makes her look more suspicious.

"Just say it."

"You act different around Lex."

"I do?" My pitch goes up the way it does when I'm

being insincere. So I nod. Because I know that she's right. It's something I'm conscious of even if I don't do it intentionally. "I do. She brings the obnoxious teenager out of me."

"I think you bring it out for her."

"Yeah, it's funny. You know, if you say cock around her, she turns beet red and looks around to see if anyone heard you say it. It's hilarious. You should try it."

"I'm sure it has more to do with the fact that you're her little sister and you probably shouldn't have that word in your mouth."

"I'm no one's little anything. And I'll put whatever the hell I want in my mouth."

"Lex acts different around you, too. She acts all...maternal."

I take a sip of my drink. "Yeah, I guess I can see that."

"It happens. It's like that with my sisters, too. I think being around family makes you revert."

"What about you? What do you revert to?"

"Me?" She grins and I know she's about to lie through her teeth. "I don't revert. I just remain...wonderful me."

"How convenient," I squint at her, "I wonder what your sisters would say?"

We have a stare down that lasts a few seconds before she yields. "Okay, fine. They might say I'm a bit extreme in my views. I'd soak a rag with my opinions and chloroform people with it, given the chance."

"Wow...and here I thought we were discussing alter

egos," I say. "What you described sounds exactly like you everyday. "

"Shut up."

"So, I got my brains fucked out of me the other night. Want to hear about it?"

Julia gives me a look as though I'm being ridiculous. "Of course, I want to hear about it!"

I laugh and give her a quick rundown on Owen. How we went to school together, how I never noticed him until he grew into a serious, panty-dropping stud. How I haven't been able to stop thinking about him or our night together. How the piece of paper with his number scribbled on it must've fallen out of my purse because I haven't been able to find it. And how none of it matters since we basically said our goodbyes that night, with no real promise of seeing each other again.

"But you're staying right?" Julia asks. "Weren't you talking with Giles about that job?"

"Yeah," I say, hesitant. "I need some time to process it all. I mean, don't get me wrong, it's really exciting to have a real job prospect. But it's also an adjustment. A few hours ago I was gearing to head back to San Francisco this weekend. A snap of a finger later, I have a real option to stay here for good. It's not even something I thought I wanted. And yet, now I do. It's strange. I can't wrap my head around it, tonight."

"Do you think this Owen guy has anything to do with you wanting to stay?"

"No. The thought of repeating the other night is exciting, but sex isn't something I'd build my future around. To be perfectly honest--and please don't say this to Giles--I don't have a lot of other options on the job front. Staying here makes sense. It's the responsible thing to do. Anyway, even if I do stay here it doesn't mean anything will come out of the whole Owen thing. We might end up being a one-night stand."

"Sure, just promise me you won't run away from the possibility of a relationship because stability scares the hell out of you."

"Oh, does it?" I give her an exaggerated, doe-eyed, attentive look, cupping my chin in my hand. "Please, go on. Tell me all about myself. Make sure to soak a rag with it first, though."

She glares at my teasing. "I think you know I'm right."

"I think you think you're right."

"Stubborn ass."

"Know-it-all."

Lex appears again and says, "Awesome, so we've progressed to name-calling?"

Julia shoots Lex a look as well. My sister brings her hands up in surrender as though realizing she walked into an armed stand off.

I tilt my head back to look at Lex. "Julia was enlightening me on the theory of the universe and everything in it."

"Again?" Lex asks.

Julia narrows her eyes at us, albeit playfully, then points from me to Lex. "Screw you guys. You two are a lost cause. I'm sending you both a bill for all of my therapy services."

"I'd be scared to see that bill," my sister jokes, sitting

down beside me.

Chapter Twenty-Two

SATURDAY AFTER CHRISTMAS, I DRIVE up to San Francisco to meet the movers I've paid to pack up my belongings and bring them to a storage unit in San Diego. I figure it's the best use of my time and money. The drive is too long and I don't want to inconvenience anyone I know with my last minute move.

Elle isn't home and by the air of neglect clinging to the bare walls of the apartment, I don't expect to see her. The living room looks strangely large with just the two-seater sofa and side table. The bigger couch is gone, as is the coffee table and television. She must have started moving out already and left behind only what I brought in. That makes things easier.

It only takes a few minutes to give the movers a walk through of the apartment and tell them what I need them to take. Afterward, I escape up to the roof to get some fresh air. There's a patio there, shared by the building's tenants, with a grill, some patio chairs, a bench, and string lights hanging from tall potted plants. No one is out here today, but it's early morning.

I press my phone to my ear and listen to the ringing. My eyes take in the view in front of me, tracing the rows of sloping rooftops that yield in the distance to a sliver of sparkle that is the waterfront.

"Emily?" Her voice is hesitancy, thinly veiled by surprise.

"Mona, hey. Do you have a minute?"

"Yes, of course. What's going on?"

"I have a huge favor to ask." Silence crackles over the phone as I take a breath and continue.

~

The sky overhead is a brilliant cobalt blue, without a single smudge of white to dilute it. Electrical purring noises swirl around me as I push the golf cart pedal to the furthest position. My hair whips in the brisk morning air and my heart pounds in my chest. There is something about anticipating trouble that I find exhilarating, fills me with energy. The kind of energy that makes me feel unstoppable.

Weaving along the dirt road path, I drive further into the course until the view of the Golden Gate Bridge, a glimmering mirage of rusty orange in the distance, is completely obscured by trees and shrubs. Lincoln Park seems to swallow up the city, dissolving it to sloping bright green fields and insulating itself from the noises of traffic and the bay until I'm sure that I'm in a different world, altogether.

It only takes me a few minutes to spot him, standing a few yards from hole four, kneeling by his ball in contemplation. Three other men, each dressed in wind jackets and khaki pants, all stand a few yards away conversing.

Bernstein's silvery white hair is as recognizable from behind as is the massive, pear-shaped bald spot on the back of his head.

The dirt road I'm on winds away from them, so I take a sharp turn and cut through the field instead. Neither Bernstein nor his companions notice the single golf cart headed straight for them. Not until I'm ten feet away and one of the men turns toward at me as he speaks. His perplexed expression melts to a look of concern when I whip closely past.

Bernstein is focused on his swing. The loud snap of the metal hitting plastic cuts through the air. And he peers up in time to see me steer the golf cart onto the putting green, taking a sharp turn to rest the cart directly in front of the hole. Bernstein's ball hits the front wheel of the golf cart and bounces back a few feet.

I give my ex-boss a small wave from where I sit and, recognizing me, his expression swings from bewildered confusion to livid fury.

Throwing his golf club aside, Bernstein charges toward me in such a frenzy, a spark of fear shoots through me that he might just kill me. Then I remember the old man can't even say the word *dick* out loud without blushing.

Ignoring the erratic pounding in my chest and my slippery palms, I step off the golf cart and take a sharp breath, reminding myself I have nothing to be afraid of.

This man isn't a god. He just thinks he is.

When he reaches me, Bernstein seems unable to speak for a handful of seconds, breathing heavily like a worn, agitated old engine. His companions come forward also, but hang back slightly as though realizing it's a personal confrontation.

"What the hell is this?" Bernstein demands, temper boiling so tangibly I expect to see his hair quivering over his head, or steam to waft from his pores.

Fixing a pleasant smile on my face, I speak loudly enough for his companions to hear. "We need to have a little chat."

"No. You need to leave."

"What's the matter? Afraid your friends will hear about your illegal side activities?"

Bernstein stiffens, and I know it's not because he's ashamed of blacklisting me, but because of the more salacious implications of my words. The men behind Bernstein shift noticeably in their footing, exchanging meaningful sideways glances. I know exactly what they are thinking because it's exactly what I want them to think.

I'm wearing a low-cut, tight dress under my leather jacket. My hair is loose and wild and my eyeliner purposefully heavy handed.

My ex-boss's reaction gives me the confidence to go through with my plan, having confirmation of what I suspected. Bernstein, for as much of a hard-ass as he pretends to be, is extremely prudish. I can't imagine what must be going through his mind at the realization his companions must be confusing me with a call girl.

Bernstein walks off, closer to the other side of the golf cart with the silent connotation I'm meant to follow him. It's not really in my best interest to make our meeting more private, so I hang back far enough to keep us visible to the bystanders.

Seeming to realize my intention, Bernstein jabs a finger at the golf cart. "You need to get in that thing and get the hell off the field before--"

"No. First, you need to stop slandering my name to potential employers."

He straightens. "I don't have the slightest idea what you're referring to."

"Drop the act, Donald." I pause at the way he narrows his eyes at my use of his first name--something I'd never dare do before. "My contacts at Harper & Lyon provided me with direct quotes."

This isn't true, of course, but Bernstein hesitates and the smug look on his face seems to require effort. "What exactly are you accusing me of?"

"I'm not accusing you of anything, yet. I'm here to let you know that the next time my name comes through for an employment verification, you're going to instruct your assistant to follow your company policy and confirm only position and dates of employment."

He takes a step closer to me, seemingly so angered by my tone he forgets for a moment his friends are watching. "Or what?"

"Or nothing," I say, baring my teeth in a forced, mechanical smile. "This isn't a threat. It's a reminder. A reminder of what you're supposed to do. Of what's ethical. Of what's *legal*." I square my shoulders and his eyes dart inescapably to my cleavage. He catches himself and seems angered with me for his own tactlessness. I go on, smiling wider, "Just a reminder. Because I've got absolutely too much time on my hands right now. To mull over and consider my options. And I'd much rather get back to work. It's probably the best way to make sure you'll never hear from me again."

Bernstein stares me down and I stare right back, unblinking.

I learned a valuable lesson over Christmas. Sometimes it's not a fight that's needed to win. Sometimes just the threat of one is enough. The look of insanity in your opponent's eye that makes you wonder if they are willing to go further than you, harder than you, longer than you. The looming realization that the person you messed with has absolutely nothing to lose and might be crazy enough to mess right back.

"Fine," he says through gritted teeth. "Now get the hell off my course."

I thrust a hand out for him to shake. "Glad we could come to a diplomatic understanding."

Chapter Twenty-Three

THOUGHTS OF A MAN HAVE never been a priority in my life. Not, ironically enough, since High School when my lame priority was being on the arm of the hottest guy on the wrestling team.

I've peeled away that innocuous part of myself a long time ago. I've never wanted to be the type of woman that hinges her existence on a man, or shapes her life around him the way my mother so often does.

But I can't deny the way I've woken up on more than one occasion twisting around in my sheets, my hips angling for a man who isn't there. Even as the sensations die away and reality bears down on me, the memories of each stroke, each touch flood my body with warmth. It's been days since I last felt his hands on me. And even with everything I own crammed into a storage unit and my future promising a life in San Diego, I'm not sure I'm ready to see Owen. Not sure what I'd say.

Hi. This is a bit awkward. Remember that whole bittersweet goodbye moment with the kiss and the stomach flurries? Nevermind all of that. Turns out, I'm staying. And not because I want you--though, I do. But because of other reasons completely unrelated to your cock. I swear.

Sunday morning, when Lex goes out to the store, I take the opportunity to email Leo Conrad back to tell him I'll indulge his sob story. The guy responds fifteen minutes later, asking to meet at a coffee shop halfway between our turfs. Only then does it occur to me I have yet to eat breakfast.

I scarf down a blueberry scone the moment I get to the coffee shop and pretend not to notice him right away when he takes a seat in front of me.

Leo waits in silence until I wipe my face with a napkin and meet his blue eyes. The sight of him makes me want to strangle something. I'm not sure why. There isn't anything about his physical appearance that could be considered offensive, quite the opposite, actually. The man is pleasing to the eyes. Sharp looking in every sense of the word. Keen, calculating gaze, perfectly groomed hair, clothes that fit him as though they are tailored to his every curve.

He's a good looking man, without a doubt, but an almost tangible energy radiates from him, filling the room and making his presence imposing. It's a confidence that borders on entitlement. And it pisses me off.

"You have fifteen minutes," I tell him.

"I only need ten."

"Well--" I circle a finger in the air "--any time now would be great."

Leo seems to bite back an insult and begins, instead, telling me how he needs my help convincing Lex to meet him on the thirty-first of December at a certain address. When I ask him why, he tells me, "That's when it will be ready."

I don't fall for the bait of asking him what 'it' is, not wanting him to think I even care. Because if I care, then he has a shot and he doesn't deserve a shot with my sister.

I read his face carefully as he tries to convince me how in love he is with Lex. How he'd do anything to get her back. I'm looking for the slightest twinge of insincerity. I can't find it, but even that doesn't help me believe him.

Simply because I already decided I don't want to.

Maybe he sees I'm ready to leave, senses I find this conversation is pointless, because his jaw tightens and his tone grows impatient. "You've never done something you regretted? You've never spoken out of anger? You've never hurt someone you cared about and wished you could take it back?"

I blink at this. Of course I've done all of these things. His gaze is so tenacious, it plows through mine and gives me the irrational suspicion he knows things about me that even I don't know. But whatever he sees in me must bring him to the realization that I'm simply not budging.

His face falls a fraction and he lets out a humorless laugh. "I don't know why I'm even wasting my time. You're so cynical."

I shrug. If that's an insult, it doesn't even sting.

He nods, as though acknowledging his statement has no effect on me whatsoever. "You think being cynical is something to be proud of? It's not. It's sad,

Emily. *You're* sad."

I shoot up to my feet. "*Fuck you*, Leo. You don't know me."

He puts a hand up and hangs his head for a second in apparent regret. "Okay, that was uncalled for. I'm sorry. You're right. I don't know you. I really don't. But, Emily, what I can see when I look at you is bravado and show. And that tells me something--"

I cut him off before his monologue grows out of control. "That's enough, Leo. We're not here for you to psycho-analyze me."

He lets out a breath, as though realizing he's digging himself further into a hole. "All right look, I know I hurt your sister. I'm trying to fix it, but she won't take two seconds to hear me out. I need your help." He looks away, then down at his hands in an uncharacteristic show of doubt. "I'm leaving, Emily. I can't work for her anymore. It's killing me. If you can stand there and tell me Alexis wants nothing to do with me, that she won't regret walking away without hearing me out, then you won't hear from me again. Neither will she. But I don't think that's true. I've been waiting for a woman like her my entire life, even when I had no idea it's what I wanted."

I'm rooted to the spot. His words ring around us like an echoing bell and they feel too honest to mock.

He seems to see an opportunity because he picks up again after the short lull. "I don't just want her, Emily. I want to make her *happy*. Don't you want that, too?"

Ridiculous.

Of course I want that for my sister, but why does he

assume he's her only chance at happiness? And why should I believe he is?

"All I keep hearing is what you feel and what you want. I hate to break it to you, Leo, but what you feel for my sister? Won't change anything. Feelings are abstract. They only really matter to the person feeling them. You."

He's silent and I know he's biting his tongue, clearly annoyed at my belittling tone.

I go on, "You know what else? If you want her the way you say, you wouldn't have dumped her the way you did. And in the end that's all that matters. Not what you want. Not what you feel. Not your words. Your actions. The things you actually do. So, what do you have, Leo? Besides your bleeding heart? Exactly," I say, nodding at his deer-in-the-headlights expression.

I secure my purse strap over my shoulder, but the hesitation on his face makes me falter. He clears his throat and, unless it's some trick of the light, he looks vulnerable for the first time since I met him. It's such a foreign look on him that it stands out, like an ugly coat he's too aware I can see.

"I bought her a house."

I start to speak. I try to say, 'excuse me?' but instead, I end up choking on my own spit. My hand flies to the base of my throat and I cough a few times. He watches me, waiting for me to finish my episode. I swallow. "You *what*?"

"I bought a house for us. I've put a lot of money into expediting the process and I'm confident the deal will go through by Tuesday at the latest."

That explains the date on his request. Still, the beginnings of a hysterical laugh erupt from me. "You can't be serious. Do you even know my sister? You two aren't even dating and you buy her a *house*?"

He nods slowly, as though my question is what's ridiculous.

"You're fucking crazy. I hope the driveway is nice and long because all you'll see of Lex are the skid marks her shoes leave on the ground when she runs off in the opposite direction. And she *will* run because...that's the worst idea I've ever heard."

The eagerness in his eyes gives me an instant pang of regret--or maybe it's pity--at the realization that I've probably crushed his ridiculous hopes. But I'm surprised by Leo's expression. There's resolve there. Pure resolve to the point that it makes me doubt my own hesitation.

He's so confident in what he's doing that suddenly, just his conviction seems to be changing what should be a crazy event to a, perhaps, understandable one.

He bought her a house.

I try to mentally shrug it off, but end up shaking my head in disbelief, instead.

"I want a life with her," he says, eyes pleading with me to take him seriously. "And I know she wants it too. I get she has a lot of baggage. I get she feels like she can't trust anyone with her heart. But she wants this with me, I know that more than I know anything. And I think you know it too. Lex wants to be with me, Emily. And she and I, we can be great together. We are great together. But she's too stubborn. Too proud. I made it so all she has to do is step through the door. Just one step to let me in."

"You do know that expression isn't meant to imply a *literal* door?" I laugh. "You're a crazy motherfucker, Leo."

The corners of his lips twist and he puts his hands up in a '*what can you do about it*' gesture.

Chapter Twenty-Four

LEX IS PISSED, AS I knew she'd be, that Leo dragged me into their drama. I'm still not sure what she'll do with what I told her. New Year's Eve is in three days and she doesn't seem inclined to give Leo another chance. I don't push the subject, though, because my intention isn't to force her into the decision but rather let her know it's not a ridiculous notion to consider.

Monday morning, I spend over an hour on the phone with Giles, talking with him about a job opportunity in the university's legal department. Officially putting my name in the hat. I'm relieved he sounds inclined to help me get the position. But when we end the phone call, I still don't have an interview. And though Giles promises me a follow up call, I'm wound so tightly with anxiety at the fear he might be my last chance at a job connection, I end up having a few drinks to calm myself.

Tuesday, Giles calls me with his colleague on the line for a phone interview. By the end of it, they ask me to come in to meet them and talk more about the position the following Monday. As I hang up, relief plunges through me, reaching my core and leaving me feeling fifty pounds lighter.

This is it; this job is as good as mine. I can feel it in my bones. And with that immediate concern out of the way, my attention shifts to the next point of worry.

Finding a place to live.

Lex wouldn't mind me staying here as long as I need to, but something in my gut tilts with the notion that tomorrow things might change for her, when--well, if--she meets Leo and he convinces her to embark on...whatever it is he's angling for. I'm still not sure.

As I contemplate a place to live, a very real image forms in my mind. A bright cozy room, slanted ceiling, the merger of the new and old, modern and antique. The ad I saw hanging on the diner's bulletin board. I don't even know if the loft is still available to rent. But there's only one way to find out.

The guy behind the counter is the fresh-faced young man Owen trained two weeks ago. Seeing this stranger taking orders and greeting customers brings a sinking feeling to my stomach. The realization that Owen isn't here. He's gone back to his usual life, his day job.

Even after I'd lost his number, I never really worried about not being able to see him when I was ready to. Somehow, I pictured it being as easy as walking in here and finding him behind the counter.

I wade through the floor of the diner, between the tables, to reach the back wall, where the bulletin board of announcements hangs. At first glance, I'm certain the ad for the loft is gone. But then I see it poking out from behind a sign about a yard sale. As I eye the bright, clean, open space, my resolve wraps around a sudden blooming hope. God, this picture is like a siren's call to me. I'm mesmerized by it. I'm *pulled* to it. This is where I'm going to live. It's still here for a reason.

Of course, for every part of me that wants this place, there's a small voice in the back of my mind warning me not to get my hopes up about it. I last saw this ad a week ago and have no idea how long it's been pinned on the board. The most likely scenario is that it's already been rented and the ad was simply forgotten.

But really, what have I got to lose by checking? I dial the number on the bottom of the page and each ring seems unusually long, long enough for the voice in my head to warn me repeatedly.

Don't get your hopes up. Don't get your hopes up.

The ringing cuts away to a clipped tone. "Hello?"

"Hello, I'm calling about the ad for the second floor loft. Is it still available?"

The line goes silent for a beat.

"Emily?"

It's Owen.

Chapter Twenty-Five

OWEN WALKS TOWARD ME, LOOKING timeless in his motorcycle jacket and dark-washed jeans, hair tousled from the helmet. His face is shaved smooth and I'm surprised at the way this makes his eyes shine brighter than before, every nuance in color, from soft caramel to jade green, rippling with intensity.

Jesus. He's even more gorgeous than I remember. I'm finding it difficult to not get excited. Impossible to not smile. I'm motionless as he approaches, though he stops, abruptly, beyond arm's length.

I point toward the second story of the building behind me. "The loft is here?"

He nods and I let out a short laugh. The loft I've been fantasying about over the last few weeks sits atop Lucas' diner. I kind of feel tricked. I almost feel glad.

Owen's hands are in his jacket pockets, but his eyes can't be contained. They take me in an insatiable way, dancing with memories of the last time we saw each other.

"You're staying in town?"

I'm surprised it's taken him this long to ask, I expected it to be the first thing he asked when we talked on the phone earlier. But now that I look into his eyes I can see why. He's too guarded to show me how pleased he is by the prospect of me staying. I recognize that brand of hesitation--it borders on a deep fear of disappointment.

"I am. I've got a job connection here," I say, a bit discouraged by the strained, unfamiliar energy between us. It's like the past week we haven't seen each other worked to reverse whatever ground we broke in getting comfortable with one another.

"And you want to live here?"

"Well, I don't know yet. I'll have to see the place. But honestly, I've been eyeing the picture for a while."

"Come on, let me show you."

Owen leads me into the diner, past the tables and down the back hall, then through a set of doors that lead back outside. Another parking lot is back there, and though it seems to belong to the apartment complex behind the building, it's accessible to someone renting the loft, as well. I follow him up the stairs running along the backside of the building.

He opens the door and motions for me to take the lead. I enter into a small living room that yields soon after to a kitchen, separated by a countertop island. Owen is still behind me and I realize too late the entrance is not big enough for him to get past with me in the way.

"Excuse me." He places a hand on the small of my back and this simple, innocent touch draws out the vivid memory of our naked bodies heaving in sync.

I move forward, refocusing my sights on the loft before me. A lightness tears through my insides. There is something very charming and feminine about this place. It's quaint and familiar in a way I can't pin point.

I love the slanted roof, the feeling of being in an attic, but with the ceiling being high enough to not render the space as claustrophobic. The windows are huge and because of the angle of the walls, they are more like skylights.

There's so much light streaming in that the place is incredibly bright. Daylight reaches every nook, causing the gray paint on the walls to nearly glow. The place feels bigger than it should. There's not an inch of square footage wasted.

The muted color of the walls makes the white trim and around the windows and doors pop. Off toward the right, the kitchen is an oasis of white tile and oak cabinets.

I can already see myself living here.

"Well?" he asks, turning to face me.

"It's...nice." Still rooted by the fear of being disappointed, I try to not sound too enthusiastic. Try to pretend I'm not already envisioning a future where I'm curled up on the couch or leaning over the counter top island, sipping on coffee.

He motions to either side of the room, toward the large windows. "This side faces west. You can see the ocean. That side, obviously, faces east. You get direct sunlight streaming in all day."

I walk over to the closest window on the right side of the room and look out. Sure enough, there's the ocean. Less than a mile away and in perfect view beyond the Pacific Coast Hwy.

I'm practically swooning.

Owen walks past me, possibly a little closer than necessary, leaving his crisp scent trailing behind him. When I look at him again, he is in the kitchen, behind the countertop island.

The kitchen is small, but it's open to the living room and there's enough room between the island and the appliances to move around comfortably.

"The countertops are new." He runs a hand over the white tiles. "The refrigerator broke down a few days ago and my father decided to get all new appliances. They'll be delivered next week. A dishwasher will be installed, as well. Lucky for you, because I had to wash everything by hand."

"Wait, you lived here?"

"I rented it from Lucas my first year of college, then I moved on campus and he moved in after he and my mother sold their house. They're divorced."

Though the place is empty and without decor, there's a sort of shabby chic air to it that makes me think of a fashionable old lady.

"Can't imagine you got laid very often here," I say.

"You'd be surprised." He pats the kitchen counter absentmindedly, but it's clear what he's implying.

I glare at him. "Oh, that's gross. Is this your sales pitch?"

He shrugs. "You're the one that brought it up."

I laugh and his lips curl up in what has to be his very first smile that I've seen today. I'm surprised by the way the unfamiliar edge in his gaze dulls away as though he suddenly remembers we aren't strangers.

One joke, that's all it took.

I cast my eyes away to take in the details of the walls. Vertical lines are visible from underneath the layers of paint. "You painted over the wood paneling?"

"I did."

I imagine what the place must of looked like with exposed wood paneling and it suddenly transforms in my imagination into a sort of man cave.

"How do you feel about the tenant painting over this gray?"

He doesn't answer right away, seems distracted as he looks down at my lips. I swear he nearly leans into them, before turning the movement into a short shake of the head. "What's wrong with the color? It's neutral."

"I'd paint it something lighter, to contrast with my dark furniture."

He raises an eyebrow, visibly surprised by my detailed plans.

"A paint job would be fine," he says, almost reluctantly. "As long as you let me help you. I don't want it getting all on the ceiling and trim."

I make a point to roll my eyes, showing him how uptight I think he is. Without preamble, I turn to follow the short hall leading to an open room.

He follows after me.

The bedroom is a decent size. I could fit my queen-sized bed in here and have enough room for my nightstands. The room has a more pronounced attic-feel than the rest of the place. The walls touch at the top like a pair of cupped hands. I envision my bed, there at the end, cradled by the walls. The room has recess lighting like in the living room but natural light pours in from the large window on the far wall.

For a moment, I'm overwhelmed by the refreshing novelty of the loft. Laced in the air is the smell of hardwood floors, fresh paint.

The smell of new beginnings.

A surge of excited energy courses through me. I've always lived with a roommate. Partly because it's more affordable, partly because I always liked knowing someone was there. But for the first time in my life, I envision myself living alone. I'm romanticizing the idea of living here, I know it. Even knowing it, I can't stop myself.

A place just for me, myself, and I.

After everything in my life felt like it was slipping away, I suddenly see a light breaking through. The thought of it fills me with butterflies and I feel like I'm in love. In love with my life. With the possibilities before me. In love with the idea of a fresh start. Starting from scratch.

New job, new friends, new everything.

I peer back and see Owen leaning against the doorway, his arms crossed, watching me as I stand in the center of the bedroom with my hands on my hips.

Suspicion seeps into me, a sudden apprehension that crowds my excitement into a corner. "Why hasn't this place rented out yet?"

He looks unsurprised by my question. "Haven't found the right tenant."

I raise an eyebrow at him. "The right tenant?"

"A place like this doesn't get family oriented people,

for obvious reasons. I get more of the college kid. And that's not going to work."

I keep my expression serious. "God forbid someone has a little fun on your watch."

He stares at me, narrowing his eyes.

"How do you know I'm not a wild party animal?" I ask, taking a few steps toward him and lowering my voice. "How do you know I'm not going to tear your place apart in a crazy binge of sex and drugs."

"Is this *your* sales pitch?"

I grin at the way he's unfazed by the crazy things that come out of my mouth. I've missed him.

He reaches behind him, pulls a wad of folded papers from his back pocket and hands them to me. "Here's an application."

I walk past him without taking it and enter the bathroom, which I've yet to explore. It's small but functional. The tile over the tub is a vibrant white, as is the porcelain sink. Owen's right behind me, still holding the folded papers.

His gaze rises up from below and I know he was consuming my curves with his eyes.

"What's funny?" he asks at the short laugh I let out.

"It just occurred to me--it might be awkward...renting from you."

He taps the papers on an open palm like a baton, still watching me. "This isn't my place. It's my father's place. You'd be sending the payments directly to him. I'm the property manager." He pauses. "Did you really decide to stay? Or are you trying to trick me into bed again?"

"Both."

He brushes a thumb along his bottom lip in a seemingly unconscious gesture I find utterly seductive.

"All right, look. You want the place? It's yours. Pending a deposit, of course." He throws the application over his shoulder and it lands in a soft thud in the hallway as he takes a step closer.

I'm half sitting on the bathroom sink, eyes flashing to the papers on the floor behind him. "Am I meant to fetch that?" I ask, amused.

"No. I'm done talking business." He tucks my hair behind my ear and my lips part in the wake of his touch.

"Now what?" I try to keep my tone cool and unaffected, but the air feels thick with him.

"Now, I ask you out on a date."

"A date?"

"Yes, tomorrow night. Unless you already have plans for New Year's."

New Year's. I was supposed to be back in San Francisco by now. And even after I contemplated staying, the days have been such a blur I haven't had the time to consider any plans.

"What about Landon?"

"He'll spend it with my sister, she's throwing a party at her house. His cousin and some of their school friends will be there. Trust me, he'd much rather be around them than me."

"And your sister won't be mad at you for bailing?"

"Not when I tell her I've got a hot date."

"All right," I say, smiling. "It's a date."

He grins, looking into my eyes as I stare into his and

try to get a grip on the flurry in my stomach.

"I've got to be honest." His breath is warm and soothing on my face. "I didn't think I'd be seeing you again. But the sound of your voice has been playing in my head, on a loop. I can't get it out."

"Is that so?"

"There's a very specific sound I'm dying to recreate."

"I'm not sure what you're talking about," I say with exaggerated confusion. "Is there something you can show me? You know, to jog my memory?"

"Something like this?" He pulls me up against him and I gasp. He's solid and inviting, and the way his bulge presses into me through our clothes is enough to shatter my pretenses. Still, I manage to tilt my head back and smile coyly.

"Sorry. It's not ringing any bells."

I glimpse the wicked smile that flashes across his face before he spins me around and bends me over the sink, bringing my nose inches from my own reflection in the mirror. "How about we let your face tell us when you're close to remembering?"

I take a sharp breath, heart pounding against my ribcage, enthralled by the unchecked desire flooding the man in the mirror. His fingers weave over the buttons of my blouse as he lowers his face onto my neck, kissing me there, waking all my nerve endings, and setting them off at once. He peels away my blouse and lowers his lips to my back. Everywhere his lips touch is blanketed by static energy, making me squirm as I relish in the sensation.

He unhooks my bra and the straps fall over my

shoulders almost on their own accord. The spot on the back of my neck he's kissing must be a pleasure center, because when he sucks on it, I cry out in surprise. My eyes shut tight, heightening the effect of his touch, his hands over my bare breasts, thumbs flicking my hardened nipples.

Lowering a hand down my abdomen, he hooks it between my legs, over my jeans. I gasp at the way his palms press against where I'm already throbbing with need.

"Take them off," he says, tugging on the front of my jeans before pulling away from me to peel his own clothes off. I yield to his request, pulling my panties off along with my jeans.

When I straighten up again, he presses his bare chest to my back and my skin flushes. I'm primed for his touch, wet and on edge, knowing the delicious pleasure that's coming and already reeling from it.

He lowers me over the sink again, bringing my forearms to rest on the cold porcelain. I watch his reflection as he straps a condom on himself; the sight of his gorgeous body behind me is enough to make my mouth water.

"Don't go easy on me," I beg, breathless.

My words elicit a hungry groan from him. His hands close over my waist, eyes holding mine in the mirror. He enters me, filling me slowly until his pelvis is pressed against my ass. I throw my head back and sigh, feeling myself squeezing his shaft. As I go to catch my breath, he starts his breathtaking, rhythmic pulsing. Pure ecstasy surges through me, my moans echoing off the bathroom walls.

"Eyes forward," he growls, voice strained.

I meet my reflection in the mirror; my eyebrows are turned up at the ends, eyes slightly narrowed and lips quivering with each breath I take. I cast my sights up to his reflection. He's biting his lower lip, staring right back at me, muscular arms securing me in place as he claims my body with delicious vigor.

His hands move up my back to close over my shoulders for leverage as he picks up his speed, driving up my need for him to an overwhelming level. Until I'm alternating between panting and moaning, my ass burning from the contact of his body slapping against it. I'm quivering from the electrifying sensations he's delivering.

Before I know it, I'm moaning out his name in a plea. As though the sound of it describes what he's doing to me. Describes the raw, intoxicating energy coursing through me. My body is fueled by this incredible powerhouse of a man, owning every inch of me until I'm buckling under him.

He curses under his breath, his rhythm falling off track momentarily, as though hearing me moan out his name pulls him to the edge of control.

Is that the sound he was dying to recreate?

My sights are on the sink, but Owen grabs and handful of my hair and pulls my head back firmly so I can meet my own reflection again, the sounds of his body slamming into mine are rivaled only by my wild moans.

My body tenses up, fingers close over the edge of the

sink as the orgasm thrashes across me like a rope, coiling and beating until agony falls away to release. I sigh his name in a hoarse whisper and Owen finishes in a long, rough stroke, followed by a groan that sends a shiver of delight up and down my spine.

I wonder how I ever thought I could leave him behind.

And I wonder if I'll ever get enough of him.

Chapter Twenty-Six

If I were desperate to rent a place, there's a dozen living situations I could've entertained. There are ads everywhere. I have friends that love me or at the very least tolerate me enough to let me live with them for a few months. The truth is, I am crazy in love with the loft. I don't know what it is, but I've never had a place give me butterflies the way it does. The thought of living anywhere else literally gives me a pang in my stomach. That loft is my home. I've felt it the very first moment I saw the notice on the bulletin board. I had no idea then the loft was connected to Owen and I didn't know when I dialed the number.

Anyway, it's done. I gave Owen the check already, first and last months rent. It put a huge dent in my savings, but that's okay. I'll have a paycheck coming in a couple of weeks. Soon I'll be back on track, financially. Soon my whole life will be back on track.

The next day, my eyes open to the brightness of Lex's guest room. It's New Year's Eve and I'm already nursing a dry mouth and minor headache.

"Seriously?" Lex asks me as I settle down to eat breakfast. "You're hung-over again? What are you going to do when you start work? You'll have to cut back on the drinking."

"I'm not hung-over," I lie. "It's just a headache. Anyway, did I tell you? I found a place to live."

My sister, who is aware of my upcoming interview with the university but not yet privy to the fact that I lost my apartment, sets her fork down, surprised. "I didn't know you started looking. Don't you have to give notice at your old place?"

"No, it all worked out," I say vaguely.

There's a lot I don't tell my sister. She worries too much about me and I decide to stow away tiny, inconsequential facts--all of which add up to an inconvenient truth--and mentally place them under the kitchen sink.

I use my headache as an excuse to keep quiet and Lex, not being much of a conversationalist anyway, doesn't seem to mind. There's an offbeat heaviness to our silence. A chunky anticipation for one or the other to mention the person whose name so obviously hangs, unspoken, overhead.

Leo.

Today is the day Lex's supposed to meet him. She's yet to give me any hint as to which way she's leaning but if my gut is right, things aren't looking good for the guy. I think Lex already made up her mind about wiping him from her life the moment he hurt her.

After hearing Leo out, I understand why he needs her to meet him in person. If he tells her that he bought a house, it won't have the same impact as if she saw it for herself and, frankly, it might scare Lex away for good.

I have to admire the guy's persistence. Any other sucker wouldn't bother with this shit. It's way too much effort for someone who is anything less than bat-shit crazy in love with my sister.

Lex leaves me behind at the condo pretty early, vague about what her plans are for the day. I wonder if maybe she plans to drive around aimlessly, as a form of distraction. A form of evasion. That's one thing we Stone women are good at. Evasion.

I go back to sleep, pulling the covers over my head, enjoying the warmth of the bed, and not waking up again until well into the afternoon. By then I feel better, renewed, able to spend the rest of the evening cleaning and organizing the things I crammed in my giant suitcase when I moved the rest of my stuff into storage.

I daydream about the loft. I'll be moving my things into it in about a week's time, once the new appliances have been installed. Most of all, I daydream about the man who promised to pick me up tonight, 6:30 p.m. sharp.

Though I try to remain busy, merely passing the time until my date with Owen, the day feels impossibly long. The minutes churn lazily until I find myself pouring a drink. Sundown still too far away and me too thirsty to wait for it.

A small voice in my head warns I've been drinking alone too often. It sounds suspiciously like my sister. I acknowledge the voice, and then tell it to kindly mind its own damn business. Still, I end up stowing the bottle of vodka under the sink. Just to avoid my sister's needless nagging.

Chapter Twenty-Seven

AIR RUSHES INTO THE SPEEDING car before I can roll up the window. My jacket is open in the front and the nippy air penetrates the fabric of the cocktail dress I'm wearing. I'm glad Owen picked me up in his car, though the cold is hardly a problem when the sight of him alone is enough to stir me until I'm warm. The sight of his profile, the jagged lines of his jaw, the smooth curves of his lips, all make me consider how silently he commands attention, how effortlessly he conveys the fact that he knows a thing or two about handling a woman.

He's sitting there, one hand on the steering wheel, the other on the gearshift, pretending he can't feel my eyes peeling away the layers of his clothes. Pretending he can't feel the way my imagination whirls to build an elaborate fantasy, one where we're both driving each other over the edge, no car in sight.

The drive is long but he won't tell me where we're going. I'm highly doubtful he would've been able to come up with anything surprising in such short notice. The day before yesterday he didn't think he'd be seeing me again.

We've been heading south on interstate five but it's

not until he clears past the exits for La Jolla that I begin to suspect we are headed downtown. It's New Year's Eve and the only reasons I'd go downtown today would be to party in the Gaslamp Quarter or to watch the fireworks show by the bay. I assume Owen is planning for us to do the latter, probably at some restaurant with waterside views.

But we veer away from downtown, crossing over the Coronado Bridge. The dark waters of the San Diego Bay glisten in the subtle glow from the surrounding buildings and the moon. It's a clear night, mere wisps of clouds dissolving into nothing before my eyes.

I don't come to Coronado often, though it's a beautiful island. Houses are worth a pretty penny and the streets on the main part of the island have an almost dainty, historical feel to them.

As I suspected, Owen takes us to eat dinner at a nice restaurant overlooking the bay. Nighttime views of downtown span out before the wall-to-wall windows.

Along with a delicious dinner, we enjoy light and fun conversation, which flows with surprising ease. Even though we don't talk about anything important, we both lean into each other's words, not wanting to miss a syllable.We end up reminiscing about high school, as though those were days we shared and not a time when we lived in different worlds.

I usually have to watch my mouth on a first date, since I tend to say outrageous things when I get carried away. But I don't have to worry about that with Owen. He counters all my quick remarks without even batting an eye.

Afterward, we walk out of the restaurant and onto to the grassy area facing the bay. Out here, the view of downtown is even more stunning. Bright, multicolored lights glimmer like squared Christmas trees in the distance.

Wordlessly, but eyes shining, Owen takes my hand and leads me down the nearby boat access ramp, which yields to a public dock further down. I look for the white flash of a boat against the dark waters, but I don't see any. Then, as we reach closer to the end of the dock, a dark wood, banana-shaped rowing boat comes into view. Waiting for us, a man stands on one end, holding the long oar he will undoubtedly use to propel us into the bay.

"What in the--" I turn to Owen and laugh in surprise. "A gondola?"

Owen nods. "Thought maybe we'd get away from the crowds tonight."

A pure, inquisitive expression comes over his face in the form of small lines on his forehead. That, contrasting with the eagerness in his eyes, makes my knees go weak. This man has no idea how utterly irresistible he is to me.

The gondolier helps me onboard and the boat, though easily fifteen-feet long, sways a little too much for my liking, too small for this vast body of water that is the bay. I've only ever seen these things in the fake canals of The Venetian, a hotel in Vegas designed to be a miniature replica of Venice, Italy. Though, those gondolas were far smaller in scale than this one.

After quick safety brief, Owen and I are provided

with a warm blanket to settle under in our padded leather seats. Owen sits behind me and I settle in between his legs. It all feels incredibly intimate. A little over six feet of dark wood separates us from where the gondolier stands, on the opposite end of the boat, paddling us onto the bay.

"This is nuts," I say, almost to myself. "I've lived here my whole life and never once heard of gondola rides."

"Glad I can be your first," Owen says. I can hear the smile in his tone. "They aren't usually on this side of the bay. The gondola company is down by the Coronado cays. But I called in a special favor to have the boat towed out here."

"Special favor, huh?" I ask, amused. Maybe he *is* in the mob, after all. I laugh inwardly and shake the thought away.

It's warm under the blanket, warm enough to shield us from the chilly air, colder here from the proximity to water. Owen's face is nestled in the crook of my neck from behind, and his hands are caressing small circles on my abdomen, over my dress.

"How'd you hear about this, anyway?" I ask.

"Google."

"What? Did you google 'panty dropping first date ideas in San Diego?'"

"Something like that. I was trying to impress you. Did it work?"

"Are you kidding? I'm not usually into sappy stuff, but I swear, if that dude wasn't standing over there paddling this boat, I'd be sucking your dick right now.

This is the most romantic thing anyone's ever done for me."

He chuckles softly as our boat weaves through the water, parallel to the shore. The twinkling lights from the buildings beyond are as seductive as they are romantic.

"Am I monogamizing the hell out of you?" Owen asks.

"You are," I say, taking in the array of sensations around me. The salty smell of ocean. The warmth of Owen's arms wrapped around me, his hard chest pressed to my back. Soothing, rhythmic sounds of water lap against the sides of the gondola. All of it grounds me in the moment in a way I've never quite experienced before, until a strange feeling presses on the walls of my chest. A fullness that reminds me a lot of gratitude but leans more toward satisfaction. But, as I consider this, the feeling is eaten away by one I absolutely recognize.

Foreboding.

The dark, ominous twinge that things, especially good things, are never what they seem. The suspicion the universe balances happiness on the thin blade of chaos.

"God, you make it hard to think," he says into my ear. "Feeling you like this. So close."

Something about staring out into the water and the view before us makes it easier to say what's on my mind. "Tell me something, Owen. Do you have a crazy ex-girlfriend hell bent on branding your penis like cattle?"

"No..." He's audibly confused by my question. "What

makes you ask me that?"

"My sister went through crazy drama and I'm not into that stuff."

"Good, because neither am I." One of his hands holds me steady against him, the other traces small circles over my belly button. All the warm air under the blanket pools between my thighs as I begin to throb with desire for him. And yet, as badly as I'd love to fuck him right now, him holding me feels good too, in a different way. In a brilliantly understated way.

"Tell me," Owen says by my ear. I shift a little where I sit, stirred by the way his breath sends a delicious flurry down my neck. "Was there someone waiting for you in San Francisco? Someone upset you didn't go back?"

"No," I say, hesitating as his hands move down to the sides of my thighs, slowly inching up my dress. I'm not sure how to react, it's not like we have a chance at sneaking in any real action with the gondolier around. But the man is facing away from us and the blanket shields the progress of Owen's hands as he pulls my thighs apart on a caress. Nothing can betray his indecent touch, except for the change in my breathing.

"Go on," he whispers, "tell me why not."

"Well," I begin, taking in a breath, slow and steady, trying to remain still as his fingers find my tender spot over my underwear. "I've had an issue with the men I've dated. The same problem every time. Men...they always want to...." I pause, trying to nail the word on the tip of my tongue. "Claim ownership over me. Like I need to be tamed or something." That word feels close to the mark, but not quite right. "Maybe I have daddy issues, but I've always had problems with authority." Owen laughs a little at this, though I'm not sure how it's funny. "A man telling me what to do suffocates me, it turns me off. I don't want to be controlled."

That's it. The word I'm looking for.

Owen brings his lips to my ear. "Except in bed."

"And how'd you guess that?" I ask with a grin.

"Because your body responds to my every command." Owen starts to rub me in slow circles. I sink my teeth into my bottom lip to keep from moaning aloud. Closing my eyes, I hone in on his touch, the ache it elicits, as he adds, "Yet you say you can't be tamed."

My lips turn up at his playful tone. "Unless I'm turned on and naked, I'm not looking to be handled--" I take in a sharp breath at the sudden, rough stroke of his finger. "So no, I don't want to be tamed. Why is that always a condition to being with a man?"

"What sorts of conditions would you be interested in, then?" His finger finds my entrance and traces the wet skin there.

I suppress a sigh of delight and ask, "Hypothetically speaking?"

"No, Emily--" He pushes his finger inside of me and begins to pulse in and out of me, slowly. "I think I've made it clear I'm not talking hypotheticals. Tell me what you want."

He knows what I want; he can feel the evidence all over his fingers. But I know he means more than sex. He made it clear he wanted more from the first night we slept together.

I take a moment to gather my thoughts, which are clinging over the edge of a blissful cliff. "I'd say...someone who doesn't want to change me, or make me something I'm not."

"That's me," he says, bringing his thumb to stroke my clit as his finger remains inside. "I can give you that."

"Owen," I breathe at the jolt of ecstasy shooting through my core. In an attempt to gather myself, I turn my face to his and crane my neck to reach his ear and whisper, "You're going to make me come. And that man's going to hear."

Owen smiles, but doesn't stop. His strokes pull on my orgasm, stringing it along further even as I desperately try to hold it back. I shut my eyes and tilt my head back onto his shoulder, gazing up at the black sky. "You're going to regret this," I hiss.

"No, I won't," he whispers.

I bite down hard on my lip again and when I take in a sudden, trembling breath, Owen releases his hold on me, pulling his hand away. It seems all my blood is pumping into my clit, which now throbs painfully in dissatisfaction.

"I fucking hate you," I whimper, grinning.

"Wait for it," he says.

"For what?"

No more than three seconds pass after my question when the sky overhead erupts into a brilliant array of colors. Being in the bay during the New Year's Eve fireworks show is like landing in the middle of an explosion. The sounds clatter and echo around us, reverberating against the buildings in the distance and rolling back toward us like waves. Owen's fingers come over me again, faster and more furious than before. The orgasm that seemed to have dissipated roars back to life in an instant. I turn my face to his again, feeling utterly helpless under his touch, unsure of how I'll keep from screaming out loud. His lips close over mine just in time, and the trembles of my long, satiated moan, trickle into his mouth, muffled and safe from prying ears.

He kisses me, long and with purpose. And when he pulls away again, hands smoothing my dress down carefully, Owen brings his lips to my ears and says, "Here it is in black and white, Emily. I've wanted you for a very long time. First, I wasn't brave enough. Then we weren't in the same place. But now we are. You're here. I'm here. And I want to be your man."

Chapter Twenty-Eight

WELL PAST MIDNIGHT AND NEARING the end of our drive back, Owen takes an unexpected exit and pulls the car over. He parks along a side-road bordered by an empty parking lot and an office building, abandoned this time of night. The only sounds are of the highway nearby.

"You doing that...is distracting me," he says in a deliciously strained voice.

"What is?" I ask.

Owen's zipper is undone and my hand is firmly wrapped over his long, hard shaft. Stroking it.

He groans and tilts his head back onto the headrest. "I can't even see the road anymore."

"Good thing you pulled over then," I say, leaning over to run my tongue over his length. He sucks in a breath and lays a hand on my shoulder, caressing me, urging me on.

"I got us a room," he says, breathing heavily. "It's not far from here. We can make it."

I peer up at him. "Can we?"

He shuts his eyes in resignation and I take him into my mouth. His body tenses and relaxes in waves as I work my mouth over him, pulsing, tasting, and using a hand to pump the part of him that I can't fit into my mouth. I'm incredibly turned on by the way his body reacts to me and, peering up, his face strains under the sensations I'm delivering.

For the first time, Owen is at my mercy. It's my turn to show him what a slow burn feels like. To squirm under the need and feel helpless in the wake of someone else's touch. I weave my tongue over him, massaging him, and guiding him deeper into my mouth at faster intervals. Until his breathing reaches an all time desperate rate.

"*Wait,*" he hisses, eyes closed. "Ride me."

I pull him out of my mouth and take him into my hand, stroking as I reach into my purse for a condom. My eyes feast on the sight of his impressive cock as my hand glides the thin, latex material over it.

The air around me is electrified by the anticipation of taking him into me as I pull off my underwear and, hiking up my dress, climb over him. Our movements are frenzied, his hands fly to my waist as I slowly lower myself down onto him, relishing every inch until my thighs touch his and he's as deep inside as he can go.

"Damn," he whispers, hands closing tightly over me as he guides my rhythm. I'm overwhelmed by how badly I want him, even as he weaves in and out of me.

He pulls one of my breasts from the low neckline of my dress and brings his mouth over it, tongue teasing over my nipples. I moan out and wind my hips.

There's something empowering about giving myself to Owen, knowing all the while he worships every second of it. Knowing I've been in his fantasies for longer than he's been in mine. Watching his face contort with the waves of sensation that part his lips and fog up his eyes as I ride him vigorously.

And I feel like I'm dancing, winding my hips so easily and freely, swaying to the sounds of the groans rumbling from his throat and the moans that rise from my own. I ride him straight into an orgasm, nearly collapsing over him in fits of moans. He's not far behind, holding me firm against him as his hips jerk toward me a few more times before he groans out in relief. And the sound is so delightful, his sudden, rough thrusts so titillating, it yanks another orgasm out of me. My hips move without my consent, rocking to the pulses of ecstasy that rip through me in a blinding glare of light.

It's not until Owen pulls my shoulders back, too soon and too abruptly, that I realize the blinding light isn't a figment of my imagination or the product of an intense orgasm.

There is a very literal light pouring into the car and illuminating every inch of our surroundings. Lights from the police cruiser parked behind us.

Chapter Twenty-Nine

I PLANT MY FEET CAREFULLY on the ground, palms clenched. The same palms that apparently turned on Owen's hazard lights. An accidental move that drew the attention of the police. But what I'm focused on is not falling over and looking like a drunk. I'm not drunk, just dizzy with nerves. Police officers in general make me anxious. It doesn't help that the cruiser's headlights bathe over me like a spotlight, shrinking my pupils and making it hard for me to see anything.

As though realizing that, the officer in front of me makes a cutting motion with his hand toward his cruiser. The headlights cut out, switching to the dimmer parking lights. I can finally see a little better without the exaggerated brightness.

The man that stands in front of me, examining my ID card under his flashlight, is a decent looking twenty-something-year-old with short blond hair and a serious expression.

A breeze sweeps in, making me hyper-aware of my panty-less state. I'm still wet and throbbing with lingering sensations. Owen is beside me now, hands hanging loosely at his sides, expression unreadable.

I think idly of how there are special kits for law

enforcement to test for gun residue on someone's hands. And I wonder if there's a kit to test peoples lips to confirm they've been mouth-fucking someone in a parked car. And, well, literally fucking someone in a parked car. Which, I'm sure, has to be a misdemeanor. At the very least, it's a charge the average person wouldn't want a judge reading out in the deafening silence of the shocked courthouse.

I plead not guilty, your honor. I was under the influence of a sexy motherfucker.

The cop fixes his stern brown eyes on me and asks, "Ma'am, do you know this man?"

I nod. "Yes. I do."

He examines my ID card again. "Have you been drinking tonight?"

"No. I have not."

"What do you do for a living?"

"I'm an attorney. Not a prostitute, if that's what you're wondering."

I shoot a sideways glance at Owen, standing silently beside me and staring deadpan at the cop, who seems to be avoiding his eyes.

And I wonder, bitterly, why I'm getting all the questions.

As if hearing my thoughts, the cop straightens and points his flashlight at Owen. Owen blinks and turns his face away from the light, visibly annoyed. My stomach sinks. I'm sure Owen's unapologetic expression is only going to make this worse for the both of us.

But the cop's lips turn up and he shuts off the flashlight. He pushes the button of the radio on his shoulder and says, "Miller, get out here. You're gonna love this."

I pull my shoulder back, feeling alert, and uneasy at not knowing what the fuck is going on. The second cop, who I assume to be Miller, approaches from the police cruiser.

When Miller sees Owen, his face lights up and his hands clasp together in feigned shock. "*Well, look at this*. Mr. Perfect caught red-handed."

Owen rubs his face, impatient. "Don't be a dick, Miller. You're embarrassing my woman."

My eyes widen at Owen's words, but Miller doesn't bat an eye and carries on as if he didn't hear him. "I was wondering what you were doing with all your leave days. Guess we finally have an answer."

The gears in my brain turn slowly as I piece together what those words mean. The blond cop, standing closest to me, begins a horribly failed attempt to suppress a growing snicker, which finally bursts out of both him and Miller in the form of hysterical laughter.

Owen looks on the verge of laughter, too, as he shakes his head. "Fuck you guys."

I think this is the first time I've ever heard Owen curse.

Miller gathers himself and addresses me for the first time, taking a few minutes to give me a sympathetic smile and a moderately chastising speech about taking sexual activities indoors. I'm only half listening to him, too preoccupied by the vision of Owen as I picture him in a police uniform. Radio at his shoulder, his thick, muscular arms on either side of him, hands lingering close to his belt, at the ready. The image fits him so perfectly that I wonder how I didn't see it before.

Owen's a cop.

I'm too distracted to listen to the conversation that follows between the men. I'm gazing at Owen, unabashed. And when his eyes fix onto mine, it's not a fleeting look. It's a full-on stare, like he's peeling away my layers and not worried about who notices. I'm consumed by those hazel eyes, which sometimes lean toward green other times toward honey.

This man brings me to my knees with the simplest of looks. He's honest and sexy and unbelievably good-natured.

This man is mine. All mine.

Chapter Thirty

I'M NOT THE ONLY ONE who has an eventful New Year. Lex doesn't come home New Year's night. I would worry if it weren't for her simple, albeit slightly cryptic text:

[Emily...thank you. See you tomorrow-ish.]

I can only take that to mean things with Leo went well. Can't say I'm not surprised. What I wouldn't give to have been a fly on that fall, hear what he could have possibly said to her to keep Lex from running in the other direction at warp speed after his grand reveal.

The weekend that follows is an intoxicating and exhilarating fog of Owen. He starts back at work on Monday after having taken a few weeks off to settle his father's business. Monday is also the day of my interview. So, since I'm not moving into the loft until the following weekend, Owen and I spend the weekend together at his apartment.

Guilt squirms in my stomach at the thought of having Owen all to myself for two whole days. But he insists it's not an issue. Landon spends nearly every weekend with his aunt. It's easy to see why Landon prefers hanging out with his cousin than with the father he doesn't know and can't seem to connect with.

Owen and I talk about all of this, on and off, never

letting the mood get weighed down for too long. Still, I read the layers of hurt underneath his casual references. He and Landon are finding it impossible to connect with each other, both pushed into an awkward and untimely relationship.

There are many other things that Owen doesn't say explicitly but I can read between the lines. It seems Landon's mother never talked to him about Owen and so the kid was left to assume his father wasn't in the picture by choice. The kid's grandparents were the ones to break the news to him that his father didn't know and that once he did, he wanted nothing more than to be part of his life. But by then, it seems, the damage had been done.

Owen's sister, Callie, is a few years older. She's an oncologist and--if the fact that she owns a house in Del Mar complete with a guesthouse is any indication--the woman's pretty well off. Lucas moved into her guesthouse after he discharged from the hospital.

Something about Lucas' recovery doesn't ring true to me. A heart attack requiring his children to rally around him with such force, making him quit his job, sell his loft, and move into a guest home to keep a closer eye on him? It all makes me suspect there's more to the story. I don't ask Owen what's really going on. Our conversations still have a layer of protective coating over them as we test the waters, tentative. Unsure yet how far into topics we can submerge ourselves without going in too deep, too quick.

I immerse myself, instead, in him, in our weekend together. Because, as he points out, we won't see as much of each other once he returns to work. His schedule is demanding and mine is about to get hectic as well.

Our weekend has a distinct feel of a honeymoon in January. And by the time Sunday evening rolls around, we accept, with a frustrating reluctance, it's time to leave our self-made paradise of his king-sized bed and face the real world.

Owen heads off to pick up his son and I stalk back to Lex's condo for the night, hoping to drop into bed early and get extra sleep before my interview in the morning.

The condo door slams shut behind me. My keys rattle noisily in my hand as I walk further down the hall. I'm making a big production of my entrance, and given the way that everything is still and quiet, I know I have good reason to. There's a car I don't recognize in the lot outside. I'm pretty sure it's Leo's. And I'm pretty sure he and Lex aren't in the bedroom preparing memos for their return to the office tomorrow morning. Sure enough, Leo comes out of Lex's bedroom not even three minutes later, wearing dark jeans and a white t-shirt. He crosses the living room into the kitchen, where I'm putting away the leftovers from the dinner Owen and I shared.

"Hello," Leo says without much enthusiasm, though his eyebrows rise in question at the way I eye his appearance.

It's not that he looks disheveled. He doesn't. It's more that he's so obviously oozing sex and it's activating my gag reflexes. Back when Lex first started things with Leo, back when she vaguely alluded to theoretical sex, I was excited for her. But now it's literal sex. It's *right in the next room* sex. And I want it to stop.

We don't speak, focusing on our individual tasks. Leo reaches for two glasses from the cabinet without having to ask where Lex keeps them. He's comfortable here. Even more so than me, now.

Leo pours himself a glass of water and turns to face me. No shame, this guy, staring me dead in the eyes as though he doesn't care what I might have overheard. My sister must be hiding out in her room, mortified at the possibility I *did* hear something. If I had, they would've found me collapsed at the entryway floor after carving out my eardrums with my car keys.

"Couldn't you guys go fornicate at the little house you bought for...what was it?" I try to recall what Lex told me about his little, bleeding heart speech. "Not to live in, right? It was for your hopes and dreams of the future or some crap like that."

He chuckles as he pours a second glass of water and sets it on the counter. "It's being shown to renters next week."

"Okay. Don't you have your own place with a bed and other sturdy surfaces?"

"This is a quick drive to the office."

I turn my head a fraction to demonstrate his point is lost on me.

"We get more sleep here. Trust me, your sister needs to rest when I'm done with her."

I cringe and hold my hand up to stop him from elaborating any further. "You two are disgusting."

Leo raises his glass as though in a toast, his lips twisting up in a small grin. "Yes. Yes, we are." He pauses then adds, "Could you remind me again where all your seething hate for me comes from?" He doesn't seem upset, just genuinely curious. "Were you team Jacob or something?"

"I was team Jacob. But also, you broke my sister."

"And I put her back together."

"*No.*" I glare at his presumption. "She put *herself* back together and decided to trust you. But if you break her heart again, Leo? I'm going to cut off your balls with a pair of dull scissors."

He nearly laughs.

"You believe me, right? You think I'm crazy enough to cut off your balls?"

"You know what? I really do think you'd be crazy enough."

"Good."

With a hint of a smile on his face, he extends a hand for me to shake.

I look at it. "No offense, but I don't want to touch your hands right now. Let's just agree we have a mutual understanding."

"Agreed."

This is the closest Leo Conrad and I will ever come to a truce. With a small nod and a glass of water in each hand, he walks off and disappears into Lex's bedroom. My sister's burst of laughter is muted through the walls. The sound warms my heart. But I'm also left feeling awkward and uncomfortable. Like a third wheel. I can't wait to move out.

Chapter Thirty-One

I'M INTERVIEWED BY ELIZABETH WILSON, the head of the legal department, an attorney herself, and my future boss. She's a tall, thin, brunette in her mid-thirties who carries herself with such an exaggerated poise, I wonder vaguely if she's secretly royalty or something. My first impression of her is that she's stuck-up, but she surprises me with how friendly she is. And though I don't feel any sort of warm, possible-friendship vibes from her, she seems sharp and stern in the ways a boss should. So I have no reason not to like her.

I can tell by her facial expressions that my answers impress her. I'm doing great, until the inevitable happens.

"You left Bernstein & Snyder after only a few months?" Elizabeth asks.

I swallow. "Yes, I did."

"That was a short time for such a big firm."

My mouth threatens to part but I sink my teeth into the side of my tongue.

She posed a statement. Not a question.

I nod and wait for her to continue, but Elizabeth watches me, clearly wanting me to offer up an explanation to a question she's yet to ask. Well, that's not how interviews work. If she wants to know what happened, she'll have to ask me point-blank. I see no need to dig my own grave just because someone hands me the shovel.

The brief silence that follows echoes between us and I resist the urge to shift in my seat. I know what she's doing. My sister does it much better. Using silence as a weapon, expecting me to blurt something out in discomfort.

Right as my pulse becomes the prominent sound in the room, Elizabeth picks up the interview as though the awkward moment never happened. I can't believe my luck and suspect her leniency might have something to do with Giles, who is her direct supervisor, putting in a good word for me.

As the interview wraps up, I say a silent prayer that Bernstein will be good on his word and not sabotage my career any further. While I'm at it, I say a second silent prayer that I won't sabotage my career, either.

Wednesday is my first full day of work and I'm dropped in the midst of a land simultaneously muddy and overloaded with detail. As though my brain relaxed far too much in the time that I've spent away from work and now I have to retrain it to focus and absorb information. It's a good thing I start midweek, because by the time Friday rolls around, I'm eager for the weekend.

Saturday morning, I bring Lex to see the loft. She and I drive in my car with boxes of clothes and lighter items while Leo and Owen bring my heavier furniture from the storage unit in a small moving truck.

Lex holds in her mortified expression when she realizes my new place is over a diner and the entrance is in the back of the building. A sort of surprised, mechanical smile freezes on her face. But when she walks into the loft, her face relaxes.

"It's cozy," she says, a genuine smile now warming her face. "Aw, Emily. This is so...*you*."

"I know, right?!" I can't contain my excitement that she sees it too, and I do a small, whimsical twirl in the middle of the empty living room before leading her around for a quick tour. Lex comments on the charm of the place, saying all the things I want to hear. How spacious it feels despite its size, how bright it is in the daytime, how quaint it feels in its attic style.

When the moving truck pulls up, Lex and I peer down at the parking lot, quietly watching our men interact, both wondering if they'll like each other or if--like Leo and me--they've gotten off on the wrong foot.

Even from a distance, it's clear to see the two men are comfortable with each other. Owen and Leo converse easily, neither man seeming to try much, giving the impression of familiarity.

"I guess it's just you, then," Lex muses, shooting me a sideways grin.

"I don't get his appeal," I say of Leo, adapting the pretentious tone of a bored aristocrat. "The man is positively petulant."

Lex nudges me. "You'll always be my number one. You know that, right?"

"Yeah, yeah," I say, pretending her words don't reach the small kid inside of me, always secretly seeking her approval.

My sister and I hang back as the two men bring in my sofa, maneuvering it around the tight doorframe. I'm staring at Owen, at the ways the muscles in his arms flex under the strain of the furniture yet his face remains relaxed and unaware of the effort.

Jesus.

I need everyone to leave right now so I can fuck this man on that very couch, right this very minute.

I shoot a sideways glance at my sister, worried she might notice me drooling, but find her staring hard at Leo, instead. He locks eyes with her and winks, his lips tugging slightly. I look away, knowing they've communicated something silently that I don't even want to imagine.

Owen wears a white crew neck top while Leo wears a black one. I find it amusing that they are dressed in contrasting colors because it's true the two men couldn't be more different. It's not that Owen's hair and eyes are dark compared to Leo's blond hair and piercing blues. It's not that Owen's bigger than Leo, with a much bulkier build, though their heights are maybe an inch in difference.

No, it's most noticeable in the way they carry themselves. Leo oozes nonchalant-ness and initiates small talk with ease. Owen is more reserved, visibly tighter wound, which turns me on because it makes me want to ride him until he relaxes in all the ways I know he can.

"You're having quite the lucky streak," Lex says to me, as we unload the dishes and place them into the cabinets. The men are in the bedroom setting up my bed.

"What do you mean?"

"Emily, you've been in town for what--just shy of a month? And you already have a new job, a new place, and a new man. Each one exactly what you want. Talk about perfect."

My response is an automatic smile. I know she's saying this to make me feel good. To make me feel accomplished and maybe proud. The truth is, her words scare me.

I can't quite put my finger on why my reaction isn't what I know it should be. It's not that I'm not grateful, I am. It's not that I don't see how lucky I've been, despite my previous misfortune. And it's not that I'm unhappy. God knows it's most definitely not that.

Things are pretty perfect. Things are stable. Every little piece in its place.

And that...makes my skin crawl with discomfort. It's like that moment of the movie when the sweet couple is driving down the road, singing and laughing, having the time of their lives, not a care in the world.

And then a tractor trailer sideswipes them right off the road.

There's a reason for that cliché. There's a reason why Hollywood directors rely on it. Every single person watching can relate. We've all felt it, that nagging fear when things begin to line up in just the right way. When everything is going right--we fear it may be the perfect time for it all to fall apart again.

I've never been a pessimist. This isn't me. I don't

have these scary thoughts about impending doom. And yet, I've been having these twinges a lot lately, right in the moments I should be feeling the opposite. Moments I should feel crazy happy and insanely content.

Owen comes out of the room and the sight of him sends a thrill running down my spine, coiling between my legs. I'd do anything to freeze this moment. Keep things the way they are in this second. With him standing there, looking at me like I'm the most beautiful thing he's ever seen. Like a man wandering the desert and coming across a fresh-water lake.

Maybe the reason I'm so terrified is that I've never had so much to lose.

Chapter Thirty-Two

OWEN WASN'T KIDDING WHEN HE said we wouldn't get to see each other as often once he returned to work. Being with someone you constantly fantasize about but can't see often is a form of torture. And somehow, it's also incredibly refreshing. I'm able to focus on my new job, spend time with my sister, and my friends. All the while feeling the inexplicable comfort of knowing someone, somewhere, is missing me as badly as I'm missing him. Counting the hours until we get to see each other, kiss, and feel our bodies slide against one another.

On the days that Owen is on the swing shift, he visits me for lunch before heading off for work. Those nights, I wake after midnight to his goodnight text, as he finally returns home.

When his days off land on a weekend again, he invites me to join him and Landon on a trip to the Air and Space museum. I'm hesitant about intruding on their father-son time, expecting Landon to be as starved for quality time with his father as I am. But the sad reality is the kid doesn't want to spend time with Owen.

Landon does nothing to engage any of Owen's attempts at conversation. Yet, for as cold and dismissive as the kid is toward his father, he's pleasant and chatty with me. This makes me uncomfortable. I don't deserve his attention; I'm not the one busting my ass to raise him.

The more time I spend around them, the more I witness how overprotective Owen is of his son. And how much it suffocates Landon. How little they talk. How quick they are to revert to cutting, snide remarks in response to simple questions.

I've never dated someone with a kid before. But common sense tells me I shouldn't get involved in their relationship. So, I bite my tongue and pretend I don't notice their dynamic, or how it weighs heavily on Owen.

The other day, Amelia asked me if it was hard dating a cop. Not seeing him when I want to, spending a lot of time alone. On the surface, it's not ideal. But then I think about how much missing him keeps things between us exciting. Our time apart keeps our relationship fresh. My stomach does summersaults when my eyes finally get to feast on the sight of him. When he touches me? My entire body lights up in a flurry of nervous energy. I'm giddy and excited, on our first date all over again, every time we are together.

Tonight is one of my nights with him.

All the furniture in my living room has been pushed into the center of the room. The sofa, the coffee table, and the television Lex gifted me as housewarming presents. I've prepped the loft for a night of painting the walls, something I've been meaning to do for two weeks now.

"What exactly were you planning to do here?" Owen asks, eyeing the large sheets of plastic I've draped over every inch of the living room floors, securing them with tape to the baseboards.

"It's to protect the floors. I'm a terrible painter--ceiling, doorknobs, trim...it's all fair game. I can't help it."

His chuckle's interrupted by the chime of his phone. Glancing at it, he says, "It's my sister. I should get this."

I nod and walk off to the kitchen to pour us some drinks.

"Hello," Owen says into the phone. "No. I already told him he's not going. Because he was a smart ass, that's why. You know what--put him on the phone." A beat. "Hello? Where exactly do you think you're going? No. I didn't say maybe. I said no."

Even from where I stand at the kitchen, I can hear the buzzing sounds erupting from the speaker. Someone raising their voice. Owen lifts the phone from his ear a few inches.

"Listen to me. You are not going. You stay where you are, with your aunt. That's right. I don't care."

More yelling. At first, I remain where I stand, taking a sip of my drink and pretending to look for something inside a kitchen drawer. I've always known he and his son don't have a good relationship, but I've never been privy to the details of a full-blown argument.

Something in Owen's expression elicits a soft tug inside of my chest and makes me want to shut my eyes for a second. I decide he needs his drink, so I walk over and hand him the glass. He shakes his head, distracted, and though he takes it, he immediately sets it down on the coffee table.

Standing beside him, I hear Landon's voice, laced with venom. "Stop acting like you're my fucking father."

"Don't you dare use that langua--" Owen's mouth is still open in mid retaliation when the line goes dead with a click.

I try to remain outwardly unaffected, as though I didn't overhear what I did. But somewhere inside of myself, I cringe. It's literally painful to see the frustration fighting through Owen's expression, the embarrassment as he meets my eyes.

This wasn't something I was meant to witness.

Owen clears his throat. "Give me a second, let me text my sister. Need to make sure Landon stays put. He's grounded. Probably for the rest of his life."

The seconds drag on until he sends the message and turns to face me again. But the frustration and anger is still etched into every line of his face so I look away, not knowing what to say.

Owen rubs his face then flashes a half-smile in my direction. "Sorry about that. Kids...."

When I speak, I keep my tone light, as though I'm unaware of the tension radiating from him, pulling his jaw muscles tight. "You know, Owen, we can paint some other night. It's fine with me if you want to reschedule."

"No," he says quickly. "It's better for everyone if I stay here with you." He does a slow turn around the room. "Where are the paint cans?"

I point to them, wondering if the rest of our night will be spent pretending he isn't in an awful mood. It's not that I blame him. I just wish I knew how to fix it.

Owen opens a can of paint and, peeking at the color,

raises an eyebrow at me. "Really?"

"What?"

"This is the color of...I don't even think anything this bright exists in nature."

I wave away his words. "Quit exaggerating, it's a pale yellow. This place is small, it needs brighter colors."

"If you say so." He glances around. "Where are the paint rollers?"

"Rollers? I thought we could make do with these." I hold up a pair of brushes and laugh when his smile falls away. "Relax, I'm kidding. Paint rollers are over there." I point to a plastic bag containing the rest of the painting supplies.

We start painting the same wall, running our rollers in lengthy strokes. There's something comforting about the action. Coating the wall with paint is relaxing. Owen's shoulders relax with each downward stroke, and he seems pleased with himself when we finish a wall. Although, I can't help but notice it takes me twice the effort to coat my section. Owen's roller leaves perfectly even patch on the walls whereas mine are uneven and a bit streaky.

"I think my roller is broken."

"No. You're not putting the right pressure on it," he says.

"Show me."

He sets his roller down in the container and comes up behind me. His arms come around, hands wrapping over mine. With that simple touch, he sets me on fire.

Bringing his lips to my ear, he says, "Like this." He pulls my hands down to guide the roller over the wall, applying firm pressure. My paint roller leaves a perfect, even stroke.

"Oh." His scent and body heat wrap around me, slowing down my thoughts.

I love when he's behind me. There's nothing like the feeling of his large, powerful build holding mine.

"Just keep applying even pressure," he says, but as he brings my roller back down again, he also presses his lower body against me and I feel something there, stirring alive.

"Like this?" I pull the roller back up, but press myself even further into him.

His voice is thick when he whispers, "Just like that."

Then he lowers a hand to my waist, setting me on fire there, too. His other hand remains over mine where my clasp on the roller's handle grows weaker. Owen pries the tool from my hand and lets the roller drop onto the plastic covered floor.

He spins me around to face him and pulls me close, so I can feel how incredibly hard he is.

"What's the matter," I taunt, "having trouble concentrating?"

"Only every time I'm near you."

I eye our drinks on the living room table. His lays untouched. I lower my voice playfully. "How about we get liquored up and have wild, drunken sex? Maybe slip into places not often ventured?"

"You know, drunk sex is overrated. Why would you ever want to dull a single sensation?"

I narrow my eyes and circle around him like a predator. "Fine. We can get drunk *after*. Dull the soreness you leave me in."

"Why is it so important we get drunk?"

"It's a rule of mine," I say, making my precondition up on a whim." I need to see you drunk. At least once. What if you're a violent drunk, *hmm*? Shouldn't I figure that out before I let you slip into places not often ventured?"

He laughs. "I can save you the trouble. Because I don't drink."

"Oh," I say, the single word carrying heavy disappointment.

He watches me carefully in the moment that passes, his expression slips against some shadow of a thought crossing his mind. He seems to cast it all away with a deliberate breath and, without warning, sweeps me off my feet. Literally. I snicker gleefully at the way he carries me across the room like I'm some fair maiden he's rescued from the forest. A fair maiden that's about to be screwed to kingdom come.

Owen sets me on the kitchen counter so that my ass is right on the edge of it. In one swift movement, he peels off my dress, tugging it firmly from beneath where I sit and dragging it over my head. Hooking a hand under each of my knees, he pulls my legs up, propping them on the counter, on both sides of me, and I fall back onto my elbows. I'm spread-eagle.

Holy hell, the ways he handles me.

His grin is sinful, as though noticing something in my expression. He runs a big, rough hand up from my abdomen to the concave between my breasts, bringing it to rest at the base of my neck, fingers curling gently.

It's a subtle move of possession, letting me know my body is his. Desire throbs through me like a pulse. His fingers trail over the exposed skin of my inner thighs and I swear all the windows in my loft fog at once.

"How fond are you of your panties?" he asks.

"They're brand new." I'm struggling to form words, but I manage to add, "I barely know them, really."

His fingers find the top of my underwear and yank on them. Hard. I gasp as the material momentarily cuts into the skin over my hipbones before the ripping sound cuts through the air. Owen casts the flimsy thong aside.

A moan parts my lips as his fingers discover how badly I want him. I tilt my head back as he rubs me. The electric storm between my legs makes it impossible to think of anything but his touch. My skin is on fire and his hands are relentless and unafraid, rough as coal and fueling my heat into a full-blown flame. I'm hurting for him to be inside of me.

Eyes shut, I have no idea what he intends to do next until his lips find mine below. I groan out. Loud. He savors me slowly at first. But his tastes turn to nipping, and then he devours me with increasing vigor. Out of nowhere, he gives my clit one sudden, sharp suck.

"*Oh God,*" I breathe out. My back arches upward, pulled by the firing nerves running up and down my core.

Reality blurs away, intoxicating lust pulls a veil over all of my other senses. All I know is his lips on me. I'm clutching the edge of the counter and twisting my hips any way I can to grind against his face and show him with my movements how incredibly good he's making me feel. Owen's waging an assault on my body, concentrating all his forces on the one small spot where the war is won.

I've never been tasted like this before. This man knows what he's doing. He knows how much pressure to put where, he knows how to weave over all the sensitive spots. When to be rough, when to pull back. He puts his whole damn head into it.

Jesus Christ.

It's like he knows exactly what I'm itching for before I even decide, scratching the perfect place every single time. His tongue massages my most sensitive spot long enough to put me on edge and then tortuously moves to another itch.

He's a fucking professional, bringing me to the brink of orgasm three or four times and somehow, defiantly, keeps me right there until I'm begging in a desperate whisper for him to make me come.

He slides a finger inside of me, all the while tasting me, and lets out a groan as I squeeze around it. His finger pulses in and out of me to the rhythm of my uneven heartbeat. One of my legs hooks over his shoulder, pulling his face further into me. He must know, somehow, how close I am, because he lightly drags his teeth against me. My eyes fly open as the sting of pain twists instantly to insane ecstasy that plunges me into an explosive orgasm. I'm sure my spine dissolved and my body is left boneless.

I laugh. That felt so damn good I don't know what else to do but laugh.

"Does that mean you want more?" Owen asks. The

look in his eyes tells me he's still starving. And I'm on the menu. "I'll give you more."

He drops his pants and pulls off his shirt. And in a low growl that nearly plunges me into another orgasm, he says, "You drive me crazy."

I wait for him to wrap himself, shutting my eyes and focusing on the way my pulse pumps furiously as a different, more maddening intensity throbs between my thighs.

He pushes inside of me and my legs twist tight around him, body heaving on the surface of the counter as he pumps in and out of me with delicious rhythm.

Owen is over twice my size, easily. He's a muscular guy, more muscles in his hands than I have in my entire body. Yet there's always been a tender, almost fearful nature to the way his hands close over me. His fingers clasp my thighs to keep them steady, but with such a contained force, it makes me suspect he's afraid he'll hurt me by mistake, break me if he gets carried away.

He's afraid to give me all he's got because he thinks I can't handle it. And the truth is, I'm not sure I can. He drives me over the edge of sanity in the way he takes me, pummeling me to the core with only moderate effort.

Maybe he should hold back. Maybe he really can break me.

Owen brings me to orgasm in a way I've never experienced from a man. Usually I'm chasing it, looking for the right stroke to stir it in the right way. Feeling it build and build and sometimes slip from me before it peaks. But with Owen, I'm on the verge the entire time.

Constantly agonizing, perpetually exploding.

Sex with him is a giant impending orgasm. A mind-blowing tease. And somehow, I'm always caught off guard when I finally tumble over that cliff. It's always more intense than I anticipate. This time my voice squeaks embarrassingly as I scream out, my hips thrashing, as he meets me in climax, leaning over to let me taste the sound of his satisfied groans.

Afterward, we head to my room and lie in bed for a while, me on my back, and him on his side, chest damp with sweat. He strokes my collarbone, seemingly lost in thought as he watches me where I lie, enjoying thinking about nothing but his touch trailing over my skin.

"What?" I ask, self-conscious. "Why are you looking at me like that?"

"Being with you," he pauses to run a finger over my cheek, "is so much more incredible than I ever thought it would be."

My face seems to forget I'm not the blushing type because my cheeks grow warm. "Be careful, Owen," I tease, "you don't want to go falling in love."

His features yield to a small grin. "Might be too late to warn me. I'm already there."

He kisses me without waiting for my response. I'm glad because I'm stunned into silence. This man. He anchors me. God knows I need that.

And in this moment, I finally understand why Owen was so guarded around me for so long. He wasn't teasing me. It wasn't a game. He was overcompensating for one simple truth. There's a chink in his armor.

And that chink is me.

Chapter Thirty-Three

OWEN IS INTENT ON WEARING me out tonight. I'm spent. Utterly spent and immensely satisfied, as I lie with my head on his chest, breathing in his scent. Neither one of us has said anything in a while and I'm sure he's fallen asleep. But then...

"I'm still curious," he says, "remember that night you came over for the photographs?"

I nod, smiling a little.

"What did you mean, when you said the cheerleading picture brought back bad memories."

I lift my head to look at him. "That's a strange thing for you to be thinking about."

"I think about a lot of things." He runs his fingers through my hair, holding out the strands as though admiring the way they glow golden in the light of the lamp. "Most of them have to do with you."

Resting my chin on his shoulder, I deliberate on what I should say. The topic is bound to ruin the mood, but I can tell he's curious enough to press me for an answer. "My mom had--has issues with addiction."

"Alcohol?" he asks automatically.

"Yes. And drugs, too."

His eyes dart across my face, trying to read my

memories so I don't have to share them. But, of course, he can't. And no matter how hard he works to keep his lips pressed together, another question parts them. "Was she violent?"

"Sometimes. Mostly she just...sort of forgot about us--about my sister and me. Disappeared for a while without telling us if she was ever coming back. Always treated us like a burden. Like we were disposable to her. Little tokens to make people pity her, look at poor Cassandra raising these two girls on her own. But it was bullshit. She didn't raise me. My sister did."

Owen allows my words to settle into a brief silence then, matter-of-factly, he says, "My father had a nasty temper when I was a kid."

"Really?"

"Oh yeah. Drank himself stupid every night." He hesitates a moment, and then, "It's not a heart attack that got him hospitalized. His heart attack was minor, but what they found is that his liver is nearly useless. He's going to need a transplant soon. That's why my sister wants him under her roof. She wants to make sure he doesn't drink himself to death."

"Jesus."

We fall silent again as I consider his words, their implication.

I feel a twitch of insecurity Owen will realize what a stark contrast he is from me. He seems so absolutely steadfast and certain in who he is and what he stands for. When I look at him, I see someone comfortable in his own skin, not just physically, but mentally as well. Someone who has reconciled what he's been through and doesn't let it define him, his relationships, or his future.

Owen's consistent. Stable. Watching the way he is gives me the impression there's a puzzle in me, one I'm meant to solve before I can even dream to reach his level of comfort.

I've never known stability, real stability. Just lulls. Moments when things go still and there are no fires to put out. But for the first time in my life, this feels like more than just a lull. This loft, my home, it fills me with a splitting joy. This man, my man, he makes me feel safe and steady. And my new job, it's exactly what I needed, just when I needed it.

But the unpleasant feeling I've been keeping at bay swirls around in my stomach, obscuring the gratitude and churning along with a low voice in the back of my mind.

You don't deserve this. You don't deserve any of it.

"Are you asleep?" Owen asks.

I lift my head, hoping he doesn't have the secret power to read my thoughts.

"What are you thinking?" I ask, before I can stop myself.

What a generic, needy question.

He doesn't seem to mind. In fact, he smiles a little as if he's glad I asked.

"I'm thinking about how I should've found the damn balls to talk to you, long before that night."

That night. The night I bothered to glance at him, but not long enough to really register his face. The night of the dance when he got the living crap beaten out of him by my ex-boyfriend.

"Shit," I say, closing my eyes. The thought of it still makes me cringe. "I hate that Jonathan hurt you like that."

He shakes his head. "I don't. I'm glad it happened. It taught me a good lesson."

"What's that?"

"If you don't want to get beat up, get bigger and learn to fight."

I run a hand over the curve of his biceps. "And become a cop?"

"That might've been overkill."

"Worked in my favor, though," I say. "The uniform. The muscles." I press my lips to his chest and feel them mold over his firm frame.

"Worked out in my favor, too. Look who ended up with the girl."

"Don't get cocky," I tease.

Owen abruptly pulls me up by the underarms, eliciting a shriek of laughter out of me, and settles me onto him until we are both sitting upright, facing each other, my naked body firmly on top of his.

I shake my head as if in a slow realization. "You can't possibly want more already?"

But even as I say that, I can already tell he's growing hard beneath me.

"You think there's a second that goes by I don't want more?" He runs a hand down my back and cups my ass, squeezing it and tugging me closer to him, his erection teasing me.

"How many more times can you possibly screw me

before your cock falls off from overuse?"
"Why don't we try and find out?"

Chapter Thirty-Four

I'VE FORGOTTEN THE NUANCES OF being with someone, dancing the line between building intimacy and withholding unflattering information. Lying by omission. Everyone does it, especially in the beginning. It's the novelty of starting something new with another person. Pretending they're a clean slate just because they're new to you, fresh to your eyes. Pretending their history doesn't matter, isn't relevant, as long as you don't bring it to light. Pretending the differences between the two of you are small, inconsequential gaps that won't widen with time.

Owen doesn't drink and, though he's never said as much, he doesn't like when I drink. His reaction is measured: eyes lingering over the glass of clear liquid in my hand, lips turning slightly downward before bringing his attention back to his dinner.

I suspect it has to do with his father, but whatever the reason, Owen resists the urge to tell me and so I resist the urge to ask. I pretend I don't notice his disapproval because I'm not doing anything wrong.

Before Bernstein fired me, I'd have a beer once or twice a week and stronger drinks at bars when I got around to partying, which wasn't often. These days, maybe driven by the boredom of living alone, I indulge in a glass or two of something stronger with more regularity. It's not even the taste I enjoy. I find comfort in the burn.

Owen will work through the weekend, but thankfully, they're dayshifts so I'll get to see him after work. Though the thought of him having days off this week while I'm stuck in the office really sucks.

I expect him to spend the night on Sunday but he leaves me early, before the sun even sets. I'm left missing him a lot more than usual and I'm not sure why. A restlessness comes over me that I haven't experienced before, a heaviness in my stomach when the door closes behind him. Dread weighs on me as heavy as the thick silence of the loft.

Monday morning, an alarm blares so loud it jolts me as though someone drove a knife straight into my brain. The sound comes from my phone, so I reach for it and hit one of the side buttons to silence the alarm.

Burying my face back into the pillow, I try to will myself to get up. I doze off for what feels like another minute or two. Lifting my head and squinting against the brightness of my bedroom, I peer at my cellphone again. My eyes widen at the time displayed on the screen. Eight in the morning. Precisely the time I should be getting into work.

Panic jars me and I shoot out of bed. If I leave right now, in the next few minutes, I will be forty minutes late to the office. Cursing under my breath, I rush into the bathroom and splash water on my face. I barely glance at my reflection long enough to smooth my hair up with my fingers and twist it into a bun. A minute later, I'm wiggling into my dress pants and pulling on a blouse. Grabbing my shoes, I slip them on my feet as I walk to the door, my keys in my hand, remembering only at the last moment to grab my purse.

I settle into my car and am relieved to see a bottle of water in the cup holder. I take it and chug down the few inches left inside, my mouth still impossibly dry.

It's not until I've pulled out onto the road that I begin to realize I'm not disoriented from being jolted awake and rushing out the door. Something is wrong, my eyes sting and the road ahead blurs ever so slightly. I press down on my brakes. A car horn blares from behind me, long and angry.

I clutch the steering wheel tighter, the blaring sound exasperating my panic. From my peripheral vision, I catch the reflection of the car that was behind me swerving into the lane beside me. A blue Honda, it speeds by, passing me with obvious flair. And when I half roll my eyes at their dramatics, the driver of the car swerves once more, pulling into the lane in front of me and slams on his brakes, as though to teach me a lesson. My foot is already hovering on the brake, but I immediately know the car won't stop fast enough to avoid colliding into the car. I'm left with no choice but to yank the steering wheel to the right and swerve onto the side of the road, slamming on my brakes once again and coming to a complete stop.

"Fuck!" I punch the steering wheel, dizzy from all the blood rushing to my head. My hands are shaking and I feel I might throw up. Laying my head on the steering wheel, I try to take deep, calming breaths.

What the fuck is wrong with people?

And what the fuck is wrong with me? God, I don't feel good, at all.

Another sound blares behind me, this time a sound that never fails to plunge me into a mild panic. Sirens chirp twice and, glancing up at the rearview mirror, I see a police cruiser pulling up behind me.

Fantastic. As though I'm not already late enough, and now I have to explain why I've swerved onto the side of the road. The cop will probably want to see my identification and ask me a few questions. This is going to take at least another ten minutes.

The man that gets out of the car isn't just any cop. It's Owen. And despite the situation, despite the uncomfortable churning in my stomach, a smile tugs on my lips as I watch my insanely sexy, uniformed boyfriend walk up to my car.

"Hey," he says when he reaches the window, which I've rolled down expectedly. "Are you okay? Is your car stuck?"

I try to speak, but have to press my head back onto the headrest as my surroundings seem to wobble. I swallow back the acid rising in my throat.

"Emily?" Owen's voice grows stiff, as though he's drawing backward in realization.

My eyes fly open at his tone. "Yeah," I groan. But even as I say it, my hand flies up to cover my mouth and I heave. Owen opens the car door and steps to the side just as I bend forward and throw up over the doorframe of my car and onto the dirt path. Nothing comes out the first time. The second time, there's some liquid.

"Jesus christ," Owen says, lowering his voice. "Emily, have you been drinking?"

I wipe my mouth with the back of my hand, fear surges through me.

Drunk? I'm not drunk.

I just woke up.

"No," I say in a low voice. I feel small, and disgusting under his critical glare. And embarrassed that he saw me vomit.

"Get out of the car," he orders, none too friendly.

I do so, careful to step around the vomit. Owen's expression is one I've never seen from him before, an anger I can't quite reconcile.

"I'm not drunk, Owen," I say. "I swear, I just woke up...and ran out the door."

"Were you drinking before you went to sleep?" He eyes my gaze in a strange way, as though testing it for sharpness.

"I...well, yeah. But--"

"How much?"

"What?"

"How much did you drink?"

"I-I don't know. That was hours ago. I went to sleep and--Owen, that was *hours* ago."

"You're slurring your words," he says, evenly. "Obviously you're still drunk."

I shake my head, sicker to my stomach than before with not just embarrassment squirming in me, but self-loathing too. I can't be drunk, can I? Not if I slept through the night. I slept six...five hours, I think.

I try to recall how many drinks I had, try to mentally pull the statistic of how many hours it takes for alcohol to work its way through a person's system. But trying to think so hard just makes everything spin again.

"Don't move," Owen says, before heading back to his cruiser, and I notice for the first time there's another person there in the passenger seat, a female cop. He talks to her for a few minutes, nodding over at me a few times. I can't tell what he's saying. I can't gauge what's going to happen next.

When he returns, Owen tells me to get back into my car. In the passenger side.

"Where are you taking me?" I ask as he pulls out onto the road.

"Home."

"What? No! Owen, I have to be at work!"

"Emily," he pauses to take a deep breath, as though so frustrated he could scream, "you have no business being at work. Do you understand that? You're intoxicated."

"That's impossible--"

"What time did you have your last drink."

"Eleven," I say immediately. Then I hesitate. I watched another movie...it might have been closer to one in the morning. Or even later. I glance at the side view mirror and in a low, guilt-ridden voice, ask, "What did you tell your partner?"

His eyes snap in my direction as though my question irritates him more than anything else. "I told her you're my girlfriend. That you have a stomach virus and that's why you had to pull over onto the side of the road to throw up."

Owen drives the rest of the way in silence. The worst silence I've ever experienced in my life. When we reach the parking lot behind the building of my loft, he pulls something out of his pocket. It looks like an outdated cellphone, a small blue device with a screen and a number pad. Except there's a small white tube sticking out of the side.

A breathalyzer.

My stomach tightens as Owen turns it on.

"Blow."

I stare at him.

"*Blow*," he says again, more forcefully.

Closing my lips over the tube, I let out a breath into the machine. It beeps a few times then a number appears on the display.

.07

"That's not too bad, right?" I ask, my voice small.

He lets out short a breath, though it does nothing to relax his posture. "You don't drive with alcohol in your system, *period*."

"I know that--"

"Is this something you do?" he asks. I frown--not so much at his words but at the way he can't seem to look at me. Hands closing tighter over the steering wheel, he presses further, "Have you ever done this before?"

"No! I thought I slept it off. Owen, I'd never get into the car knowing I was drunk. I don't even feel drunk, I just feel sick...."

I can't remember the last time I ate.

My words fall away awkwardly. I press my lips

together, realizing every word I speak paints a worse picture of me.

"Emily, you need to get inside. Drink water and sleep it off for a few more hours. I need to borrow your car to get back to work. I'll bring it back tonight."

"What do I tell my boss?" I ask, almost to myself.

"*I don't care.*"

I wince in surprise at the force of his tone. I've never seen him this way. He's incredibly intimidating, not just in uniform, but when his displeasure is a beam aimed in my direction.

Shutting his eyes, Owen pinches the bridge of his nose. "I didn't mean to yell. I'm just frustrated you would let this happen. You shouldn't have been on the road. You could've hurt someone, do you realize that?"

"It was a mistake, Owen." I take a breath, hating the way my eyes burn, hating how angry I am at everything. At myself. Hating how much mental effort it takes me to keep my words coherent. "I thought I was fine."

He considers me, his expression softening by a hair, and then nods in the direction of the loft. "Emily, go home."

"Are *we* okay?"

A beat passes. One long, heavy beat.

"We'll talk about this later. Just get inside, I've got to get back to work."

I hesitate, wanting so badly to lean in and kiss him on the cheek. Needing to feel some sort of familiarity, connection. But I think better of it. Something's shifted between us. I suddenly feel we are on shaky ground, ready to topple over.

Chapter Thirty-Five

IT'S ONLY MY FOURTH WEEK on the job and I have to call my boss and tell her I've had an incident on the road and will not be able to make it in today. Four weeks isn't enough time to establish yourself as a dependable employee.

Elizabeth's usually friendly voice stiffens as she accepts my vague description of the emergency that kept me out of work today. But really, I know she's rolling her eyes and wondering if she's hired someone who isn't dependable. A flake. A drama queen. Someone that will constantly complain of unfortunate events that might hinder her ability to follow through at work. Coming in late, missing days, leaving early. All of this is the silent implication in her brief pause before she tells me she hopes everything is all right.

I'm not sure the sickness in my stomach is the alcohol anymore. It's more from disgust in myself. I crawl into bed, almost paralyzed with embarrassment.

Owen brings back my car later in the evening. By then, I'm so painfully sober, the night air presses onto my face and stings every inch of my skin. Owen doesn't come in, he stays on the landing of the front steps, and quite frankly, his tone is clipped. It's obvious he's still upset with me. I get it, I do. I just don't know what to say to make him not be mad at me anymore. 'I'm sorry' just isn't cutting it.

He drops the keys in my hand, mumbles something about his sister waiting for him downstairs. She followed him here in order to give him a ride back. I ask if I can meet her and his response is so quick, it slaps me on the face.

"No. I told her you're sick. You'll meet her some other time."

He says goodnight but when he goes to turn away, I pull him back and kiss him. His lips don't part right away, but then they do. And as his hands move to my waist, his mood yields ever so slightly to his craving for me.

I ask him to come inside, to spend the night with me, but he says he's tired from a long day and just wants to go home, his disappointment in me still evident on his face.

"Hey," I say, "this won't happen again."

"Okay." His simple word plunges through me. It's shaded with doubt.

The next morning, my alarm is set to go off earlier than usual and I'm at work long before anyone else. I sit behind my desk, catching up on emails and making notes of all the things I need to take care of for the day.

My boss comes up to my door; she's an ice queen frosting over everything in her wake. I don't blame her. I blame myself. I'll have to work ten times as hard to prove to her that she didn't make a mistake by hiring me.

I'm willing to do whatever it takes.

Owen and I don't get to see each other over the next few days. It's his week to work the night shift and our schedules leave us missing each other by mere minutes. This doesn't help my efforts to make things right between us.

We talk on the phone when we can but with each passing day, I sense him gradually resisting the urge to warm up and let our silent, passive aggressive fighting finally be over. I start to just wish he'd truly believe me in his gut when I tell him it isn't going to happen again. His quiet reluctance just fills me with uncertainty about myself. And I hate it. I hate how important his opinion is to me. I hate how much I care.

I've been anticipating these consequences. Before I knew what could go wrong, I knew that something would. Once again, I'm unsure of everything in my life. Feeling as though I'll never be able to prove myself worthy again. Feeling as though maybe I'm just not worthy of all the good things life has given me, at all.

Chapter Thirty-Six

SHORTLY AFTER NINE O'CLOCK ON Friday night, I'm sitting on the floor of my living room, sorting through the boxes I've yet to unpack. The television is on low, just a discernible rumble throughout the empty loft.

When a soft knocking sound reaches me, I lift the box I'm holding and scan the floor, thinking I've dropped something. The second knock is purposeful and my eyes dart to the front door. I'm not expecting anyone.

When I pull open the door, I'm greeted by the sight of a slouchy, grumpy-faced Landon. He's wearing a dark jacket with the hood of a gray sweatshirt pulled up around his head, a backpack strapped to his shoulders.

It's chilly out tonight and I'm in a tank top. So, I motion for him to come inside before I even say anything. I shut the door behind me, dreading the questions I need to ask because I already suspect the answers.

"What are you doing here? Did you just rob a bank or something?"

"No. I just need a place to crash for tonight. Can I stay here?" His expression falls even further as he notices the instant hesitation forming on my face.

"Never mind." He tries to push past me to open the door but my hand lands on his shoulder.

"No, wait--" I have about four questions that attempt to erupt out of me at once, causing me to falter in my speech. I pick the most important of them. "Does your dad know you're not home? Does your aunt?"

"They'll know when they can't find me."

I throw my head back and pinch my nose.

Landon says, "My aunt's out of town and I can't be home anymore. It's just constant yelling and fighting."

I bite my tongue, not wanting to ask who is doing all of the yelling and fighting because I'm sure it's Landon.

I'm resisting the overwhelming urge to tell him he's being a brat. But I remember what it's like to be that age. To think that problems were so heavy and permanent. To feel as though all you want is for someone to tell you it's okay to feel the way you do. Tell you it's okay to *not* feel okay.

Right now, I have two options. I can scold the kid and demand he goes home, or I could give him what he's looking for right now: a safe-haven.

I rub the space between my eyes. "You can take the couch. I'll go get you a blanket."

Relief floods his face as he rushes to take his shoes off at the entryway, setting them down beside mine. I leave the kid behind and start dialing Owen's number before I even close my bedroom door.

"Hello?" Owen's voice is pulled taut, so tense it pulls me with it.

I lower my voice to a whisper. "Landon's with me--"

"*Jesus Christ*, this kid's going to kill me...I'm on my

way--"

"I can drive him back."

"No--I'll head over now."

"Owen..." I hesitate. "Maybe he can stay the night? I'll make sure he doesn't get into trouble."

"That's not necessary. You don't have to do that."

"No, I know. I just...he's on the run and came to *me*. He trusts me. I feel awful turning him into the authorities."

Owen laughs a little, albeit reluctantly.

I go on, "At least you know where he is. Maybe a little time apart will help you two cool off?"

He takes a measured breath. "Are you sure?"

"Yes. It'll be fine. Come in the morning."

Owen thanks me and we end the call. When I go back out into the living room, Landon is watching television, but the volume is still low. The remote is nearby but I sense he didn't feel comfortable touching it without asking permission first.

"I was about to put on a movie," I lie. "Want to join me?"

"No. Thank you. I just want to sleep."

I glance at his cellphone on the coffee table. The power is off.

He takes the pillow and blanket I hand him, mumbling his thanks. I motion for him to scoot over and sit on the other end of the couch, facing him.

He's looking at the television, avoiding my eyes.

"Landon, I know it's none of my business but...what's going on?"

He opens his mouth then closes it again. Then he

shakes his head, running his hands through his hair.

It's clear he isn't going to answer me. "Okay. How about this? I'm just going to throw out a few theories and you stop me when I'm warm. California is lame and you want to go back to Arizona."

He shoots me a look, half amused, half annoyed.

"You and your dad don't get along because you both think you don't have anything in common--" I pause, noticing how he starts to drum his fingers on his arm, impatient. "Your school is too--"

"Just stop, please," he says. "You don't know what it's like."

"So, why don't you tell me?"

I can tell he's surprised by the genuine question. I wonder how often he's asked anything at all versus being *told* things. That's part of why kids end up so angsty. While growing up, they are constantly told what to do, what to feel. No one really listens to them because, really, what the hell should they know about anything?

He hesitates, takes in a sharp breath, and lets the words out quickly. "One day everything is fine, the next everything's taken away."

"By everything, you mean your mom?"

He doesn't respond.

I look down at my hands. "I'm sorry. It's not fair that you lost your mother so young."

Again, he doesn't respond right away, staring out into a spot below the television screen. I know he's listening but it's too much for him to give me his full attention. I'm still formulating what I should say next when his next words take me by surprise. "There's no part of her here. Nothing. It's like she never existed."

A beat passes, followed by a few more--until the silence grows so big I'm afraid to break it.

"You're wrong," I say.

He scoffs and though he doesn't *say* I don't know what the hell I'm talking about, I know that's what he's thinking.

"You're wrong," I say again. "Your mother's past is here. It's in Owen. He knew her at a time you didn't, long before you were born. Don't you ever wonder what she was like back then?" I hold the reluctant gaze he gives me. "I think you and Owen have more in common than you believe. You just have to take the time to get to know each other--" He looks away again and I hurry to finish. "You just have to try."

Silence blankets us again. I feel extremely awkward, unsure why I thought I had a right to speak on things I really know nothing about. I run my hands through my hair. "Are you hungry?"

His eyes say yes, but the words that leave his lips are, "I'm okay."

I get up and go to the refrigerator. "I've got some sushi I made earlier. Do you like sushi?"

He shrugs and I take it to mean he's never tried it before. "You make it yourself?"

"Not always, but I did for lunch. Why? Are you worried it won't taste good?"

"No." He gets up and joins me at the other side of the small countertop island. "Just seems complicated."

"It's actually pretty easy and...kind of relaxing. I can

show you?"

He gives me a hesitant smile. "Sure."

Landon helps me pull out the ingredients and we set up a sushi making station on top of the coffee table. We sit on pillows on the floor and work on slathering the sticky rice on the seaweed rolls. We go slowly at first, until Landon catches on and his attention becomes divided between the task and the movie playing on the screen in front of us. I witness the kid warm gradually; the giant block of ice he was burrowed in slowly melts away to a kid who smiles more easily than he frowns. A few times, I'm doubled over laughing at his sly commentary.

When I leave him behind to go to sleep, a halo of worry falls over me. Landon is probably idolizing the idea of me. Just like I idolized the idea of Lucas. It's easy to look up to someone when you don't know half of who they really are, easy to get attached to anyone who seems to get you.

Chapter Thirty-Seven

I WAKE UP TO MY cellphone vibrating against my chest. Apparently, that's where I left it when I fell asleep for the tenth time last night. Blinking a few times against the light of day, I look at my phone.

[On my way.]

At first, I don't understand the message. Then the hazy fog lifts just slightly, enough for me to remember Landon is asleep on my couch. It's only 7 a.m., but I guess Owen doesn't want to wait a moment longer to pick up his son.

My body is heavy. I had a hard time falling asleep last night. And when I did fall asleep, my dreams were uneasy and tense. My reflection in the bathroom mirror is an adequate representation of how rested I feel. Which is not at all. My eyes are slightly puffy and I can't seem to open them past a squint.

I finish brushing my teeth and go back out into the living room to stand over Landon. He's peacefully asleep and I hate to wake him.

"You should probably get up now." I nudge him with my foot.

He groans in disapproval, then peers up at me with sleepy eyes and says, "Is Owen on his way?"

I go to answer him, but hesitate. How does he know?

Landon sits up and answers the question I didn't verbalize. "I heard you on the phone last night. You whisper really loudly."

It's hard to not laugh. So, I do. "Sorry, kid. I couldn't let your dad worry without knowing where you were."

"I know."

When Owen shows up at the door, the cold air that rushes into the room from outside is rivaled only by the look he gives Landon.

"Go wait in the car."

"My bicycle is downstairs..." Landon keeps his eyes cast downward, his tone serious but not combative.

Owen hands him the car keys. "Put it in the trunk. Pull down the back seats if you have to."

Landon nods and walks out of the loft, only glancing back to make eye contact with me for a second. He doesn't say anything to me, but I can tell what he's trying to communicate.

"Thanks," Owen says, arms wrapping around me in a hug. My hands come up to his sides, fingers molding over the familiar muscles. His body reacts as mine does, tensing before relaxing. Needing a moment to adjust to the realization we haven't had real time together all week, with Owen's schedule and the looming threat of the unresolved argument hanging over us.

I know he can't stay with me now, but I'm in no rush for his arms to leave me.

Owen looks over his shoulder, making sure his son's out of earshot. "I just wish I knew why he's so angry all the damn time."

"The kid's not angry." The words leave me before I realize how presumptuous they are.

"What is he then?"

For a moment, I'm sure I'll brush away my statement, not wanting to get any more involved in their argument. Even though I know a thing or two about a young person hiding emotional baggage behind obnoxious behavior.

Owen waits for my answer with such a measured look of interest that betrays just how much he wants to hear my opinion.

Pushing up on my tiptoes, I plant a kiss on his lips. Softening the topic that I'm about to approach.

"It's been hard for you both. I get it. Landon lost his mother and he's taking it out on you because...you're the only person left to be mad at. He's not angry. He's hurting."

"What am I supposed to do? I'm trying to be here for him, but he won't let me. He acts like I made all of this happen on purpose. Like I don't care that she died."

"Do you?"

He lets out a breath, his body almost coiling against mine. The evidence is subtle, but he's stressed. "Of course I care. But the truth is she is--was a stranger to me. We weren't even a couple. I know nothing about her, the person she became, what her life was like."

"Well, why don't you ask him?"

A pause.

"What?"

"He lost his mother and had to move his entire life to another state. I bet he feels like he didn't just lose her but that every trace of her is being erased from his life. Maybe that's what he wants--to talk about his mother. To remember her. Ask him about her."

He stares at me for a moment too long then kisses me again. "I never thought of that." A beat passes before he adds, "Landon really likes you."

"He's a good kid."

Even before the words leave my lips, I catch Owen scanning the room behind me. I don't like it. It's a calculated, searching way. Something catches his attention because his eyes narrow almost imperceptibly and his arms loosen their hold on me.

"That went fast," he says in a low voice I've heard only once before.

I turn to see the bottle of vodka. It's the same one I poured a drink from the last night Owen and I had dinner together earlier this week, and is now nearly empty with just an inch of liquid left in it.

Owen's hands are already by his sides and I take a step back to look at him properly, crossing my arms and instantly irritated by the implication of his tone.

The silent judgment. The heavy, disapproving glare.

"I'm not driving drunk, if that's your concern."

Owen rubs his forehead. "I can't believe you haven't slowed down your drinking at all."

"Was I supposed to never have a drink ever again?"

"Did you drink all of that yourself?"

Heat rises to my face. "I didn't give any to your son, if that's what you're asking."

Resentment turns my veins to ice. He's keeping mental dibs on my drinking. Making me explain myself even when I'm doing absolutely nothing wrong.

Trying to reel in my annoyance, I take a deep breath. "I'm in the privacy of my home, Owen. Can't I enjoy a drink every once in a while? Or is that a crime?"

He stands up straighter at my words. "You can do whatever you want, Emily, but I have my son to consider. He likes you and, I think, he's even starting to look up to you."

I set my jaw at the way he says it, as though Landon looking up to me is a parent's nightmare.

"I like Landon. I really do. But I'm in no position to play mother figure."

"No kidding." Owen's jab is cruel, whether or not he intends it to be. "No kidding," he says again, as though needing to drive the point home.

My arms wrap tighter around me like a straight jacket, steadying my rising temper. "Let's cut the bullshit, Owen. I get what you're insinuating. But you're wrong. Do I drink? Yes. I do. Do I drink *every day*? No. I don't."

"Okay, Emily." He half turns from me, eyes focused on the stairwell beyond the open door, clearly exasperated. Noises from the outside begin trickling into the silence that follows. He goes to leave, but I catch his arm, forcing him to meet my eyes again.

"Is this how you want to leave this conversation?" I ask.

A car honks from below. Landon, growing impatient.

Owen pulls his arm from my grasp and takes another step outside. "I've got my hands full with my son. I can't deal with this right now."

"Fine," I say, "then don't." My hand throws the door forward until it slams shut.

Chapter Thirty-Eight

I'M LIVID. EACH BREATH I let out feels more like puffs of steam. I can't remember a time I've felt so angry. So frustrated. So...*livid.*

Fueled by the restless animosity pumping through my veins, I start cleaning frantically. Peeved by everything that dares be out of place. I don't intend to go on a spree. It starts small, me deciding to straighten out the living room, which looks like a makeshift guest room after Landon slept on the couch. But before I know it, I'm pushing my hair out of my face with the back of my hand as I scrub every square inch of the kitchen countertop.

When I reach the bottle of vodka to lift it out of the way, I hesitate. Then I move it and continue my relentless war against the invisible grime I'm suddenly convinced covers my entire loft.

I can't believe Owen's nerve. I'll take responsibility for my mistakes. But him? He's making a mountain out of a molehill. I'm irritated beyond belief that he would accuse me of having a drinking problem.

That's absolutely ridiculous.

I made one mistake. One. And he is holding it over my head, ready to scan my surroundings to find anything that proves his suspicion.

I'm not a goddamn alcoholic.

The word alone causes memories to flash in my mind. Memories of my mother swaying where she stood, eyes foggy and words slurred. Yet always easily incensed into a fit of rage, throwing out a hand that sometimes connected with my face if I was close enough.

That's an alcoholic.

That's an addict.

Me? I just fucking like the occasional drink.

Dammit, why am I even trying to explain this to myself?

What, so, he owns my orgasms and all of a sudden thinks it gives him a right to control every aspect of my life? Fuck that. I promised myself I wouldn't ever allow a man to make me feel this way. And I'm not about to start now.

As soon as I'm done in the kitchen, I head to my bedroom and gather up the clothes from the floor of my closet to start a load of laundry. It doesn't help my irritated state that my arms, regardless of how hard I try, don't serve as an adequate laundry basket on their own. Clothing items slip through the nooks and slink onto the floor no matter how carefully I try to contain the pile I'm carrying. I'm forced to double back multiple times. First for a stray sock. Then underwear, and again for a bundled-up shirt. Until finally, I shove all these items unceremoniously into the machine and slam the lid harder than necessary.

The machine roars to life, churning and sloshing

around the clothes against the water. The mechanical hum is soothing for a few seconds until the silence beyond reaches me again. An intense, eerie silence that cuts through everything around me.

The bottle of vodka flickers in my mind's eye and I let out a humorless laugh. I'm sure Owen thinks I'm hitting my liquor stash right now. I bet he thinks I have a collection of bottles hiding in my cabinet. If that bottle is sitting out there in display, it's obviously because I have nothing to hide.

I strip off my clothes and get into the shower. By the time I'm clean, clothed, with my hair blow dried, the anger has subsided into mild irritation. I glance at my phone and see it's not even ten in the morning yet. Heaviness settles over my stomach, a twinge that grows the longer I hold my phone in my hands.

Slamming the door on Owen was a petty thing for me to do. He didn't deserve that. He deserves a bit more understanding, considering he was already in a bad mood from the issues with his son. My fingers slide across my phone screen as I draft a message to him.

I'm sorry. Let's talk...

My thumb hovers over the send button as I consider the abruptness of his answer when I suggested I could drive Landon home last night.

No--I'll head over now.

In retrospect, there's a sort of panic in his response. Was Owen afraid I was going to drive his son home while drunk? I wasn't even drunk last night. And obviously I would never knowingly get behind the wheel intoxicated--with a kid in tow, no less. The fact that

Owen even thought I was capable of this revs the anger back to life right in the pit of my stomach. It seethes there for a few seconds, feeding on itself.

Owen doesn't trust me and will continue to hold my one mistake over my head, looking for any evidence to back up his suspicions of me. That's the problem with preconceived notions; people will always find proof to back up their beliefs.

Perceptions have a way of bending the world backward to prove themselves. That's what Owen is doing. He's painting a truth that matches his convictions and ignoring anything that contradicts them. How can I win against that? The answer is, I can't.

Deleting the message, I start a call to my sister, instead.

Simmering noises fill the air, punctuated by the smells of sautéed chicken wafting overhead. Leo stands in front of Lex's stove, making us all lunch.

I extend my arms across the countertop to reach the stray pack of gum lying there. Lex sits beside me, telling me about the trip to Europe she and Leo are planning for the end of the year.

"I imagine you're scheduling out every minute of the trip obsessively?" I say to my sister. My jaw relaxes at the motions of chewing the gum and I sense a reprieve to the anxious energy bubbling inside of me.

"No, Leo is. He won't even tell me where we're

going."

I stop chewing to stare at her. To anyone who doesn't know my sister, this statement would hold no weight. But I happen to know Lex doesn't just take the backseat when it comes to *anything*.

"Seriously?" I ask her. "You're just letting him take the wheel?"

Leo glances over his shoulder at us and he and Lex share a knowing glance. Being around them makes me realize how much can be said without the need for words. Lex and Leo have entire conversations with simple glances, fleeting touches, slight smiles.

"Why not?" Lex says, sounding uncharacteristically laid back. "It'd be fun to be surprised."

"Right," I say sarcastically. "You've *always* loved surprises."

"I'm starting to warm up to them. I guess I have no choice, if I'm going to date this guy."

The word *date* almost makes me laugh. Is that what they are doing? Dating? Seems like much more than that to me. I stare down at my fingers where I'm fiddling with the gum wrapper, folding it and unfolding it.

"What's up with you?" Lex asks, grabbing a plate of food from Leo and moving over to the dining room table behind us.

I take the plate he hands me, where a beautifully browned chicken breast lays, topped with herbs and complemented by bacon-wrapped asparagus and white rice. "You know what, Leo?" I say to him as I settle down at the table beside Lex. "I think I'm finally starting to get what my sister sees in you."

"Be nice," Lex warns as Leo opens his mouth to retort. His lips twist up into a smile and he bows his head as though yielding to his queen.

He doesn't sit on the other side of Lex like I expect him to, instead settling down in the seat across from us. It's clear he does it so Lex and I are paired, and I don't feel like the third wheel.

"Answer my question," Lex nudges non-too subtly.

I start cutting the meat on my plate into bite size pieces. "What do you mean?"

"What's up with you? You're all...fidgety."

Leo gets to his feet and asks, "You want a drink?"

"*No.*" My response is too quick, too sharp, and too defensive.

Both Leo and Lex go still and share a brief look. Embarrassment floods me as I realize Leo asked out of courtesy because we don't yet have anything to drink on the table, and not--as I instantly assumed--as an intentional jab at Owen's insinuations about my drinking problems.

"Sorry," I say, awkwardly, avoiding their eyes to place the napkin over my lap. "I'll have some water, please."

Leo walks off to the kitchen and I'm left with no alternative but to look up and meet my sister's analyzing gaze.

Lex lowers her voice to a whisper, "Do you want to go into the other room so you can tell me what the hell is going on with you?"

"No, it's fine."

"You need to start talking, Emily."

A brief moment passes where I contemplate if I have a choice in the matter. But I don't, my sister is a hound dog that's caught the scent of a problem. She won't let loose until I tell her.

"Owen and I are fighting."

"What's going on?" Lex leans in to place her hand on my knee.

"We're not seeing eye-to-eye on some things. Plus...he has his hands full with his son. And then there's his schedule. We just can't seem to get enough time together to say what we need to say."

"I get it. It's hard enough to get on the same page with someone, let alone reconciling a kid and a demanding job as well."

"I thought he'd be good for you," Leo says, coming up behind me to set a glass of water beside my plate. "Thought maybe he'd make an honest woman out of you. Or at the very least rein in your crazy."

"My crazy doesn't need reining in, thank you very much," I tell him, though I'm not sure he even hears me.

Leo slips his arms around Lex's chair to set a glass of orange juice in front of her. She tilts her head back and he kisses her forehead, as though it's something he can't help but do.

Watching their interactions is like being on an alien planet for me. I always thought people in love were idiots. Their cloudy, awestruck expressions. But seeing my sister in love really shifts my perspective. This wasn't how Lex was with her ex-husband. With her ex,

Lex never really let her guard down. The energy between them was a constant tug of war between two people trying to get their way. Each word he spoke seemed double-edged; each response Lex gave was measured and pointed.

But with Leo, Lex is visibly resigned. Visibly relaxed. Visibly...Lex. That's it. I haven't been able to put my finger on it until just now. Leo took crazy leaps to pry off her armor, to secure a future with her, and now, he nourishes what's underneath and she lets him. Lex is letting someone in for the first time, all the way.

After lunch, Lex pulls me into the guest room under the pretense of showing me something she purchased. But I can tell by the sideways glance Leo shoots her that it's about something else altogether.

"Close the door," she says as she walks up to the dresser.

I do so and when I turn back to face my sister, my heart lodges in my throat. She's holding a nearly empty bottle of vodka. For one wild minute, I think it's the same bottle that sat on my counter just a few hours ago. But it's not. There's been more than one bottle over the past two months.

"Emily, I found this under the sink."

"Yeah," I say. "I put it there."

"I gathered as much." Lex stares at me as if she expected me to deny it. "But what I want to know is why?"

I shift my footing, my fingers fidgeting over themselves. "You were keeping tabs on it when I was staying with you. Kept bringing it up. I didn't want you worrying for no reason."

"That doesn't make sense."

"This conversation doesn't make sense, Lex," I say, throwing my hands up. "What's your point?"

Lex lowers the bottle to her side, her face falling somewhat. "Emily, are you having issues? With...alcohol?"

My first instinct is to yell back, '*No!*' but the word lodges in my throat. I shake my head and even as I do so, it feels like a lie. "I don't--No, I don't."

"I'm worried you do." My sister's eyes flicker downward then back to my face. "I don't know what things were like in San Francisco, but ever since you've been back, I've noticed you were waking up every morning, hung over. Taking aspirin, needing to sleep in. Every night, another glass in the sink reeking of alcohol."

"That's not true. I don't drink every night."

"Nearly every night, Emily. Come on. Too often and you know it." Lex inches closer and it's as if I grow smaller with every step she takes. "Just tell me. What's going on with you?"

"Jesus," I snap, "I can't believe I'm having this conversation with you, Lex. Really? Are you going to ask me if I'm on drugs, next?"

I'm furious in a way I don't quite understand as I storm into the living room and grab my purse from the armchair. Leo looks up at me from the couch as Lex follows behind.

"Thanks for lunch," I say to him, glancing his way just long enough to register his small, noncommittal nod before I storm away.

"Emily!" my sister calls out.

I turn at the door. "Lex, just lay off, okay? I'll call you tomorrow."

She presses her lips together, holding back whatever it was she wanted to say. I walk outside, hoping the outside air can dilute this toxic anger because I'm barely able to breathe with it seeping out of my pores.

Chapter Thirty-Nine

Back in the loft, I lie in bed staring at the screen of my phone. I'm battling the urge to call Owen. Pushing back the need to hear his voice. I'm not even angry anymore. I'm just sad. I want him beside me.

The time displayed on the screen is obscured by an incoming phone call.

Owen, pulled by my thoughts.

The sound of the phone ringing cuts off to silence, then his voice is in my ear. "Hey."

I let it wash over me, hearing him is like taking in a breath of air.

"Hey," I say.

Every crackle of static over the phone intensifies the strain between us.

"Are you home?"

"I am."

"Good. I'm outside."

My breath catches in my chest. I hang up the phone and stand, motionless in my room as nerves wrench my stomach.

When I open the front door, he's there on the landing, looking so defeated and deflated it tears my heart in two.

"I hate this," he says, "I hate fighting with you."

"I hate it, too."

The space between us feels like miles until his hand comes up to stroke my cheek, so tender. The hairs on my arms prickle awake as I lean into his touch, taking a step toward him. He wraps a hand around my waist and pulls me closer, resting his forehead against mine.

His touch strikes the flammable surface of our desire. His lips are on mine before I can take another breath.

We kiss away our frustrations. The door slams shut behind him as he guides me backward into my living room. Until I take the lead and nudge him down onto my couch. He sits back, looking up at me, eyes hooded by the need burning behind them.

"Emily," he starts, half-heartedly.

In his tone, I hear the weight of everything we need to say to each other. But I shake my head.

Let it hang overhead; let it wait.

I peel away my blouse and throw it to the side. Owen rushes to undress himself, too, as I pull my pants off slowly, giving him a show, enjoying the way his face loses every edge and softens under the heat.

Naked, I walk over to him and sink my knees onto the cushions on either side of him. His skin sears the surface of my palms as I press my hands against his bare chest, and my hips down onto where his hardness pushes back from beneath his underwear.

"It's been a while," I whisper.

"I know," he breathes, as his lips brush over my collarbone. I lean back, letting his mouth taste the skin of my breasts, his tongue flicker over my nipples. "How do you do this?" he asks, almost to himself. "Your smell...drives me crazy."

I can barely hear his words, feeling them instead. Feeling his warm breath on my breasts as he kisses them between deep inhales as though getting high from my skin.

He teases my nipples, even as I turn my upper body toward my side-table, reaching into my purse for a condom. I prop myself up on my knees in front of him, his lips brushing the skin just under my breasts as he removes the last bit of fabric separating us. All without pulling our bodies away. The thought of separating my body from his, even by a centimeter, hurts in ways I can't explain.

Our mouths find each other again, tongues caressing and chests touching, as I lower myself onto him. I melt around his length until I'm weak by how delicious he feels and how completely he fills me.

He breathes out, letting his head fall back somewhat, eyes threatening to close but holding onto mine. Then I start weaving my hips over him, his warm hands gripping me, helping my movements. I'm on the edge of orgasm almost as soon as we begin. I keep myself right there, enjoying the incredible urge for release.

The air around us chars my lungs and singes my skin. My eyes drift down his gorgeous, sculpted chest to where our bodies connect, absorbing the sight of him sliding in and out of me. I pick up my pace, grinding furiously against him as his fingers burrow into my hips in warning that he's close.

My breathing grows heavier and our moans grow wilder. As I'm thrown into bliss, my body shivers and reels from the sensations just as he bites his lip and allows his orgasm to bring forth a low groan that carries over me. My body goes limp over his, my head collapsing over his shoulder, nose at the nook of his neck. I breathe in his scent, and the effect it has on me, even with my lust sated, scares me a little. It fills every part of me, making me miss it even as I inhale it.

Owen takes us to bed but as he lies down on his stomach beside me, a heavy silence falls over us. We are no longer distracted by the lyrical sounds of our breathing and moans or by the storm of desire between us.

He strokes my hair and, though he's looking right at me, the expression in his eyes is distant. When he presses his lips to mine, the guarded way he kisses me ties my stomach in knots.

This isn't right. Something isn't right.

"I want you to stop," Owen says into the silence.

"What?"

"Drinking. I want you to stop drinking."

I smooth out the sudden tension between my eyes and a streak of defensiveness roars to life so quickly, I'm powerless to stop the words that burst out of me. "I didn't have a dad growing up, Owen. And I don't need one now. I don't need you telling me what to do."

Silence.

I cover my face with one of my hands. Regretting my tone. Regretting how Owen and I are tainted by something I can't get a grip on. Things haven't been the same since the morning Owen found me on the side of the road.

We can't shake it off. The grime I spent all morning trying to scrub away from every surface of our loft covers our entire relationship. No, it's all over me.

He pulls his hand away from my hair, his jaw flexing, though he keeps his tone even. "You had your mom. Is that who you want to be?"

That's a low blow and he knows it. He lets out a breath, as though acknowledging his lapse. I sit up in bed and he does the same, the sheets around our waists, our bodies no longer touching.

"We're not okay, Emily. I don't know how to fix it, but we're not okay."

"If you're looking for a way out--If you don't want to do this anymore..."

He hesitates. "The problem isn't that I don't want to. Don't you get that? The problem is that I do. The problem is that I can't resist you. And as long as I give in to you, you'll never see a reason to change."

My head pulls back in surprise. "There it is. I need to be something different for you? I thought you said I didn't."

"I meant that. I meant you could stop pretending for me. That stuff last week, all this drinking. It's you pretending."

I have no clue what he means, but his words pick at scabs I didn't realize I had. It's the implication of one of my deepest fears. That I'm not good enough. That there's something really, deeply, and fundamentally wrong with me.

I'm torn between my pride screaming at me to defend myself and the painful swelling in my chest.

"Do you know why I don't drink?" he asks.

My response is a slow head shake.

"Like I told you before. I went through a bad phase after high school. I was heartbroken and reckless. Then college came around and I was drinking way too much. You know, the way a lot of college kids do. But there's something no one told me. My father being a chronic alcoholic? It meant I wasn't like everyone else. I had a predisposition, halfway to being an addict before I ever had my first drink. Things got out of hand pretty quickly for me. Didn't realize how much I was drinking until I put myself in the hospital, needed to get my stomach pumped. Before then, I thought I had it under control, I thought it was just fun. But there I was, an alcoholic at twenty-two."

"You were an alcoholic?" The revelation stuns me and yet makes perfect sense all at once.

"No," he says, "I *am* an alcoholic. You don't stop being one just because you stop drinking. And you don't stop drinking until you admit it to yourself."

"Why didn't you tell me?"

"I guess I didn't want you looking at me the way you are now."

I blink. "Sorry, I...."

"It's fine, Emily. It was selfish of me not to tell you sooner. I guess I just like the way you look at me, like I'm--" He cuts off for a beat, then starts again. "Look, I'm telling you now so that you understand why this conversation is important to me. It's not that I can't be around people that drink, I can. But what you're doing? Watching you go down this road? I can't, Emily. I can't be part of it."

"You think I have a problem?"

He pauses a moment. "Do you think you have a problem?"

"Honestly, Owen, I don't." I shut my eyes, realizing my words don't do anything to help my case. "Look, I can cut back on my drinking if that's what bothers you so much. But I can't admit to a problem I don't have. I'm sorry."

"You're just not getting it."

"What am I not getting?

"If it were just me, I'd get in the mud with you, Emily. I'd fight for as long as it took. But it's not just about me. I can't have my son around you when--"

"When what?"

He hesitates.

My teeth grind together as I wait. "Say it."

"When you hit rock bottom."

He looks me dead in the eyes when he says it and something about that causes his words to stab at something mean and ugly in me.

"I'm sorry, but this is ridiculous," I snap. "You're projecting your issues onto me, connecting dots that don't exist."

"I don't think I am."

"So, you're done?" I ask. "Just like that, huh? Got tired of fucking me so quickly?"

"Damn it, Emily." Anger darkens his eyes at my

words. "That's enough. Don't you see? If it weren't for my drinking, I might've been told about my son from the beginning. I might've been in his life all along. And who knows, maybe if his mother would've told me, it might've been enough to pull me out of it. I just want you to understand. This...it can make you lose everything you care about. But I can't force you to see that."

We stare at each other until he shuts his eyes in dread at my lack of response. I know it's dread because I feel it too; it pours out of us both and makes my eyes burn.

He's going to walk away. He's going to leave me. And I'm not sure if I should stop him.

Some relationships are toxic. Trying to maintain them for the sake of it is like allowing a disease to eat away at you when you hold the antidote.

That's what it boils down to, isn't it? I'm going to ruin this. I *am* ruining this. Because I'm just like my mother. I set things on fire just to watch them burn, pretending not to know how the match lit in my hands.

"I'm trying to make things right with Landon," he goes on. "Every decision I make, every person I bring into my life, it affects him. It impacts his life."

"You should go," I say.

"Emily..."

"Owen, let's not make this harder than it has to be, okay? I get it, I really do. Your son needs to be your priority. I don't hold that against you. I just...please, go. Let's just end it now." The words come out hoarse and desperate. A pang of embarrassment accompanies them because I realize how much they hurt me to say. My pulse quickens and I turn my back to him, bringing my legs over the opposite end of the bed so he can't see my face. I'm terrified he'll see it all written there, everything I feel. Everything I am.

The only sounds are the rustling of clothes as he gets dressed. I shut my eyes tight when I sense him go still, hovering somewhere on the other side of the bed as though trying to think of what to say.

I hear him fumbling over items on my nightstand. Paper ripping. The unmistakable sound of pen scratches. Then, nothing. The silence stretches out for what feels like an eternity. Each second packs onto the next, compacting into something dense and solid, until I'm sure when I look at Owen again I'll see a solid block of ice separating us.

But I don't look. When he finally walks away, each one of his footsteps is a punch right to my gut.

I sit there, facing the wall, until I hear the front door close, then I turn to see what he left on the nightstand. There's a white envelope. On top of the envelope, there's a small, satin black box, shielded by a piece of torn paper.

I reach for the paper and read the word scribbled there. Just one word.

Always.

Not knowing what to expect, I open the black box and see a glint of silver, or maybe white gold. A necklace. The pendant on it is a small, curving shape I recognize immediately.

My thought erupts from my mouth. "Is this a

fucking joke?"

As I say it, I realize what today is.

Valentine's Day.

My body shakes with laughter, somehow, my brain disconnected from the laugh, not finding an ounce of humor.

Snapping the box closed, I take it, the unopened envelope, and the piece of torn paper, and shove them all into the nightstand drawer, slamming it shut.

Chapter Forty

My dreams are uneasy and I toss and turn all night. Sunday I occupy myself in any way I can. Cleaning. Organizing. Tackling the last few moving boxes I've neglected to unpack. When there's nothing left to do and my thoughts start bouncing around my head, gathering traction as they go, picking up more things that just intensify each one, I grab my keys and head out the door.

Calling Lex on the way, I ask her if I can go through the boxes in her storage shed. She and Leo are out somewhere having lunch. Her tone is overly formal and pulled taut. She's upset with me for the way I stormed out yesterday. But that's just another thing I'm trying not to think about today.

For hours, I pour through boxes of inconsequential items from my past. Things that bring me no comfort but keep my hands busy as I sort and pull aside what I want to take with me, not allowing my body to slow down long enough to catch up to my thoughts again.

In the evening, I gather items for trash collection, which comes on Monday's every two weeks. Pulling back the lid of my recycling container, a sobering sight crashes into my world.

There are bottles, lots and lots of bottles. Beer bottles. Have I not been counting beer? When I think back to the nights I drink, I seem to only consider the nights I drink vodka. Which isn't every night. Somehow, I seem to have filtered out the fact that, judging by my vast collection of empty bottles, that I have at least three beers a night. *Every single night.*

A cold feeling envelops my stomach and nausea rolls through me. Heart beating fast, I take the bottle of vodka from my counter and dump the remaining liquid down the kitchen sink. I throw the empty bottle into the bin so hard I hear it crack. I pull open the refrigerator, yank out the newest pack of beer, and pour each of the bottles down the drain before chucking them in with the others.

Taking the large bag of clinking bottles to the dumpster outside feels like a walk of shame. I'm overwhelmed by how absolutely pathetic I am, carrying a huge bag of empty bottles. When I go back inside, I lie face up in bed with my pulse still quick in my ears. My stomach churns with disgust at the very discernible dryness in my mouth. At the way my mind's eye still envisions all of the beer pouring down the drain. At the sickening way I wish I hadn't done that. Because I want one. I want a beer so damn bad, I'm tempted to drive to the store and get a new pack.

And that's when I realize I do have a problem.

I can't believe I allowed this to happen. How could the need to drink have rooted in me? Just a few months ago, back when I lived in San Francisco, I'm certain I wasn't drinking this regularly. This started after I was fired. I see that now. I tried to numb my nerves, my restlessness, bending the world around me to match my perceptions. Lying to myself.

How long does it take to build a habit? Twenty-eight days? I think back to how many days since the night I opened the first bottle of vodka at Lex's condo. Over sixty days.

Jesus.

I've been drinking every single day for the past two months. No wonder I'm missing it. I've trained my body to expect it. To need it.

My phone is heavy in my hands. Warm. It's silently luring me to call Owen. My eyes sting and the urge to hear his voice overwhelms me. It's stronger than my urge to drink. I want him so much it scares me. Everything feels better with his arms around me. But even as my finger hovers over his number, ready to call him, a realization trickles in, cold and thick.

Owen was wrong when he said we're finally in the same place. We're not. We're in completely different places. Our priorities are different. Owen's priority right now is his son. And me? I'm just another complication. More weight for him to carry on his shoulders.

How could I possibly fit into the picture, the way I am now?

I like Landon. Really, I do. He's a good kid and his issues with Owen are misunderstandings and overreactions on both their parts. But I'm not in a position to be anyone's role model. Except that's the problem--I *can't* be a neutral person in Landon's life. Not if his father and I continue to be involved to the extent that we are. The deeper I get into things with Owen, the deeper I bind my commitment to Landon, as well.

That scares me. No. It *terrifies* me. The responsibility of it. The hypocrisy of it. To go along pretending I'm this put-together adult. To allow him to confide in me in a way he can't even confide in his dad. To build a connection with him that could influence him for the rest of his life. I know what the kid is looking for because I was looking for the same thing when I was his age. Someone to trust. Someone to look up to.

But how can I have Landon looking to me for answers when I don't know what the fuck I'm doing myself?

I can't fix things with Owen and I shouldn't want to.

Not until I fix myself.

I have a problem.

The phrase leaves my lips and my sister holds her concerned look, though I know she's relieved to hear me say it. Lex goes into crisis mode, overwhelming me with information and suggestions and a plan. A solution. It seems she's collected a lifetime of information on managing addiction, everything she's ever wished she could do for our mother, and unloads it on me instead. All at once.

I'm grateful. I'm overwhelmed. I'm exhausted.

It's too much. Too soon. I tell her that I'm still

processing it all. She seems hesitant, but agrees that perhaps I should take it a day at a time and see how I manage.

Time crawls to a near stop in the week that follows. Days are longer than before. Maybe because I don't drink. Not a drop. And though I expect myself to feel better with each day, I feel worse.

More and more miserable. Anxious. Restless.

When the sun is out, thoughts of Owen crowd into a corner of my mind. I make my job a priority. I've been skating on thin ice since my misstep. I overcompensate, as much as I can. Taking on more work and more responsibilities.

But every night, thoughts of Owen creep over me with the moon. And my phone ends up in my hands as I stare at the screen for long periods of time. The metal body heavy and warm in my palm. Daring me to call him. Every part of me itching to feel the comfort his voice will bring me.

Even as the ache for Owen presses against my ribcage, I almost savor the pain.

You're hurting? Good, the voice in my head taunts. *This is what you get. This is what you deserve.*

That voice has grown increasingly loud over the last week, since I stopped drinking. It whispers things that make me feel small. And somehow, the mean voice stirs awake another instinct in me. The instinct to fight. A fierce anger that wants to silence the voice. Prove it wrong.

I'm in a battle with myself. Stubbornness and pride versus weakness and listlessness. I'm not sure who will win, but both forces are equally relentless.

All of this? What I'm feeling? It has nothing to do with Owen and everything to do with me. With something that's wrong with me. Something I've yet to really put my finger on. And that's what I remind myself in order to find the willpower to set my phone down every night.

I can't fix things with Owen. Not until I fix me.

Every morning, Elizabeth, my boss, walks by my office and seems increasingly less frigid toward me. And when Friday morning rolls around, nearly two weeks since the day I missed work over my drinking, Elizabeth stops at my door. I meet her critiquing stare.

The woman carries herself like someone with a steel rod for a spine. For some reason, her posture alone intimidates me. Her perfectly manicured fingers close over the doorframe as she addresses me from the threshold. "You've been coming in earlier than usual."

"Yes, I have."

"Staying late, too," she adds.

I nod.

"You've been doing a great job here, lately. I just wanted to let you know I notice."

"Thank you," I say, unsure how else to respond.

"Keep it up." She gives me a small smile, possibly the warmest gesture since the incident.

I pour myself into work partly as a distraction but mostly because I'm truly enjoying the work. When I close my office door at the end of the day, I don't feel worn thin or my abilities underestimated the way I did when I worked for Bernstein. In this job, I get to be a small part of securing the ground-breaking research going on at the university. And though the work is paperwork intensive and often tedious, my colleagues make me feel like it's significant and, therefore, worth every painstaking ounce of effort.

Friday night, I get home and I clean, the way I've done every night this week. I find it hard to sit still, like my thoughts live under my skin instead of in my head. Of all nights, I'm dreading this one the most. The end of the week. The start of a weekend without my job as a distraction. The first weekend since Owen and I broke up.

Sometime after eight, just when I'm starting to feel exhausted by my futile attempts to avoid my own thoughts, I get a call from Amelia. I haven't spoken to her in a few weeks, aside from the stray text message where we check in on each other. She's been busy with work as well.

Amelia invites me out for drinks. The urge to say yes is overwhelming. But the words 'I can't' leave my lips, instead. And that simple act cuts off the head of one of my demons. I've just resisted temptation.

But Amelia has no idea what's going on with me. "You can't?" she asks, concerned. "Why not? Did something happen? Did you get fired again?"

"I can't because I apparently have a drinking problem."

She laughs, but quickly falls silent when I don't join her. "Seriously?"

"Yeah. Seriously."

Silence.

"Damn. Emily, I didn't know."

"Yeah," I say, loosening my grip on the phone a bit. I'm relieved she isn't dismissing what I've revealed. Somehow I feared having to defend the realness of my issues, as ridiculous as that sounds. "I just recently got the memo, myself."

I hear rustling over the other end of the phone.

"You want to come over?" Amelia asks, her words washing me with a deep sense of gratitude and relief.

Chapter Forty-One

AMELIA LIVES IN THE GOLDEN Hill section of San Diego, just south of Balboa Park. Her apartment building is an old, two-story Victorian manor that now houses numerous apartments. As I cross the road from my parked car, I glimpse the way B Street slopes downward, cutting through the residential neighborhoods and disappearing toward downtown.

I adore this area. The merger of the cold, modern architect of downtown, a mere collection of lights this time of night, with the more rustic, historic feel of the houses lining this portion of the road, their windows glowing amber.

It reminds me of San Francisco, but even if I weren't so enamored with the loft, I wouldn't really consider an apartment down here. Even if it would mean a shorter commute for me to UCSD. Moving back to San Diego County reminded me of how much I love Carlsbad. It's a slower pace in the northern cities of the county, more laid back.

Amelia meets me at the front door. I expect there to be an awkward strain between us, after my recent confession. But she's her usual, aloof self, dressed in loose fitting clothes and making small talk as she leads me down the wide hall and up the stairs to her apartment.

We settle in front of her flat screen television, which casts us both in a bluish light. Our eyes train on the tense, overwrought scenes playing before them. Landscapes, yielding to shots of an empty home. Room by room. Eerie music in the background. We both lose interest fairly quickly and talk whenever the actors are busy sharing ominous glances or creeping slowly down darkened hallways.

It's small talk at first, everything but the real reason I was relieved she invited me over. Amelia doesn't push the conversation, allowing us time to settle in comfortably, allowing it to unravel organically.

"Whatever happened with that guy you were dating?" she asks, eyes on the movie. "The mobster from the bar?"

The phrase turns up my lips. "Shut up. He's not a mobster. He's a cop." My smile melts away, as the movie's soundtrack kicks up into a frantic, eerie pace. "And we broke up."

Amelia grabs the remote and pauses the movie, right as the actor's hand closes over a doorknob. "Shit. What happened?" She puts a few pieces of popcorn into her mouth.

Reluctantly, I give her a summary of the past few weeks. She listens and when I reach the end of my story, she waits for more, eyebrows rising in a silent prod for me to continue.

I put my hands up, signaling I'm done.

"That's it?" She frowns. "That can't be it."

"That's it."

"So, now what? He'll just sit on your shelf for a while?"

Having no clue what she means, I merely squint in response.

She pushes the bowl of popcorn toward me and I reluctantly pick up a few pieces and fling them into my mouth.

"I told you," she says, "you put your problems up on shelves. And now? You're shelving Owen. And for what? You think he'll be waiting for you when you're ready?"

I chew instead of answering, though her words make my throat feel too tight to swallow. Of course I don't expect him to wait for me. A part of me counts on the fact that he won't. Because Owen's everything I don't deserve and I'm everything he shouldn't want right now.

"I don't really see how we can work out. I'm not right for him."

Amelia gives me a weird look at this. "Because of the drinking thing? Okay--Fill me in on this whole drinking problem. What's that about?" Her tone is unassuming, the way it always seems to be even when approaching a potentially serious topic. It's as though we are talking about the issues of a different person, who isn't even in the room with us. The topic isn't weighted by judgment or impending disappointment, and I find I don't mind talking about it for once. The way I mind talking to Lex about it.

"I don't know. I guess I have a predisposition for addiction, or something." I think back to when Owen used the term, realizing now that he was throwing me hints. "But honestly, it's not so much the drinking I enjoyed. It was the...knowing I shouldn't have been drinking. Knowing it was growing too frequent. Knowing it was a bad idea." I rub my eyebrows. "I know...that doesn't make sense."

"Maybe it does. You were drinking because you knew it would fuck everything up? Because you secretly wanted to?"

Gathering my thoughts, I run my hands through my hair, collecting it up and twisting it only to let it fall again. Fidgeting. "Fucking shit up is apparently my specialty so...yeah. I think so. But even now, even after I stopped drinking...I don't feel like I'm getting better. I still feel...like something's wrong with me."

Amelia considers me in the beat that follows, her eyes softening with sympathy. Then she sits up the way she does when she gets an epiphany. "I had this roommate a few years ago. She had this constant headache and she kept popping aspirin to dull it. Because the pain was a symptom of the headache, right? So, every day, she treated the headache with pain killers, going through bottles like you wouldn't believe. One day, I tell her, 'Mia, you really should get that checked out. It's not normal. You could have a brain tumor or something.' Hang on--" Amelia holds up a finger at the way I snort at this. It's so like her to assume the worst, a headache being brain cancer. "Listen to this. So she went to the doctor and guess what? She had some sort of severe vitamin deficiency and the headache was just a symptom of that." Amelia points at me as though drawing me into her explanation. "The drinking? Maybe it's a symptom. Of something else, unrelated to alcohol. So treating it--cutting out the alcohol--it helps with the headache, but doesn't treat the root of the problem. The deficiency."

There's an innate truth to her theory, I feel it in my bones. In the way the room swells slightly. Or maybe I shrink where I sit. All I know is I try to keep my voice from revealing how important my next question is, and how badly I hope she has the answer. "What's the deficiency, then?"

"You're asking me?" Amelia pulls her eyebrows in. "How am I supposed to know?"

Chapter Forty-Two

THIS PLACE DOESN'T BRING ME comfort anymore. The bell over the door makes a shrill sound that sets me on edge. Yet I come here every morning, if only for a few minutes. It would be easier to get my coffee at the shop on campus. Easier for the part of me that sinks in disappointment every time the new guy greets me from behind the counter, instead of Owen. Caleb, I think is his name.

It's Friday again, going on two weeks since I last saw Owen. Two weeks and not a word from him. Not a word from me, either. It's ridiculous I keep expecting to see him. Ridiculous I hold my phone in my hands every night willing myself to call him and warning myself against it all at once.

I shouldn't hope to run into him, anyway. Seeing him, having to pretend we are friends--or worse, strangers--would just twist the dagger in my stomach.

When I come up to the register and put in my coffee order, I don't bother to glance in the direction of the stool where I used to sit. But a head of dark hair catches my attention from the corner of my eye.

"Landon?"

The kid swivels his seat to face me and if he's

surprised to run into me, he doesn't show it. I walk over to him, sensing his presence here is no coincidence. He hasn't been back since Owen returned to work. I suspect Landon was forced to come to the diner every morning, probably so Owen could keep a closer eye on him.

"Hi," he says. "So you and Owen broke up?"

"Cutting right to the chase, are we?"

He tilts his head to me as though recognizing my aversion tactic. "Answer my question."

"We did break up."

"Why? He won't tell me why."

I hesitate. "Reasons, kid. Sometimes people realize they aren't a good fit. Thanks, Caleb," I say, as the new guy hands me my cup of coffee.

"That doesn't make sense," Landon says.

Pulling sugar packets from the stack in front of Landon, I flavor my drink. Quicker than I normally would. Speaking to Landon makes my stomach clench but I don't want him to think it's because of him. "Why doesn't it make sense?"

"You two are perfect for each other."

The packet of sugar slips between my fingers, landing inside of the coffee. "What makes you say that?" I ask, peeling back the soaked paper.

"He's better since you two started dating. Easier to talk to. Not as serious, I guess. And that morning he picked me up from your place? I don't know what you said to him, but he's been so much better since then. We're not fighting so much anymore."

"I'm glad to hear that," I say, ignoring the first half

of his statement.

"You two are perfect for each other," he repeats, slower this time as though making sure the meaning sinks in for me.

Concern is etched in Landon's light-brown eyes. So intense it takes me off guard. A question leaves my lips before I have a chance to stop it. "You really care about your dad, don't you?"

"Of course."

"He has a lot on his plate, you know? Make sure you tell him you love him every once in a while."

A beat.

"You should tell him, too."

Damn. This kid, he sees right through me. His words wrap around my heart, squeezing tight in pulses opposite to my natural beating rhythm.

Clearing my throat to segue, I change the subject because I'm getting ready to leave but don't want to seem harsh about it.

"How are things with the girl?"

It's been a while since we talked about it and I don't even know her name, but I'm sure he'll know whom I mean.

"It worked." He glances down and I think it's so I don't see the smile in his eyes. I wait for him to elaborate but he doesn't.

"That's awesome." I don't push the subject, securing the lid on my cup and taking a breath to prepare my parting words.

Landon heads me off, continuing as though we never stopped talking about Owen. "You should go see him. He's off tomorrow."

I'm already gearing up to leave.

Landon slides off his stool, too. "And I'm going camping in Mount Laguna with my aunt this weekend. Until Sunday. Emily--"

"Sorry, kid, I've got to head out. Work, you know? Good seeing you, though."

Disappointment overtakes his features. I know he wants me to say something else. Something real. But I can't.

"Tell your dad I said hi," I add, over my shoulder, my chest tightening again.

The shelf I've been stuffing with my thoughts of Owen? Son of a bitch is more of a large, overflowing bookcase. Seeing Landon threw its center of gravity off kilt. Boulder-sized pieces fall on me at random times during the day. It takes twice the amount of energy for me to focus on my tasks at work. And after I eat dinner and run out of things to clean, I pick up my phone a few times, only to set it down again.

The side lamp on the table is the strongest light source in the living room, its amber glow a contrast to the television, an indecipherable collage of voices and faces. My legs are tucked under me where I sit, but my index finger taps at my knee.

I want to be alone, tonight. It's been a long day. A long week. A longer two weeks. I'm just not sure how to calm the discomfort in the pit of my stomach. The silence around me feels different. Strange, even. Like there's noise weaved into it, static that needs tuning. I look around, getting the odd sensation there's something I'm supposed to be doing. And for the first time in weeks, I don't think it's my usual restlessness.

On my side table, the cover of a paperback novel draws my eyes.

In the Dead of Night.

It's the book Owen lent me the first night we slept together. I've never gotten around to reading the book. In all honesty, I just forgot about it. But tonight it seems to glow in the light of the lamp, almost humming in the silence, begging to be read.

I ignore it, turning to the television to continue flipping through the channels. But my eyes keep darting to the book. I can't remember the last time I felt the desire to pick up a book. I'm not sure why I'm resisting the urge to do so now.

I shut off the television and pick it up, glimpsing the first few words. Then the first few pages. Soon, the words and pages melt away and I see a movie playing before my eyes. The night wears on and I read completely unaware.

I'm not sure what I expected--but it wasn't this. The protagonist is a detective in the middle of a murder investigation. But the case draws parallels to her own personal demons. The story is dark, graphic, and disturbing. But it's also funny and even a little sexy at times. I shovel grapes into my mouth and nibble on half a leftover sandwich, barely realizing what I'm doing as my other hand holds down the pages that my eyes dart across. And as the story wears on, it's obvious the character's desperation to solve the crime is rooted in something else altogether. One passage in particular grips me. So much so, I go back and read it again.

She saw it all the time. Random acts of violence, calculated bits of evil. Good, innocent people whose lives would never be the same because they made a seemingly simple decision to turn left instead of right. To walk in when their gut told them to back away.

She witnessed these things and wondered how she managed to escape it all of her life, even while being right in the middle of it. It didn't make sense. She never considered herself a good person. It's not that she'd done anything unimaginably terrible to anyone--she hadn't. But the truth was, she'd never done anything to merit admiration either. Nothing that took her out of her comfort zone. She'd always taken the easier road. Pushed people away, lived just for her. The reason wasn't that she felt better than the people around her. On the contrary, she secretly considered herself unworthy.

When I finish the novel, flipping past the obvious last page as though hoping to find another secret chapter, a deep disappointment fills me at the realization the story is over. There's no happy ending for her. She never gains more than a superficial understanding of how her unhappiness is a symptom of her feelings of unworthiness.

The symptom...

A paralyzing halo of self-awareness settles over me as my own truth finally clicks into place.

Chapter Forty-Three

MY KNUCKLES RAKE AGAINST THE cold wood surface and the hollow sound breaks through the morning air. Leaning against the stair railing, I tilt my head back as I exhale. I'm not sure what to expect or how to calm the frantic pulse of my heart at my temples.

There's not a single smudge of white to be seen in the rich blue sky this morning. The California sun seeps into my pores and releases endorphins that cover me like a blanket. But the warmth can't reach the cold nerves in my stomach.

I close my eyes and take a deep breath. Then another.

What am I doing?

"*Emily*? What are you doing?"

My eyes snap forward and land on his.

I go to speak, but somehow forget how to make a sound, distracted by the sight of him. Seeing him with fresh eyes for what feels like the first time ever. He's wearing a white t-shirt, tucked into navy blue pants, as though he'd just been removing his uniform when I arrived. His clean-shaven face, bright hazel eyes. His frame, the outline of his muscles under his shirt. It all makes my heartbeat kick into a frantic pace in my ear.

My lips part again, but words don't come out fast enough. "I--you were right."

He waits.

"You were right," I repeat the words slowly. "I have a problem. It's not just the alcohol--though I cut that out the night after we broke things off. The real problem is how I sabotage good things in my life."

My words leave an awkward ring in the air. The aftermath of the quick, almost choked way I say them, afraid my brain might try to filter the rawness out of them. The truth.

Owen looks frozen where he stands. He blinks a few times then gestures inside. "You...want to come in?"

He notices the way my fingers clutch the strap of my purse to keep my hands steady. I've never felt more intense nerves. And fear. The fear of realizing what's keeping me from everything I want, but not knowing if the realization is too late for me to get those things back.

Owen follows me into his living room and closes the door behind him.

When he turns to look at me, I falter.

"You look good," he says.

"You too."

We stand a few feet away from each other. His posture is stiff. Feet shoulder width apart, hands behind his back, face as serious as ever. The air between us is tense, accusatory even. We're both upset. Both secretly looking for someone or something to blame for keeping us apart. And there's no one to blame but the people in the room.

He scratches his forehead and I decide it's on me to break the ice. I made this mess. I need to clean it up.

"You were right," I say for the third time. "And as soon as I realized it, I stopped drinking. Weeks ago. But, things still didn't feel right. Then I realized the drinking was just a symptom. Of me feeling like I didn't deserve happiness. Good things. My job. My life. *You*."

My palms grow cold by the way he watches me in silence. I can't help but search his face for a hint of his thoughts. His expression is like a foggy glass wall, leaving the sensation that if only I stare long enough I will make out details. But all I see are shadows and blurry shapes of what lies behind it. I remind myself he deserves to hear this and push past the anxiety of baring myself to him. To anyone.

I go on, "It's like...this urge to keep myself right on the edge. When I'm standing at the height of everything I want, I feel a pull right behind my bellybutton. To jump. Standing too close to the edge and temping fate to take it away and give it to someone else. Someone who deserves it."

I can't deny the way his eyes dull under the compassion flooding them. "What made you realize this? What changed?"

My hands are a bit shaky as I reach into my purse for the book and hand it to him. "You," I say, simply. "You happened. You opened my eyes and made me realize I didn't want to be that way anymore. And so I stopped...because I want to change. I've started going to meetings."

He opens his mouth to speak.

"And I miss you," I cut in, the words bursting out of me desperately. "I guess that's where I'm going with all of this. I miss you, Owen. I want to be in your life--and Landon's life, too. Being with you makes me happy and I don't know why I'm fighting it. I want happy. I deserve happy. And, yeah, maybe there's a happy without you--but that's just the thing. I don't want it. I don't want a happy without you. I just don't."

My breath catches at the base of my throat. I'm certain I'm standing stark naked. Not because his eyes are ravenous--they aren't. They're curious and maybe hesitant. What I feel is a vulnerable sort of naked. The going to school without your clothes on naked. The standing on a stage and forgetting your lines naked.

I've got nothing left to say and he's not offering anything in the silence that follows. I get the urge to run back out that door, to the fresh air my lungs scream for. But, as though sensing my impulse, his hands close over mine and pull me to him with such force, I'm certain I slip right under his armor.

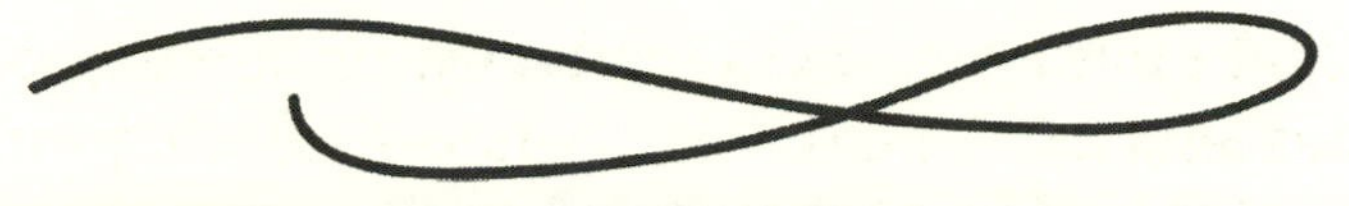

Chapter Forty-Four

Owen

She stumbles into our kiss. A kiss so good it's almost painful. Lips weaving over mine, her taste filling my tongue while her words continue to drum on me in just the right way.

My arms fold over her small frame, holding her in place, and I remember how hard it is for me to resist her and why I forced myself to stay away. Pulling back from our kiss, I look into her eyes.

"These last few weeks? They've been hell, Emily. I was a selfish asshole every night. Wanting to hear from you. Writing you messages--"

"What?" An alarmed expression crosses her face. "I-I never got any messages."

"That's because I never hit send." When her lips turn down, I rush to explain, "Wanting to talk to you, to feel you, to hear your voice--it was selfish. I knew it would pull your attention to me and away from where it needed to be. Which is yourself."

Those green eyes of hers grow increasingly translucent, but the struggle of what to say next is evident in the way her mouth opens, closes, and then opens again.

I have more than my share of things I need her to know. The sober, practical side of me itches in warning as I consider my words. "Emily, things are different now, you know that, right? Quitting alcohol isn't something you do once and never deal with again. It's something you do every single day. For the rest of your life."

"I know. I've been...lurking around some support group forums, online. The stuff on there...Jesus, it scares the shit out of me. Knowing how much worse things can get." She takes in a breath. "I swear, Owen. I'm ready to own up to this. Every day."

I resist the urge to smile because it seems out of place with her own face so grim. But there it is. Everything I've wanted to hear her say. She's acknowledging the struggle. Expressing a desire to face it.

Her body stirs in my arms when I lower my face into her neck and breathe in deep. "I've missed you, too," I say, pulling her tighter against me. "How you smell. How you feel."

Her frame curves into the gaps between us until every inch of our bodies is touching. I bring her against the door, flattening her body with mine and her gorgeous eyes dilate in surprise.

Every inch of her contained, this is how I like her best.

Her scent envelops me again, making my mouth water. It's an intoxicating, peachy smell that warms to vanilla and sweetens to caramel, somehow morphing into an actual taste. Making me want to take my time and savor her. I grow hard in my pants and, wanting her to know this, press my lower body onto her. She shivers, her hands closing over my sides, holding tight to my clothes as though afraid I'll pull away.

"God, I've just missed you," I say and as the words leave my lips, I lower them onto hers and demand another kiss. This kiss grows heavier and more frantic than the one before, our bodies already on edge, unwilling to wait any longer. "There's just one thing," I tell her, as her hands tug at my belt, undoing it. "I got called into work a few minutes ago."

She lets out a sudden breath of disappointment, arms dropping to her sides. "Oh, Okay. Really, I understand."

My chest constricts. I want nothing more than to stay here with her all morning, touching every part of her and hearing my name part her lips. But I can't and she's instantly understanding of this. All the time we were together, she was incredibly patient about my unpredictable schedule. One of the many reasons I know she and I have a real shot together.

I take her hands in mine and set them over my belt again. "It's just until this afternoon. Then I'm off the next two days. And right now?" I tug at her hips. "I've got an hour before I have to leave."

"Sixty whole minutes?" Her lips curl. "What are you going to do with that?"

"If it's all right, I was planning on doing you." My lips tease the skin just below her ear, as her body grows weaker in my arms.

"There's just one thing," she says.

"Yeah?" Already pulled under her spell, I bring a hand to the other side of her face.

"I'm in love with you," she says.

Every cell in my body responds to her words, soaking them in. I bring my lips over hers. "That?" I ask, smiling uncontrollably. "You finally figured that out?" She glares at me and my smile widens. "You already know how I feel about you." My hand slides down the curve of her neck then freezes as it brushes her bare collarbone. "You're not wearing the necklace?"

"Owen, you gave it to me after you dumped me. On Valentine's Day."

I shake my head. "Technically speaking, you dumped me. But did you look at the note? The one in the envelope?"

"Sorry, not yet. It was too hard for me."

"Oh, well," I taunt. "Then I guess you don't know how I feel about you."

"Why don't you just tell me?"

"We only have fifty-five minutes now." My fingers move on their own accord, unbuttoning her jeans, slipping between the materials until my palms meet her heated skin. "Wouldn't you rather I showed you?"

"Yes, please," she says, quickly. "That'd be nice..."

I laugh, gripping her ass and, as though anticipating my move, she jumps up, wrapping her legs around me. I carry her to the bedroom, her mouth trailing kisses over my neck until I lower her onto the bed. The moment we separate, our eyes lock and we peel away our clothes, an almost ritualistic feeling to our movements, as though some primal instinct in our subconscious propels us to tear our clothes away, our bodies screaming to feel the flesh of the other.

I can't take my eyes off of her. She's always fascinated me in a way I can't quite explain. Watching her, wondering what she's thinking, burning constantly to touch her.

A certainty splits through my gut and I know without a shadow of a doubt that this beautiful creature right here, this woman, is everything I want. What I've always wanted and what I'll always want.

I'm completely undressed before she's done unhooking her bra. I put on a condom, all the while taking in her every curve and sloping plane, the hollows, as her fingers work between her glistening skin, rubbing.

The way she looks up at me, expectantly, turns my next breath into a low groan. She's enticing in the ways only a woman like her can be. Eliciting from me a deep desire to be beside her. On her. In her. To make her body twist into stunning curves under my command.

I lower myself onto her and she pulls my face to hers, kissing me hard. Her legs wrap around me and her hips tilt to meet mine and...damn. She wants it so bad I slide in insanely smooth. She's all velvet and heat, searing through the condom and clenching tightly around me.

Soon she's moaning uncontrollably. And as much as the fire coursing through my veins makes me want to shut my eyes, I keep them fixed on her. Because there's nothing in this world quite like watching this woman melt underneath me.

Nothing more intimate than the way her eyes, glossy with desire, take in my expression as I thrust into her. The roughness in my strokes only an indication of how desperately I want her. How insatiable I am for her.

Among the sounds of our clashing bodies and coarse breathing are the desperate whines of delight drifting from her throat. She moans and coos, until her body buckles as she comes, squeezing me tight. And as her hips rock, she purrs out my name. My dick throbs painfully and I have to slow, not wanting our hour to be up so soon. Her face splits into a grin.

Because she knows.

She knows exactly what she does to me.

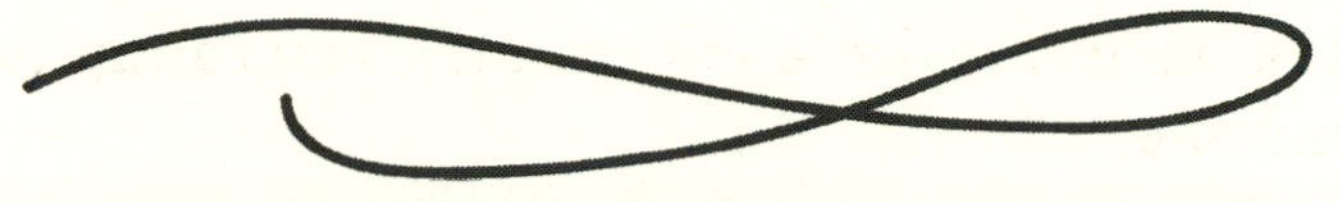

Chapter Forty-Five

Emily

MY DOOR SHUTS BEHIND ME and I barely slow to drop my purse and keys on my way to my room. I sit on the bed and pull out the envelope from the drawer, setting the black jewelry box on the nightstand. The envelope is worn, something I didn't notice the first time. The edges are frayed and the sheet of paper inside is visible. I slide a finger through the sealed flap, tearing it open.

The first thing my eyes land on is the date written in the top right corner. I close my eyes and do the math in my head. It's dated the summer before my junior year of high school. His senior year. Months before he'd slip his jacket over me outside of the prom.

Emily,

You don't know me and that's probably my fault. I

can't seem to find the right time, the right place to tell you what I need you to know. So, I thought I should write it, instead.

I've overheard things I probably shouldn't have. Heard you telling my father how alone you feel. How no one really knows the truth. How you feel like a fraud. Because you're poor and your mother's an addict and you feel cold and empty inside. How you feel like a bad person. Because no one's really showed you what it's like to feel safe.

I heard everything. And I want to say, I'm sorry. I know I wasn't supposed to hear it. I know those words were private and not meant for me.

But please don't be embarrassed. I want to tell you it's okay. Everyone feels like a fraud. I feel like that, too. I'm a fraud for carrying around these feelings for you and not having the courage to even talk to you face-to-face. I tried to work up the courage about a dozen times, but never followed through.

Here it is in black and white.

I see you. I notice you. Not the parts of you other people see. Not the swagger and the sarcasm. Not just your body or your beautiful face. The real you. The you you're scared to show people because you think it's ugly.

I want you to know, the real you is beautiful.

I want you to know I'm in love with you.

Maybe that's crazy. Maybe I'm crazy. But it's how I feel and no matter how much I try to convince myself it isn't true, or isn't smart, or possible, it just doesn't change.

So there it is. I'm in love with you, Emily. And I hope you'll seriously consider giving me a chance to prove it. I promise it'll be worth it.

Owen

—

A teardrop falls onto the center of the page. "Shit," I say, rushing to blot it with the corner of my blouse, relieved the ink doesn't smear.

My breathing is uneven as I lay the letter down and pick up the little black box, opening it. The necklace is a recent purchase. I know this not just because the box is as sleek and new as the item inside, but because there are four diamonds dotting the curves of the pendant. Owen wouldn't have been able to afford it at the time he wrote the letter. The letter, of course, is more than enough. But this necklace? The infinity symbol hanging from it?

It's more than just a symbol. It's a promise. The promise he scribbled on that torn sheet of paper a few weeks ago.

Always.

I pull the chain over my neck and the metal cools the skin of my collarbone. My fingertips come up to my lips as I laugh, realizing I had it wrong before.

I'm not the chink in Owen's armor. He's the chink in mine.

The weeks that follow are wonderful and sometimes terrible. Realizing just how much I've come to depend on drinking, especially at night. Having to admit to Owen when I feel particularly tempted. Acknowledging that blatant weakness in me, isn't something that I like to do. But it's necessary and Owen understands. He's patient and caring and supportive.

This town is familiar and somehow feels brand new. Something in me shifts with every passing day. Whatever it is, it's *good.* I'm aware of it even when I'm trying not to be. And if I ever feel my focus waning, I bring my fingertips to the infinity charm at the end of the necklace. A reminder I need to work on myself every single day. A reminder someone is counting on me. I'm not accountable just for myself anymore. The things I do, they affect Owen and Landon.

These days, my life is fresh with possibility as the grime I allowed before washes away slowly, but surely.

Things really are changing. I'm starting to like myself more and more, learning not to pick at scabs, allowing the lightness to be real and not an act.

One night, I wake up alone in bed. My loft is silent, streaks from the moon cut through the window behind my bed. A certainty tears through me like a beam of light. It finally feels real.

This is my new beginning.

The real beginning. It's not weighted by the constant fear of impending doom, or the subconscious desire to pull on the threads until things unravel. I'm wrapped in a sensation of worthiness. Standing on top of everything I've been through, everything I've earned, and no longer teetering near the edge, feeling the urge to jump. No longer needing to fear the things that come my way.

Those things should fear me.

Because I am determined and a force to be reckoned

with. And if, even for just a moment, I ever question which way is north, I'll anchor myself with the help of my compass.

The good things in my life. The good people.

And, of course, myself.

The End

You've just read ENTICE, the third book in The Hearts of Stone series (a series of standalone novels). But don't stop now! There's a spin-off to Entice called Reckless Touch, which features Emily's journalist friend Amelia. **Want a FREE preview?** There's one ahead!

Thank you for reading!

Please consider leaving a quick review.

Don't stop now...

Read the trouble Emily's friend Amelia gets into in RECKLESS TOUCH. FREE PREVIEW AHEAD!

The Hearts of Stone series

ALSO BY VERONICA LARSEN

Now, a preview of...

RIVETING. SEXY. SUSPENSEFUL.

Amelia

The air is thick with a mixture of sweet and musky notes. Wall-to-wall mirrors run along the back wall. Reflected in them is a group of half a dozen elementary-school-aged kids donning white karate suits. Their instructor's a twenty-something-year-old man with prominent brow bones that add a strong and domineering quality to his face. This isn't the guy I met with yesterday. Travis. He's here somewhere, though. He's the one that called me and asked me to come in this evening to arrange private lessons.

Walking into the studio brings relief that threatens to relax my shoulders, but I resist. I rub my face and try to remind myself of the urgency that propelled me through these front doors. It's been a day full of unsettling revelations. The jarring suspicion my attack was premeditated and the terrifying fact that the police are no longer looking for the person who tried to harm me.

I stare at the class of white-robed students as their instructor guides them in a routine. On my right, I pass the wall of framed pictures and awards, the studio's history in photographs. I didn't pay attention to these the last time I was here, but seeing them now bolsters my confidence in my decision to come back. The pictures show groups of adults as well as groups of children. The students all stand tall, faces beaming with pride.

Movement reflects off the glass as someone steps beside me.

A shriek bursts from my lips. The noises in the studio die down, the class disrupted at my yell of surprise. A few students stumbled mid-kick to look back at me where I stand. The instructor struggles to regather their attention.

Embarrassment blasts my face as I bring my attention to the man beside me. His powerful posture and build stand out before the rest of his features, causing a lag before recognition hits me.

"Jesus," he says. "I didn't mean to startle you."

I falter, blinking in bewilderment. "*Detective Reed*?"

I almost don't recognize him. He isn't dressed in the business attire I've seen him in. His jeans and black t-shirt are in stark contrast to his stern posture.

He doesn't seem surprised I'm here and I figure it's because he referred me. In turn, I bite back my own question of what *he's* doing here.

Instead, I say, "I'm looking for Travis, he asked me to come in."

"Of course, follow me."

Reed leads me down a narrow hall and into a

small office crammed with a couch, desk, and filing cabinet. The place sets my nerves on edge. I look around at the pieces on the walls. Frames stuck up without rhyme or reason, all different sizes, shapes, and colors. Pictures, awards, and other random martial arts related items strung up as decoration. Aesthetically, the place is a clusterfuck.

Reed motions for me to have a seat and, after squeezing past the filing cabinet, settles down behind the desk. I'm left looking around, puzzled, halfway expecting Travis to pop in and ask the detective what he's doing behind his desk.

"I'm sorry--am I...is my meeting with *you*?"

"Ms. Woods--"

"Amelia," I remind him, my brows still furrowed in confusion.

"Amelia, I'm sorry, I thought Travis explained it to you. This is my gym. I haven't taught any classes for a while now, but I offer private lessons from time to time."

Oddly, what surprises me isn't that he owns this gym.

"You're offering me private lessons?"

"I am."

"With you?"

"Yes. With me."

Thinking, I fold my hands over my lap and his gaze falls there. When I pull a hand back up to tuck my hair behind my ears, his gaze rises there, too. He's watching me so closely it's making me wonder what he's searching for.

"Detective--"

"Please, call me Reed. Or Sebastian, it's my first name."

Sebastian.

A guy like him couldn't have just any name. It had to be a name that stirs your tongue. The way his appearance stirs your eyes when you look at him.

He stares right back, patient as always.

"Have you looked into the gifts being left at my desk?"

"You've only just told us about them this morning. You'll have to give us time."

Fair enough.

"But you will look into them? You'll handle my case separately?"

He looks out toward the door behind me, undecipherable thoughts fleeting past his expression. Seeming to come to some deliberation, he meets my gaze again.

"That isn't my call," he says, plainly. "Your case is still part of the investigation on the string of assaults. And that investigation is coming to a close."

"So, why did you call me here?"

He sets his hands down in front of him and brings his fingertips together. All the while, he takes in my features more freely than before. With more open appreciation than before.

His lips part slow and hesitant. "I'd like to offer you peace of mind."

"You know what would bring me peace of mind? You catching the guy who did this to me." I zip down my jacket to reveal more of the bruises peeking out from under my V-neck t-shirt.

Reed looks at me with a steely focus I couldn't break if I tried. At the sight of my bruises, something darts past his eyes like a fleeting shadow. Anger. He shakes his head as though to clear it, glances down at his hands then back at me.

"We've got our suspect in custody. He's not cutting loose anytime soon. He's our guy. We've got him."

Small tendrils of anger shoot through me.

"With all due respect, fuck your certainty, Detective."

First, he looks surprised, but then a struggle forms in his eyes, as though he's keeping himself from saying what he really wants to.

"*Amelia, listen...*"

I take a quick breath. There's a delicacy to the way he says my name. A fragility that hints at how he sees me, like he has to handle me with care so that I don't fall apart suddenly in a spectacular show of neurotic emotions. Because he knows. He has the file, a window into one of the worst times of my adult life.

I get it now. I get why he called me here. Why he's offering me these classes.

The careful tone of his voice, the pity in his eyes, it all sets my teeth on edge. I'm reminded of all the times I've been looked at like this. *Poor little girl with no one to vouch for her, no one to be outraged on her behalf.*

I've been victimized in the past. I've been

underestimated. I've been made to look crazy and seem like a liar. I walked through these doors because sitting alone in my apartment tonight made my skin crawl. I came here because learning to defend myself rose to the top of my most urgent needs. But I recognize the expression in Reed's eyes. He's straddling a white horse. I came here for strength, not to let someone who only sees me for my weaknesses handle me. The pain and soreness in my body are on such a low frequency, my thoughts about it all perfectly numbed.

"You know what?" I say. "Never mind. Never mind this whole thing. Thanks for the offer, Detective. But none of this is for my peace of mind. It's for yours. It's so you can battle with the guilt of knowing you're sending me out there, alone. Someone out there is antagonizing me, at best, and trying to kill me, at worst. It doesn't matter if you choose to believe it or not. If you won't help me, I'll have to find a way to help myself."

I turn from him, but right before I do, I could swear he wants to reach out to stop me. I hesitate, in the same way he hesitated yesterday, eyes glinting with a hope he couldn't bring himself to say aloud. I wait for him to ask me to stay. But he doesn't.

So I leave. I walk away from him, out of the studio, and into the crisp night, all alone, where every single shadow makes me jump right out of my skin.

<<>>

Acknowledgements

First and foremost, I want to thank *my readers*, from the bottom of my heart, for taking a chance on this new author and embracing my stories. You have no idea the difference your words of encouragement made on me during the writing process of this novel. I'm not going to lie. This book kicked my butt. It was hard to write for so many reasons. In the moments I felt like giving up on the story, you'd lift me up again by expressing your excitement about reading it. Your support lit a fire under me to push past the last walls and deliver.

A huge thanks to ALL of the *Bloggers* who have read/reviewed my books and/or offered to help spread the word. I truly appreciate your passion for books and all the time and work you all put into your blogs and Facebook pages on a daily basis, helping stories find their audience.

There's a group of incredible women who I'm blessed to call my friends, and who offered their invaluable insight to help me bring Entice to it's fullest potential. *Ariane*, you're my twin-soul and this novel is proof of that. *Stephanie*, just when I was starting to lose sight of the story, you shone a light that served as my beacon back to my narrative voice. *Courtney*, you're just always there to tuck my sanity back in. *Karyn*, your last-minute, top-secret beta-read made all the difference.

There are also some hardworking, talented women

who have stood behind Entice and propped it up onto it's proverbial legs. *Lea*, you took amazing care of this story. Your genuine passion and talent for editing blew my expectations out of the water. *Neda*, your vote of confidence means so much to me. Thank you for believing in my story enough to represent it. *Julie*, thanks for being my last pair of eyes, making sure this baby is ready for the limelight.

To *my sister and mother*, thanks for showing me what strong women are and for promising to never read my sex-ridden stories. I love you guys and can't possibly imagine a world without your relentless teasing.

My husband, this novel wouldn't exist without your unconditional support and encouragement. I don't know what else to say. You are simply everything.

I like to include a section in my acknowledgments where I mention any conscious influences the novel might have derived. As with Entangle (Hearts of Stone, book 1), this book drew inspiration from Brene Brown 's TedTalks. This time, her insight on what she refers to as 'scarcity' was what unlocked what I identified as the root of Emily's issues. I should also mention that the entire time I was writing Entice, I listened to Taylor Swift 's album '1989' on repeat. I believe the tone of her album shaped the tone of Emily's story. The songs that come to mind at the moment are *Wildest Dreams*, *This Love* and *Clean*. Along with the bonus tracks: *You Are In Love* and *New Romantics*.

Last but not least, when Owen scribbles a single word onto a piece of paper, it seemed natural for the word to be *always*. But as soon as I typed it, I was reminded of Snape and Lilly, from the Harry Potter series by JK Rowling . I almost deleted the word to think of something else, because I knew other fans of the series might draw the same parallels. In the end, I decided to keep it in, as a homage. Because Snape was my favorite character in that series. And I really wish his story would've ended differently. I wish he would've gotten the girl.

80221469R00216

Made in the USA
Lexington, KY
30 January 2018